ANITA'S REVOLUTION

For St. Michal's University School —

— with best wishes!

Shirley Langer

Copyright © 2012 by Shirley Langer

Published by *Shirleez Books*:
www.shirleylanger.com
www.anitasrevolution.com
shirleylanger@gmail.com

Library and Archives Canada Cataloguing in Publication

Langer, Shirley, 1935-
  Anita's Revolution / Shirley Langer.

ISBN 978-0-9812538-1-7

  1. Literacy programs--Cuba--Fiction. I. Title.

PS8623.A5248A75 2012   C813'.6   C2012-901088-X

Cover image: © pressurepics - Fotolia.com
Book Layout and Cover Design: SpicaBookDesign (www.spicabookdesign.com)

Printed and bound in Canada

ANITA'S REVOLUTION

SHIRLEY LANGER

SHIRLEEZ
books

OTHER WORKS:

Road's End: Tales of Tofino
Tofino Time magazine: monthly articles

*remembering Marjorie Moore whose
enthusiasm about Cuba's literacy campaign
and her hopes for what would be achieved
inspired me to tell the world about it*

ACKNOWLEDGEMENTS AND CREDITS

O ccan Books granted the author Rights to use archival photo graphs of the *Campaña de Alfabetización* published in the pages of the book *In the Spirit of the Wandering Teachers*. These photographs and hundreds more are available to be seen at the Literacy Campaign Museum in Havana, Cuba. The editor of New Internationalist magazine granted me permission to draw extensively from the on-line article, A Brief History of Cuba, Issue 301, published May 5, 1998.

Names listed in the book (partial list) of those who died during the Cuban Literacy Campaign, were taken from the book CUBA TERRITORIO LIBRE DE ANALFABETISMO, published by Editorial de Ciencias Sociales, Cuba, 1981.

The author is indebted to Marjorie Moore Ríos, (now deceased) who was generous in communicating so much information which provided the foundation for this novel. Marjorie served as a supervisor in Cuba's National Literacy Campaign in the Bainoa region. Her eleven-year-old daughter, Pamela, taught basic literacy to seven adults. Interviewing the adult Pamela provided me with many engaging details about the campaign. Pamela today works in Cuba as an expert in Good Manufacturing Practises.

I am indebted to the following people whom I interviewed. Marieta Bosco, whose vivid recounting of her experiences made the writer's job easier. Carlos Isaac Garcia not only shared his experiences as a *brigadista*, he also let me read a detailed journal he had kept throughout the campaign. Dr. Antonio Pasco, an orthopaedic surgeon, was thirteen when he volunteered. "When I set out to teach, I was a mere child, but by the end of the campaign I had developed some character." By the end he had also outgrown his uniform. *Señora* Esperanza Caridad Bracho y Perez was sixteen when she and three other young girls landed in Arroyo Negro (Black Creek) to teach literacy to two adolescents, five men and three women. She loved teaching so much she became one and enjoyed a long professional career.

Thank you Anne Millyard, one half of the founding and publishing team (now retired) of Canada's Annick Press, for stating emphatically that the world needs to know this story. Thank you David Floody for your fearless literary sensibilities. I am grateful to three particular teens—Liam Eady, Ava Hansen and Carina Pogoler—who read the story as a work-in-progress and provided me with useful feedback. I thank my Clayoquot Writers Group colleagues whom I asked to comment now and then on various sections. They were always forthcoming and encouraging. Thank you Dayle Getz for providing invaluable editorial suggestions, and Valentina Cambiazo for eagle-eye proofreading services. I'm grateful to my Langer family for bearing with me as I fretted about this book over the years. Special thanks must be given to my great friends, husband and wife Lina de Guevara and Celso Cambiazo, who urged me to be true to my vision of the story rather than comply with certain current trends.

CONTENTS

PREFACE

*A*nita's Revolution is a work of historical fiction inspired by the success of the Cuban Literacy Campaign which took place in 1961. The book is about how Cuba began educating its masses of illiterate people, people long ignored by successive governments and society. It's about how the social classes of Cuba, so long separated, were united. It's about how illiterate people were introduced to the world of words thereby changing each person's future and the country's future. A dear friend who participated in the campaign provided the basis for much that transpires in the story. Some characters who people the pages of *Anita's Revolution* share qualities with some real-life persons. All other people within its pages and some parts of the plot are imaginary.

I lived and worked in Cuba almost five years during the mid-sixties, a few years after Cuba's National Literacy Campaign had accomplished its initial goal of basic literacy. Everywhere I went, I saw classes taking place: in the lobbies of hotels, in workplace cafeterias, in apartment building vestibules, even outside in parks. Adults who had achieved basic literacy in 1961 were studying throughout the years I was there to achieve elementary school levels. Public education in Cuba, including acquiring university degrees, was then and has remained a priority and is completely free.

Cuba struggles with many problems, but illiteracy is not one of them. 2011 was the 50th anniversary year of having reduced illiteracy nation-wide from 25% of the population to 3.9%. Cuba never slipped back. Today as I write this, organizations such as UNESCO and The World Bank state that Cuba enjoys a literacy rate of almost 100%. It all started with the decision in 1961 to make Cuba "a territory free from illiteracy". How it was done is an amazing story, one that most people I encountered over the years knew nothing about. This book then, not all fact but not all fiction either, celebrates the campaign, the people and the spirit that ended almost five centuries of ignorance when, on December 22, 1961, Cuba raised a flag declaring itself "A territory free from illiteracy."

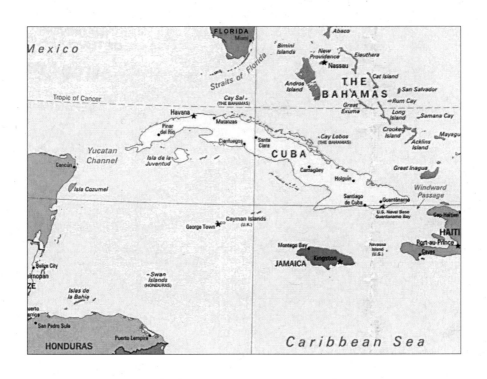

A BRIEF HISTORY OF CUBA

Before the conquest by Spain

The Siboney people, aboriginal hunter/gatherers, were the first inhabitants of the island we call Cuba. They were followed by the fierce Taino, who settled most of the Caribbean islands. When Christopher Columbus reached Cuba on October 27, 1492, it is estimated that there were a half-million indigenous people living in small villages farming yucca, yams, peanuts, avocados and tobacco.

The time of occupation

The Spanish occupation began in 1514 when Diego Velasquez landed near Guantánamo Bay with 300 men. Smallpox, brutal treatment and malnutrition quickly decimated the native people. Thousands committed suicide rather than submit to the Spaniards. The entire indigenous population was wiped out by 1542.

Slavery, plunder and sugar from sugar cane

The first Africans were brought as slaves to work the mines and plantations of Cuba in 1522. Sugar cane, which eventually became a huge export crop, was first planted in 1512, but it was tobacco, a plant native to the island that became the first important commercial crop. The sugar industry exploded into importance in 1791 when French planters fled a slave revolt in Haiti and settled in Cuba. Sugar cane blanketed the island and 700,000 Africans were bought to Cuba over the next 40 years. Eventually, Africans outnumbered whites. Cuba was the world's largest sugar producer, and the newly-independent United States was its biggest market.

Wars of Independence

Criollos—persons born in Cuba of Spanish descent—were becoming wealthier and dissatisfied with Spanish rule. The US twice tried to purchase Cuba from Spain, in 1848 and 1854, but the colonial power refused to sell. Pressure for self-rule began to build and erupted in a war of independence in 1888. The independence movement was exhausted by great expenditures and loss of life, forcing the leadership to sign a peace treaty. Spanish landowners were also bankrupted by the war. US investors took advantage, snapping up plantations being sold cheaply. By the late 1890s, 70 per cent of land in Cuba was in US hands, and 90 per cent of the country's sugar went to the US.

The second uprising against Spain began in 1895. Due to an incident arising between the Spanish colonial government and the US in February of 1898, the United States declared war against Spain. A few months later, in July, the Spanish surrendered and Americans occupied Cuba.

In 1902, the island finally gained its independence after being forced to accept a made-in-USA constitution. A clause, the Platt Amendment, gave the US the right to intervene in Cuban internal affairs whenever it was deemed necessary to protect American interests. It also allowed for a US naval base at Guantánamo Bay which remains to this day.

Dictators and gangsters

The next five decades were dominated by corruption and increasing American control of the economy. Tourism boomed along with gambling and prostitution as mobsters from Miami, Florida and New York moved into Havana. Poverty and unemployment increased. The countryside and its agricultural working people were virtually ignored. In 1933, a young mulatto army sergeant, Fulgencio Batista, seized power and ran the country until ousted in 1944. Batista staged another successful coup in 1953. Elections were cancelled, and for the next six years Batista and his cronies lined their pockets by opening the arms of the government to organized crime. Order was maintained by the army and secret police. Hundreds of government opponents were tortured and murdered.

The revolution triumphs

In December 1956, a young Fidel Castro and 82 cohorts sailed from Mexico in a small yacht called *Granma*. The Cuban revolution had begun. Of the 81 original men, only 12 survived the landing in Cuba. Betrayed by a guide, the rest were ambushed and killed by the army. The survivors established themselves in the Sierra Maestra mountains in the eastern part of the island, and slowly gained support among the rural *campesinos*, the peasants. Underground resistance grew in the cities. Protests were staged and new recruits joined Castro's guerrilla fighters. As popular support for the guerrillas spread throughout the island, Batista's troops became demoralized. When the army collapsed, the dictator Batista fled to the Dominican Republic on New Year's Day 1959, reputedly carrying $40 million.

Fidel Castro arrived in Havana on January 8, 1959. Now 33, Castro was named prime minister, and on January 25th over a million Cubans filled the streets to hear Fidel Castro define the goals of the Revolutionary government. The new government immediately nationalized all land-holdings over 400 hectares. Racial discrimination was abolished, rents slashed and wages increased. Some land was redistributed to landless peasants and the rest was turned into state farms where agricultural workers were given secure, paid employment for the first time. Fidel Castro and his close colleague in arms and friendship, Ernesto "Che" Guevara set out to build a utopian state that included a complete shake-up of the economy, a ban on all forms of private enterprise, and the intention to create an enlightened "new man" and "new woman" to fulfill the revolution's goals.

Thousands of volunteers were needed to teach one million illiterate Cubans to read and write. It is at this juncture of Cuba's history in 1961 that the story *Anita's Revolution* begins.

THE WARNING

U ntil now, Anita thought that murder happened only in the adult world. The newspaper article beneath the stark black headline—**Volunteer literacy teacher captured and murdered by rebels**—said counter-revolutionaries had grabbed literacy teacher Conrado Benitez on a mountain path when he was on his way to teach and had hung him from a tree. Anita's stomach lurched imagining Conrado dangling from the end of a rope. *Why had they done that? What had that boy ever done to them?* Her father was a news editor at Cuba's largest daily newspaper, El Diario, The Daily News, so she knew about counter-revolutionaries, how they wanted to sabotage the work of Cuba's new revolutionary government. *But this!*

She moved the newspaper spread out on her desk aside and tried to focus on her algebra homework. Heaving a great sigh, she raised her eyes from her homework and looked again at the picture of the murdered boy in the newspaper, but the room was now too dim to see it clearly. How long had she been sitting at her desk, staring at the page? Long enough for day to become almost night. When the sun sank into the sea off Cuba's shore, it was as though it dragged the darkness right behind it. The floor in front of the windows was striped with bars of last light seeping in between the *persianas*, the polished louver boards of the shuttered windows. Anita got up to turn on the light, but instead, opened the shutters and leaned out the window into the cooling air of the Cuban twilight.

Lights were turning on throughout the wide streets of Miramar, the suburb where she lived. Just a few blocks from her house lay the sea, the Caribbean. Only the western horizon flared orange and magenta in a sky the colour of ink. The sea itself was already swallowed by darkness. Anita looked eastward, where the great city of Havana, sparkling with a million pricks of golden light, stretched as far as the eye could see.

Anita closed the shutters, screwed the *persianas* closed and turned on the light. Blinking, Anita surveyed her bedroom. A little messy, but nothing like her brother's. She glanced at her reflection in the full-length mirror of the closet armoire. Tall for a Cuban girl, she took after her father—slim and wiry. Her shoulder-length chestnut-coloured hair and full arched eyebrows were her best features. People told her she was pretty, but she knew she'd never be beautiful like her mother, a petite, buxom, always elegant woman who spent a lot of time taking care of her looks. Anita's eyes rested on the armchair she loved to curl up in and read. The book she had just started, Anne Frank: The Diary of a Young Girl, lay balanced on one armrest. The armchair and the book beckoned her, but she returned to her desk, to her algebra homework.

Still, her eyes kept sliding over to the newspaper. Anita stared at the picture of the murdered youth again. A couple of days ago hardly anyone in Cuba knew anything about Conrado Benitez. Now, his face was everywhere, in all the papers, on TV, on posters—Conrado staring out of the grainy black and white I.D. photo. He had been at her school assembly a few months ago speaking about the importance of literacy; promoting Cuba's pilot literacy program run by volunteer teachers. The presence of the young black man in her all-white school was quite a novelty. Inspired by his talk, Anita had hurried up front to talk to him before he left.

"I'd like to teach literacy someday," she told him. He had been so serious during his talk that she was relieved when he smiled.

"That's great!" he said. "Cuba needs people like you."

They had talked a while more before she had to return to her classes. The stark black and white photo in the paper showed an unsmiling young black man who looked older than his eighteen years and revealed nothing of Conrado's personality. Anita shut her eyes to recall his big-toothed smile, his contagious enthusiasm for teaching. Now he was dead. She opened a desk drawer and fished out scissors. She cut Conrado's picture out of the newspaper and taped it to the wall above the desk, right at eye level. Giving up on homework, Anita flipped her algebra book closed and ran downstairs, heading for the patio.

"Where are you going, Anita?" mamá called out as Anita passed by the living room. "Dinner will be ready soon."

"I need some fresh air," said Anita.

Her mother and father put down their evening cocktails, got up and came toward her.

"You're feeling upset about the murder, aren't you?" said mamá, placing her hands on Anita's shoulders.

"Yes. Aren't you? Isn't everybody? He was so young, and doing such good things." Anita fought back tears.

"Yes, he was," mamá said, pulling Anita close to embrace her.

"He was a real child of the Revolution," her father said thoughtfully.

She and her father had had a few good conversations recently about the revolution. Only last week her father had tried to explain what made counter-revolutionaries tick; why they were constantly doing awful things like blowing places up and sabotaging machinery.

"What alarms these people most," her father had explained, "is the new government's program of nationalization—that means the government taking control of banks, large businesses, land, mines, the fishing industry . . . of many, many things. You know that the newspaper I work for was nationalized. That made the owner angry, very angry. He could have stayed on, continued as the boss, but he didn't want to be an employee of the government, so he left the country."

"Why does Fidel want to nationalize everything, papá?"

"He says the wealth of the country belongs to all the people, not to just the few who use wealth and power to benefit themselves. Fidel says that having the resources of the country in government hands will make things fairer for everyone."

"What do you think papá? Is Fidel doing a good thing?"

"It could be good, Anita. Cuba is a poor country, and for many years there has been terrible corruption. Government has ignored Cuba's poor. So we need change. But these kinds of changes have made a lot of people furious—especially the very wealthy people who were used to sharing the loot gained from government corruption. Some people are so furious they are prepared to do anything to get things back to the way they were before the revolution."

"Furious enough to kill people?"

"Yes, Anita. Furious enough kill people."

Hearing those words then, Anita had shuddered, and she shuddered again now. They had killed. Anita wanted to talk more about all this with her father, just not now. She felt she would suffocate if she didn't get outside. Pulling away from her mother's embrace, Anita bent to kiss her rouged cheek, then headed through the dining room on her way to the patio.

"*Hola chica. ¿Cómo está Anita la cubanita?*"

Even though she was a head taller than Tomasa, the family maid, Tomasa still used this affectionate nickname she had given Anita when she was a toddler—*Anita la cubanita*, Anita the little Cuban girl. Anita didn't mind. She adored Tomasa. She flashed Tomasa a smile, slid open the patio door, grateful for the cool air that enveloped her.

Anita wandered around the patio, kicking a seed pod from the *almendro* tree across the flagstones, thinking about what her father had said about Conrado being a child of the Revolution. *La revolución!* That was practically the only thing everyone ever talked about since the Revolutionary government took control just two years ago. Before that, there had been years of violence and struggle in Cuba. Until recently though, Anita hadn't been paying a lot of attention to the ups and downs of *la revolución.*

Even at school *la revolución* was like a school subject. Photographs of Fidel Castro and all the other revolutionaries who had fought along with him to get rid of Cuba's dictator hung in the halls and in every classroom of her school. They studied *la revolución:* how it was fought; how it was won. School field trips to observe new government programs first hand were frequent. The agricultural and fishing cooperatives her class had visited had been kind of dull, but the brand new daycare centre they went to see was interesting. Hundreds of day care centres were being set up because *la revolución* was urging women to enter the workforce or get more education.

Last week her class had gone by bus to see a newly constructed junior elementary school in a small village outside Havana. The students—mostly mulatto or black—had never been to school before. Some of the kids were barefoot. She had tried not to stare at their dirty feet. Anita remembered feeling strange, feeling . . . too white. Afterwards, her teacher had explained many parents were simply too poor to buy shoes, but that she knew the government was importing shoes so that no child would have to go to school barefoot. *How could anyone find fault with that?*

Anita leaned against the mango tree, thinking about all the people deserting Cuba because they thought Prime Minister Fidel Castro was ruining the country. Six months ago her uncle Eduardo, her father's brother, had left for the United States with his whole family. The faces of her cousins rose in her mind and she wondered if she'd ever see them again. Neighbours had left, and lots of other people her family knew. She didn't want to ever leave Cuba—especially not leave her friends—but knew she would have to leave if her parents decided to. Anita thought back to the evening, not long ago, when she and her parents were out strolling in Banyan Tree Park after dinner. She had suddenly decided to test her parents about this, so skipped in front of them and started walking backwards.

"You wouldn't ever leave Cuba for good, would you?" she asked.

Her mother remained silent, but after a moment her father began speaking. "You know, Anita, several months ago your mother and I thought we should leave Cuba. I was feeling that adjusting to all the changes going on since Fidel took over was too overwhelming. Everything felt so unstable. I speak decent English . . . I'm an experienced newspaper editor, so I was thinking I could earn a good living in the United States. My brother leaving suddenly with his family really shocked me—especially since he had just received a promotion at the hospital. And I suspected that many of my colleagues at the newspaper were planning to leave. In fact, since that time, many have left."

"But here we are, so that means you and mamá have changed your minds, right? What made you change your minds?" She glanced at her mother who still hadn't said a word.

"We have changed our minds . . . at least, for the time being. Do you remember the reception at the newspaper we all attended a few months ago?"

Anita nodded. How could she forget? Fidel Castro was to be the guest-of-honour. People arriving were invited to sign a guest book, and after signing she had turned to hand the pen to the person waiting behind her to sign . . . and there he was! Fidel had taken the pen from her hand, looked at her signature and said, "Thanks, Anita." She had bragged about this for days afterwards.

"That evening," papá continued, "Fidel described his vision for change in Cuba. If you remember, Anita, he spoke at length about Cuba's poor who have been ignored by government and society for centuries. I've always felt rather self conscious about being part of the haves when there are so many have-nots. So . . . well, I was really impressed. He's very convincing, you know. I decided then that we should stay; that we should give the new government a chance and help make Cuba a better place."

"Great!" said Anita. "Because I want to help make Cuba a better place too. I never want to leave. What about you, mamá?"

"We'll see," was all her mother said.

Anita wasn't surprised. Her mother was crazy about everything American. She always dressed in the latest American fashions, she was a fan of American movies and movie stars—she never missed a film starring Marilyn Monroe. She was always looking for opportunities to speak English, embarrassing Anita by striking up conversations with visiting English-speaking tourists. Family and friends were always teasing her about loving the United States so much. "The stork delivered you to the wrong country, Mirta," they would say.

Since that conversation in the park, Anita had relaxed despite hearing people talk about the waves of people leaving or wanting to leave. *But now, there was this awful murder! Would this kind of violence by counter-revolutionaries affect how mamá and papá felt about staying in Cuba? Especially mamá?*

Anita slumped onto a patio chair, shivering as her back pressed against the cold metal. She could hear the clatter of pots and pans as neighbours prepared dinner. Voices and music from the radios of neighbouring houses drifted out through open shutters mixing with the chirping of crickets sounding from the shadows. Underneath all these sounds floating on the evening air, Anita could hear the rumbling of the ocean at the bottom of her street as waves surged onto the rocks and retreated.

The radio was on in her house too. Tomasa always kept the radio tuned to stations that played popular Cuban music. She could see Tomasa moving between the kitchen and the dining room, not dancing exactly, but sort of shuffling in tempo to the rhythm as she set the table. She wondered if her parents were talking about Conrado. Being murdered had turned the young literacy teacher into a hero. Already people were calling him a martyr. She had looked the word martyr up in the dictionary:

Martyr: one who suffers keenly, especially for a cause or principle.

"Anita . . . dinnertime," mamá called from the doorway.

Everyone was already seated around the glass dining room table when Anita entered, blinking in the light. Mamá was serving out a traditional Cuban dish of black beans and rice. Her long, crimson fingernails flashed as she spooned out the food and handed the heaped plates around. As usual, her brother Mario was already wolfing down his dinner.

"Anita, even though it's only January, it's time to start thinking about your *quinceañera*, your coming-of-age party," said mamá. "We should get started on the invitation list and look at patterns for a dress. I'll call the Country Club tomorrow to reserve the dining room."

"Almost fifteen, and never been kissed!" said Mario, his mouth full of rice. Anita kicked him under the table.

"I'm not sure I want to have a *quinceañera*, mamá." The words seem to have spilled out of Anita's mouth and she felt her face burning. Everyone stopped eating, and looked at her as if she'd turned into an iguana.

"What an idea, Anita! All Cuban girls have a *quinceañera* party when they turn fifteen," said her mother. "It's an important Cuban tradition."

Anita twisted and untwisted her napkin.

"Why don't you want to celebrate your *quinceañera*?" papá asked. "I thought you were looking forward to it." He spoke in a quiet voice, continuing to eat, but her father's calm voice and reasonable manner often unnerved Anita more than her mother's temperamental ways.

I was looking forward to my quinceañera, Anita admitted to herself. She began pushing her rice and beans into a hill in the middle of her plate, then began dividing the hill into smaller mounds. *What did make me say that?* As soon as she asked herself that question, thoughts came flooding randomly into her head.

"Cousins and some kids from school I would have invited have taken the ninety," she said.

"Taken the ninety?" said mamá. "What's that mean?"

"What planet are you living on, Mirta?" said papá, laughing. "It's the ninety miles between Cuba and the tip of Florida. "Taking the ninety" is the slang expression used when talking about people who have left Cuba for the USA."

But mamá was too concentrated on Anita at the moment to be amused.

"It's true that some of your friends have gone," she said, "but many others are here, including Marci, your best friend. You are planning to go to Marci's *quinceañera* in July, I imagine, so there must be something other than friends "taking the ninety" behind this."

Anita pushed her food around on the plate, but didn't eat. *Only the other day Marci and I spent hours talking about details of our parties, looking forward to being debutantes for a day. So what has changed?* As she sat thinking, it seemed to her that her feelings had something to do with the death of Conrado Benitez, something to do with *la revolución,* but she didn't know what exactly.

Everywhere—at school, in stores, on the street, on the bus—there were heated discussions about *la revolución.* People were either enthusiastically for it: "Fidel and his people will end corruption and give Cuba back to ordinary Cubans," or they were violently against it: "That man is destroying the Cuban way of life. He has no right to change everything without our consent!" People either loved Fidel Castro, or hated him—both with a passion. And now, some people who were against *la revolución* had killed someone who was for it. She felt her mother's eyes burrowing into her.

"Anita, we're waiting for an answer." Papá's voice had sharpened a little, and he had removed his glasses, which always made Anita nervous.

"I know papá. I'm thinking."

"It seems to me you are stalling more than thinking," mamá said.

"Mamá, if I could explain, I would . . . honest," Anita replied, rolling her eyes. "It's just . . . it's just that the idea of a fancy *fiesta* seems wrong somehow. It seems kind of . . . kind of . . . frivolous."

"Frivolous! Did you hear that, Daniel? The child is telling us we're *frivolous*."

"Mamá, papá, I didn't mean to be disrespectful, but why aren't we talking about why Conrado was murdered instead of my *quinceañera*?"

Her parents just stared at her. Mario stopped eating, his fork suspended in mid air.

"I don't know why I blurted that out about the *quinceañera*," Anita continued. "It just doesn't seem right to be talking about having fancy parties at the Country Club when Conrado's parents are probably crying their eyes out this very minute. And I bet they are poor people who have never even seen the inside of a country club!"

"You're talking nonsense, Anita! One thing has nothing to do with the other," her mother said.

But the rest of the meal was eaten in silence.

At school the next day, Anita and some of the students in her class asked the teacher if they could talk about why counter-revolutionaries had murdered Conrado Benitez. Why him? they wanted to know. He wasn't a celebrity or some important person.

"I could tell you what I think," responded the teacher, "but I want you to try to come up with some possible answers to that question yourselves."

The teacher drew a circle on the blackboard, and inside the circle wrote the words: Why did the counter-revolutionaries kill Conrado Benitez? Then she drew lines like the rays of the sun. "Each one of these rays is a possible answer to the question. Who will start?"

The answers came faster than the teacher could write.

"Because he was black and they were racists. People who hate the idea of a black person teaching their kids."

"Sabotage! They were showing their hatred of any program started by the Revolutionary government."

"If all Cuba's poor people become literate, they will have more choices about where to work. They could ask for higher wages."

"It was a dramatic warning to stop the pilot literacy programs—to scare people so they wouldn't volunteer as literacy teachers."

The teacher turned to the class with an approving smile. "All of your answers are probably correct. His murder was a violent warning that if literacy programs continue, more literacy teachers will be killed," she declared, her voice trembling with emotion. "We will watch with interest to see how the government responds to this warning." The classroom conversation continued in earnest until the bell signalling the end of class rang. As Anita walked to the next class with her friends, they continued talking about the murder.

"I had nightmares about it," said Marci, Anita's best friend.

"*¡Caramba!*" exclaimed Anita. "Murdering someone just because you don't agree with what they're doing . . . Especially a teenager! *¡Qué horror!* How horrible!"

"I bet there won't be many people volunteering to be literacy teachers now," said Marci.

"That's just what the counter-revolutionaries want to happen," said Anita. "They want to ruin everything that is changing things. If people let that happen, then the counter-revolutionaries win."

"Since when did you become such a red-hot little revolutionary, Anita?" said one of the girls.

"And why shouldn't she be?" said another, placing an arm around Anita's shoulders and giving her an affectionate squeeze. "Aren't we all supposed to be super revolutionary these days?"

Anita noticed that Marci said nothing.

Anita had finished her homework and was just coming downstairs to watch TV when she heard her mother call out to her father, "Daniel, come see this! Hurry!"

A program about the literacy campaign usually came on every night at this time, but an announcer was saying the usual program was being replaced by a special broadcast. Anita was disappointed. She loved watching the nightly literacy program. She was fascinated seeing how *campesinos* lived in the countryside and remote mountain regions, seeing their huts called *bohíos*, the tiny country villages, the sugar cane and coffee plantations, *campesinos* on horseback, the slow-moving zebu oxen pulling carts, their flabby dewlaps hanging down from their chests swaying heavily as they plodded along dusty roads.

Fidel's unmistakable voice snapped her attention to the TV.

"Last September, I announced at the United Nations that by the end of 1961, Cuba will be a *territorio libre de analfabetismo*, a territory free from illiteracy. The Revolutionary government asked the Ministry of Education to develop a program that would make that pledge a reality. To achieve that, the Ministry of Education is enlarging the current pilot literacy program to make it a countrywide campaign. Thousands of young volunteer teachers are needed to join special student brigades we will call Brigadas Conrado Benitez in honour of the young hero. Members of these volunteer brigades will be called *brigadistas*."

Anita felt her whole body start to buzz.

"When the current school term ends," continued the Prime Minister, "volunteers will be given a special teacher training course. Some *brigadistas* will go to live in the *campesino* homes of those they will be teaching to read and write. Others will be assigned to teach in towns and villages, and will be billeted in homes and community centres. Supervision and services for the health and safety of student volunteers will be provided by teams of responsible adults."

The buzzing in her brain increased with each word Fidel said. *Could I become a brigadista?*

At the end of the broadcast, Fidel said, "Young people of Cuba, make history by helping your country eliminate illiteracy. Volunteer now! Become a *brigadista*!" *Would her parents let her volunteer?* Even as she was thinking these words, her question was answered.

"Is Fidel crazy?" her mother said, raising her voice over the TV. "Who would let their kids volunteer since that poor boy was killed? And what parents in their right minds would consent to let their sons and daughters go and live for months with strangers in *bohío* huts with dirt floors, thatch roofs over their heads, no electricity, no running water, chickens and dirty barefoot kids running around. And where would they sleep—in hammocks? Literacy may be important, but sending kids away from their homes for months in these troubling times? Fidel must be dreaming!"

"Calm yourself, Mirta. I doubt that many parents will let their kids go," her father said, returning to his armchair and book.

Thoughts of being a *brigadista* zipped around in Anita's head all evening. Sitting up in bed, she rested a blank diary she had received for Christmas against her knees and wrote her first words.

January 7, 1961

Dear Diary,

> *Volunteering for the literacy campaign is a chance to do something adventurous, something important, like Conrado did. Of course there is the danger of being kidnapped by counter-revolutionaries! My friends tease me about being super revolutionary, but I don't want to do anything stupid. And what about my quinceañera—the whole coming-of-age thing? Mamá and papá would be really disappointed if we didn't have a celebration. But what exactly is one coming-of-age for? The day after the quinceañera, it's life as usual, whereas helping make Cuba a territorio libre de analfabetismo—now that's really important! I'll have to think this over carefully. I don't think I should mention anything about volunteering yet because obviously mamá and papá think it's too dangerous. They don't want their darling little girl having to sleep in a hammock in a bohío. Oh Diary, just think—as a volunteer I might get assigned to teach in the Sierra Maestra Mountains where la revolución started. Or maybe go to Guamá where there are crocodiles and giant sea turtles to see. Just having an adventure away from home would be GREAT! I have decided that my diary-signing name will be the more grown-up form of the nickname Tomasa gave me when I was a little girl.*

> *So long for now,*
> *Anita la cubana*

Anita wandered around her room looking for a good place to hide the diary. *I don't trust my mother . . . Papá never comes into my room . . . I don't have to worry about Tomasa because I don't think she can read anyway. And Mario? He'd never be that sneaky. At least, I don't think he would.*

She tucked the diary behind the tallest books on her bookshelf.

AN IDEA IS HATCHED

After that first broadcast about the National Literacy Campaign, Anita saw signs announcing it everywhere, and there were announcements on TV and radio many times a day. Everyone was talking about the call for student volunteers except her parents—or so it seemed to her. When the announcements came on, they ignored them. Her mother didn't even rant anymore.

One night after dinner, Anita wandered into Mario's room. He was sprawled across his bed reading *Deportes*, his favourite sports magazine. The room was a mess of scattered clothing and sports equipment. Although Tomasa aired and tidied the room every day, it still stank of dried jock sweat. Many posters were pinned up on the walls— Yogi Berra and Mickey Mantle in batting position, Muhammad Ali crouched in fighting position with boxing gloves on. Anita's favourite poster was of Pelé, the Brazilian soccer star, when he was playing at the 1958 World Cup in Sweden. Though her brother was a merciless tease, she adored him anyway. He was smart, a natural athlete, handsome, a gifted mimic. . . . How he could made her laugh imitating Fidel Castro making a speech! She just wished he wouldn't treat her like such a kid. But then, she knew such arrogance was typical of seventeen year-old boys.

She flopped down on the bed.

"What's on your mind, little sister?"

Anita got right to the point. "Are you thinking of volunteering, Mario?"

"For what?" he said, not looking up.

"You know," she said, keeping her voice low.

"What do I know?" he said, flipping pages.

"Are you thinking of volunteering to be a *brigadista*?"

A sign-up sheet for volunteers had been posted on the school bulletin board the day after the first announcement. Anita watched the list growing longer every day. And yesterday she had seen Mario looking at the list.

"I'm considering it," said Mario. When Anita didn't say anything, Mario looked up. "What's the matter?" he said, poking her playfully. "Don't you think I'd make a good teacher?"

"It's just . . . It's just that I've been thinking that I'd like to volunteer too."

"Are you crazy? Mamá and papá will never let you volunteer. You have more important things to do—at least, in their opinion."

Anita knew what he was talking about. Her *quinceañera* was to be a lavish affair. Her mother's dressmaker would make her a fancy designer dress, and she and her mother would go shopping to buy special accessories. Her mother would insist on having her hairdresser create a special hair-do. Her parents would rent a limousine to drive her and her closest friends to the party. Her father would escort her to the head table. There would be musicians, wonderful catered food, gifts, and a professional photographer to record it all for the family album. She'd be allowed to drink some champagne. What girl wouldn't like to be the belle of such a ball? Anita stood up.

"I think volunteering to teach literacy is more important than the tradition of a *quinceañera*. If mamá and papá let *you* go, it will be because you're a boy."

"Tradition, tradition," chanted Mario.

"To hell with tradition!" Anita blurted.

"Whoa, little sister! Tell *them* that."

Anita and Marci always walked home from school together. They often did their homework together too, and today they had arranged to do it at Marci's house.

"You're awfully quiet these days, Anita," said Marci, as they walked. "What's up? Does Anita have a secret . . . ? Maybe a crush on somebody? C'mon . . . Confess."

"It's nothing like that, Marci."

"Then what? We're best friends, right? Whatever it is, I promise not to tell."

"It's about volunteering for the literacy campaign. I didn't want to talk to you about it because of the way your family feels about *la revolución*. I'm pretty sure Mario is planning to volunteer, but my parents are dead set against it. It's not only the Conrado Benitez thing. They say it's not a job for kids, especially girls. And they keep talking about the importance of my *quinceañera*."

"If you volunteer, you probably wouldn't be here in July for my *quinceañera* either," said Marci, suddenly downcast.

"I know. That's another reason I was nervous about talking to you about this."

Both girls were silent for a moment.

"My parents talk about the literacy campaign as if it were a total waste of time," said Marci. "You know what they're like about anything to do with the revolution. They talk as if people who can't read and write are dumber than mud, especially black people. My father says all blacks are good for is grunt work. That's the word my dad uses—grunt work."

"That's awful, Marci."

"I sounded my parents out about volunteering," said Marci, "but my father said I'd be grounded forever if I even so much as mentioned it again. At least your parents aren't like that, Anita. Mine don't give a damn about anybody or anything outside of this grand neighbourhood of Miramar," she said, flinging her arm in a wide arc. "And all they talk about is wanting things to be just the same as they were *antes*, before *la revolución*! I'll tell you a secret, Anita, but you mustn't tell anyone." Marci's voice sounded strangled in her throat. "We'll be leaving Cuba . . . going to Miami . . . soon after my *quinceañera*."

Even though Anita knew Marci's parents were known to be *gusanos, worms*—slang for Cubans who hated and bad-mouthed *la revolución*—this news that her best friend was going to disappear from her life was shocking. Anita burst into tears which made Marci start to cry too. They walked with linked arms, their heads down, weeping until their tears dried up. "I think it's great that you want to volunteer," said Marci, wiping her eyes. "I hope you get to go, even if you won't be here for my *quinceañera*."

As they were turning in at Marci's gate, Marci's neighbour and her two daughters greeted them. Anita had seen the woman before but had never met her. Marci made the introductions. From the way she spoke Spanish, Anita could tell *señora* Moore was an *extranjera*, a foreigner—probably a *gringa* from the Unites States.

"You may call me Marjorie," she told Anita. "The girls and I are just returning from signing up as volunteers for the literacy campaign. I told them I couldn't volunteer my services unless they allowed me to bring Pamela and Suzi wherever I was assigned, and they agreed. Not only that, but Pamela wants to teach too, and they said if she was able to do the advance teacher training, she would be allowed to teach—or at least, help teach. So we are pretty excited, aren't we girls?" Suzi and Pamela both started to talk at once, making everybody laugh. Pamela wanted to know if Marci and Anita had already volunteered.

"Not yet," said Anita, hating how lame that sounded. Marci just shook her head.

In the house, slurping guava smoothies before starting their homework, Marci told Anita what she knew about Marjorie Moore. "She's from the US, New York City I think, and her husband, Luis Ríos, is Cuban. She teaches English to medical students at the University of Havana. She's really nice."

"She's pretty, too," said Anita. "Do you think her hair is naturally blonde, or does she bleach it?"

"Bottle," said Marci, making Anita laugh. After that, all Marci had to do was look up from their homework and say "bottle", and they would both have a fit of laughter.

When Anita got home, she knew as soon as she opened the front door that neither of her parents was home because the radio was blaring. She entered the kitchen.

"*Hola,*" she shouted.

"*¡Caramba!* You scared me," said Tomasa, her hand on her heart, scurrying to turn down the volume of the radio. "Your mother called to say that she and your father are going to eat out with friends tonight. And Mario has gone to a baseball game. So, *Anita la cubanita*, you will be eating by yourself tonight."

"I'd like to eat with you, if you haven't eaten already," said Anita.

"What would you like for dinner?" asked Tomasa.

"Your choice," replied Anita.

Tomasa wouldn't sit at the dining room table. "That wouldn't be proper," she said, so they sat at a small table in the kitchen. Tomasa had prepared something Anita loved—rice with fried plantains, avocado and tomato salad, and for dessert, freshly grated coconut with sliced mango.

"Tomasa, this is scrumptious!" Tomasa beamed. She had lived with

Anita's family since Anita was a baby. As they ate, Anita started thinking about Tomasa. Even though this woman was like a second mother, she realized she knew very little about her.

"Tomasa, tell me about your childhood. What did you like to do?"

"Whew, you're asking me to remember things from so long ago, child! You know that I was raised in *el campo*, the countryside. What did I do? There wasn't much time to play because I was the oldest, so I had to help my mother. My father would leave early in the morning—he worked at *El Cobre*, the copper mine—and never got home before dark. My mother did everything—cooked, cleaned, sewed our clothing, tended the garden, repaired things when they broke. I remember she even shoed our horse."

"What about going to school?" Anita asked.

"When I was nine, my parents sent me to live in town with an aunt so I could go to school. I missed home, but I was very happy to be going to school. But then mother had another child, her sixth . . . " Tomasa was pensive for a moment, looking off as though she were seeing something far away, then continued her thought. "Mother needed me to help her because she wasn't well, so I returned home. I was in school for only one grade." Tomasa sighed, rising to clear the table.

"Did you learn to read and write that year?"

Tomasa laughed, her plump belly heaving up and down.

"Child, if I did, I forgot everything in the mess of diapers and dishes." Tomasa lifted her apron and hid her face for a few seconds before lowering it. "No, Anita. I'm one of those *analfabetos*, those illiterate people they are always talking about these days on the radio and TV." Anita didn't know what to say. Tomasa made herself busy filling the sink with water.

"Would you like to learn?" Anita asked finally.

"Me! Learn to read and write now! Anita, child, your Tomasa is too old and too dumb to learn now. As the saying goes, you can't teach an old dog new tricks. Now, you scoot so I can finish cleaning up the kitchen."

Anita kissed Tomasa's soft caramel-coloured cheek. She had suspected that Tomasa couldn't read or write. Now she wondered about the other servants—Gladis, the laundress and Fernando, the gardener. *Were they completely illiterate too?*

Anita's father drove cautiously along the Malecón, the broad oceanside drive that bordered a good part of Havana's coastline. The street was slick with seawater breaking over the sea wall with a great booming sound. The windshield wipers slapped back and forth, working furiously to clear off the salt spray. Anita and her parents were on their way to see the movie, *The Diary of Anne Frank*.

"Papá, please pull over for a minute so I can look at that billboard," said Anita, her voice urgent. The brightly lit billboard showed a young teenager wearing a beret sitting at a table alongside an old black man. The teenager—it was hard to tell whether it was a boy or a girl—seemed to be guiding the man's hand as he wrote in a workbook. Their heads were almost touching as they bent over the page, concentrating on the task. Anita read the words under the huge picture.

Young men and women, join the army of young literacy workers. A family that can neither read nor write is waiting for you now. Don't let them down!

Her father stared at the billboard, then turned to look over his shoulder at her. "What is it that attracts you about this campaign, Anita?" Her mother swiveled around. Both parents were looking at her expectantly. Anita looked back at her parents indignantly.

"Isn't it obvious? Poor people, those "have-nots" you once spoke about don't have much of a chance in life if they can't read! And I seem to remember you saying you wanted to help make things better."

Her father sighed. "Those are noble reasons, Anita, but as I said before, this campaign is not a job for children. You have no experience in dealing with poverty. Believe me, life in a country *bohío* is no picnic. But most of all, with rebels around who kidnap and murder literacy volunteers, it's just too dangerous!" As her father pulled the Studebaker back into traffic, Anita craned her neck to look at the receding billboard. She decided the young teacher was a girl—a girl just about her age.

When she went to bed that night, Anita lay awake thinking about the movie. *What an amazing girl Anne Frank was!* Anita tried to imagine what it would be like having to live in hiding, never able to go outside, always fearful that the secret hiding place would be discovered.

Anne's only real companion during that whole time in hiding until they were discovered and taken away to the concentration camp was her diary. When Anita finally fell asleep, she dreamed of Anne Frank writing in her diary. Then Anne changed into Anita writing in her own diary, and then Anita became the teenager in the billboard, guiding the old man's hand, helping him learn to read and write.

★

"I've made an appointment with the dressmaker this coming Saturday, Anita. We'll choose a pattern, then we can go shopping for the material." Anita opened her mouth to speak, but nothing came out. Her mother had spoken from the top of the stairs, and now bent over the railing.

"Did you hear me Anita? I said . . ."

"I heard you mamá."

"Then why didn't you respond? And why that tone of voice?"

"Because you keep talking about the *quinceañera* and ignoring what I really want to do, which is volunteer for the literacy campaign. And if I volunteer, I won't be here for a *quinceañera*." Her mother had descended half way down the stairs as Anita was talking.

"For the love of God, Anita, enough of this nagging and nonsense! Your father and I will not sign a consent allowing you to volunteer, and that's that. I don't know what's gotten into you!"

"Lots of students who have signed up are my age, and most of them are girls. Their parents consented. And lots of those girls will miss having their coming-of-age parties." Anita swung her school bag over her shoulder and started out the door. "You might as well cancel that appointment," she called out, "because I won't go."

Heels pounding the sidewalk, she muttered, "I'm not giving up. I'm not!"

February 20, 1961

Dear Diary,

Some of the kids who have signed up to volunteer say it's because Cuba needs to make what Fidel announced at the United Nations about ending illiteracy by the end of this year come true. I overheard some teachers saying it can't be done. Other kids have signed up because they say it will be great fun. I sort of feel both things. I want to put my

name on the list so badly, but mamá and papá are being impossible.
But I haven't given up, Diary. And I've been thinking more about why
I don't want a quinceañera party. I think it's because that tradition is
part of the old Cuba, and I want to be part of the new Cuba, like the girl
wearing the beret in the billboard picture. I want to be a child of the
Revolution, like Conrado Benitez—but not a martyr, of course!

Anita la cubana

Anita stood staring at herself in the mirror in the school bathroom. The image looking back was frowning. "I'm *not* a child," Anita said aloud. She angled her body a bit sideways and pulled down on the blouse of the mustard-coloured uniform all the kids at her school wore. Even though her breasts were small, her friends told her she looked at least sixteen. She combed her hair, refastened her tortoise shell barrette and put on some lipstick which she rarely wore because it made her lips feel weird.

The bathroom door opened and Marci stuck her head in. "C'mon gorgeous, you can preen and admire yourself later. It's time to go outside for the general assembly."

Juniors, seniors, teachers, the school secretary, the janitor—all were gathered outside. Sprawling on the ground, the students were in constant motion, fidgeting, yelling to friends and horsing around while waiting for the guest speaker to appear. A boy sitting behind Anita tugged at her neckerchief. She slapped his hand away. The girlfriends she was sitting with bent their heads together, gossiping about teachers and school romances, but Anita wasn't listening. She pulled her blouse loose from her pleated skirt. There were a few large trees around the school, but her class was sitting in the full sun. "*¡Caramba! ¡Qué calor!* It's so darn hot!" Anita complained, lifting her hair away from her neck and fanning herself with a notebook.

"Anita . . . Anita . . ." Mario's voice. She looked around, but couldn't see him. A shrill whistle. "Anita . . . over here . . ." Now she saw him; he had risen up on his knees several metres away. "Catch," he called, and threw a balled up piece of paper. She caught it neatly. *Meet me after school. I need to talk to you about something.* Just then, a buzz of voices rippled through the crowd as the principal appeared with a slim black woman wearing the olive green pants, shirt and cap of the civilian militia. Speaking into a microphone, *señora* Sanchez called for silence, then introduced the speaker.

"Students, this is *compañera* Lourdes García, a member of the Federation of Cuban Women. She is here to talk to you about the National Literacy Campaign we have all been hearing so much about. I know what *compañera* Lourdes has to say will interest and inspire you. Please give her a warm welcome." When the clapping died down, *compañera* Lourdes began to speak.

"Of the six million people in Cuba today, almost a quarter of the adult population can't read or write. Many are the descendants of former slaves. Working mostly in agriculture on sugar cane and coffee plantations, they live in poverty and ignorance as they have for hundreds of years. Then there are the half million children or youth your age who have never gone to school—either because there are no schools where they live, or because their parents pulled them out of school because they need them to work to help put food on the table. These poor, illiterate men, women and children are the forgotten people of Cuba."

As *compañera* Lourdes gestured with her hands, Anita saw she had long nails painted scarlet, just like her mother. *What would mamá look like in that uniform*? she wondered. She pictured her mother as a paper doll; imagined dressing her in the full militia-style uniform, even the boots. No matter how hard she folded and pressed the tabs to hold the clothing on, everything kept falling off.

"Cuba wants to give these forgotten people a chance," the *compañera* was saying. Anita felt a flush different than the sun's heat, feeling ashamed that Tomasa and the other household servants couldn't even print their own names.

"You know that Prime Minister Castro announced to the United Nations in New York that Cuba would be a territory free from illiteracy by the end of 1961. It's already March. What can we do?" The *compañera's* voice became intense, speaking slowly, emphasizing each word. "Anyone who can read and write can become the teacher of someone who wants to learn. But even if hundreds volunteer, that's not enough to teach a million adults to read and write before this year is over. To teach that many people we need tens of thousands of volunteers." Again she paused, her eyes sweeping the crowd. Anita stopped fanning herself and held her breath. Everyone around Anita leaned forward a little, drawn to the *compañera's* voice like iron filings to a magnet.

The *compañera* paced back and forth, speaking slowly, pronouncing each word with great emphasis. "Each one of you can be a teacher, yet many of you have not signed up. We know your parents fear for your safety, but you can reassure them everything within our power will be done to guarantee your well-being and safety." She began pointing at random, her polished fingernails glinting in the sunlight. "Will you volunteer?" the *compañera* asked. "Will you? Will you?"

Anita knew that people who bad-mouthed the revolution would make fun of this kind of speech-making. Even her parents would probably call it propaganda, but she didn't care. She wanted to shout, "I will volunteer," but she couldn't. She bit her lower lip and crumpled the note in her hand. All around her students were rising to their feet, chanting *¡Viva Cuba!* Long Live Cuba! Anita jumped up and joined in the chanting. *¡Viva! ¡Viva! ¡Viva!*

In the crush of students heading back into the school, Anita had only one thought: *How can I get mamá and papá to agree to let me go?* No one could concentrate in class the rest of the day. The big excitement was the news that school would let out early in April, and that Varadero Beach Resort would be the volunteer teacher training centre. She felt sadder than ever, thinking that so many kids she knew would be going and she would be left behind.

When school let out, Anita hesitated in the doorway. Groups of noisy students streamed past her as she scanned the yard for Mario. She spotted him leaning up against a tree, alone for a change. He tweaked her ear in greeting, and they headed off toward the ocean a few blocks away. Young banyan trees lined the sidewalk. Their deep shade provided relief from the heat that rose off the pavement which was heaved up crookedly in places by the trees' twisting, swelling roots. Anita waited for Mario to begin, but she already had a good idea what he wanted to talk to her about.

"Anita, I've definitely decided to volunteer as a *brigadista*. I'd like to get away from home for awhile."

"How will you get them to consent, Mario? You know how they feel."

"The murder of Conrado Benitez was one horrible incident," Mario said. "Not everyone who hates the revolution will go around killing literacy teachers. And you heard the *compañera*. There'll be tens of thousands of volunteers—safety in numbers, Anita. I know mamá and papá will give me a hard time, so that's why I wanted to tell you first.

I need you to back me up, to confirm what the *compañera* said about guaranteeing our safety."

Anita picked up some twigs and began breaking them into small pieces.

"Do you think they will let both of us go?"

"Give it up, Anita. Celebrating a daughter's *quinceañera* is a big deal, so they're set on it. Besides, fourteen is pretty young!"

"Young! You sound just like papá. And you're always treating me like a child too. The *compañera* didn't say anything about age restrictions, did she?" She stopped walking and grasped two thick air roots descending from the branches of a banyan tree, the vines twisted around each other like giant dreadlocks. Leaning backwards, she let herself sway.

"Mario, if you want me to stick up for you, you're going to have to help me too."

When they were almost home, Mario asked Anita for a straight answer. "Will you back me up, or not?" Anita stopped and placed herself directly in front of him.

"Do you agree that men and women should be treated equally?"

"I suppose so."

"Then do *you* think I should be allowed to volunteer?"

"I guess so."

"Then let's make a deal," said Anita. "We both go, or neither of us goes. What do you say?"

"Do I have to sign in blood somewhere, little sister?"

ROADBLOCKS

"**N**o! And that's final!"

Mario didn't get past saying "Anita and I want to seriously discuss volunteering . . . " when their father interrupted with those stern words. Mario stood up from the dining room table so abruptly, his chair tipped, crashing noisily as it hit the terrazzo floor.

"That's unfair. No discussion, no nothing! If you don't give your permission, I'll find a way to go without your consent!" he yelled, his face red with anger. He left the table and stomped upstairs.

"Mario is right," said Anita. "You're being very unfair. Don't you care how we feel or what we want?"

"We know your feelings are sincere, Anita, but our duty is to protect you and Mario from harm. We can't allow you to put your lives in harm's way just because you *want* to do something," her father reasoned.

"We'll probably be the only students who don't volunteer, except for *gusano* kids. People will probably think *we* are *gusanos*." Anita's eyes flashed lightning bolts at her parents.

"Anita, what a terrible thing to say!" blurted her mother.

"Maybe you are *gusanos*!" Anita shot back as she fled the dining room.

"Anita! Come back here right now!"

Anita ignored her father's command and ran upstairs, flinging her bedroom door shut. She half expected one or both of her parents to follow her upstairs to bawl her out and demand an apology, but no one did. *They must be really angry*, Anita thought. *But I'm angry too.* "I'm not going to apologize," she announced to the closed door.

When her anger had cooled, she tiptoed down the hall and poked her head into Mario's room. "Mario, let's take it easy it for a couple of days, then try again." Mario didn't look up from his *Deportes* magazine, but he nodded.

It was a fine February day, warm and sunny, so the family was having lunch on the patio. Nobody had much to say to each other. Everyone was feeling the tension. Even Tomasa seemed to be tiptoeing around as she served the table. The clinking of cutlery against plates sounded embarrassingly loud in the awkward silences, so Anita was taken by surprise when Mario asked mamá and papá to wait just as they were rising from the table to go inside.

"Papá, I can understand your concern for our safety if we joined the campaign, but . . ."

"Mario, where is this conversation leading?" demanded their father, sitting down again and taking off his glasses.

"To the fact, papá, that thousands of kids from all over Cuba *have* signed up as volunteer teachers, which means *their parents* have signed consent forms. And I'm sure those parents are just as concerned about their kids' safety as you are," said Mario. Papá started to say something, but Mario interrupted him.

"Please, let me say what I want to say, papá. It's natural for parents to fear for their kids, but a *compañera* from the Federation of Cuban Women spoke at school the other day. She said many thousands more volunteers are needed to do the job if Cuba is to become a literate country. She said that everything possible would be done to protect us from any danger, isn't that right, Anita?"

Anita didn't get a chance to answer. Their father laughed—a cold, humourless laugh.

"Don't be ridiculous, Mario! Those are just words. It's not possible to protect you at all times." He turned to confront Anita. "And you? Would you really disappoint your mother and me by not being home for your *quinceañera*?"

"Is the party for you or for me?" Anita asked, looking pointedly at her mother. She could see that her words hurt her mother, and regretted having been so cheeky. She rushed to apologize. "I'm sorry. I know the *quinceañera* is important to you both . . . the tradition and everything. But at school, they say the country needs us. Isn't that more important than all the fuss and fanciness of one girl's coming-of-age party?"

Mamá had been letting their father do the talking, but now she stood up abruptly. Signalling them to wait, she went into the house, her high heels clicking on the flagstones. When she returned she held up the morning paper, pointing to the front page headline.

Bomb destroys section of El Encanto department store

"Practically every day there's news like this about counter-revolutionary activity," she said. "Last week it was an explosion near the Pepsi-Cola plant. Do you really expect us to let you be exposed to such danger?" Mamá levelled a stern look at both her offspring. "It may seem to you that we're out of step with the revolution, but regardless of what other parents are doing, our answer is the same as before: N - O."

"Consider the matter at an end," said papá quietly, putting on his glasses and leaving the table. Anita and Mario sat at the table, not looking at each other, not looking at anything.

"They'll never consent, Anita. They've made up their minds absolutely."

"We can't give up yet, Mario. There are things that we can still do to convince them."

"Like what? Have you got a magic wand that changes minds?"

"*Señora* Sanchez told me she would talk to them, and maybe *compañera* Lourdes would be willing to speak to them."

"Papá will tell them to mind their own business, and then they'll be even more furious with us," countered Mario. With that, he stood up and went inside. Anita heard the front door slam as Mario left the house.

Anita was still sitting at the table thinking when Tomasa came out to clear the lunch things away. As Anita stood up to leave, Tomasa spoke to her quietly while stacking dirty dishes onto a tray.

"Anita, come into the kitchen for a minute."

"Anita, you and Mario can't blame your parents for worrying about your safety. That's no reason to be so nasty." Anita felt embarrassed, remembering the words accusing her parents of being *gusanos* flying hotly from her mouth.

"But both my parents are way out of step with things Tomasa," Anita said, "especially mamá . . . her country-club life and the things she cares about."

"I don't hear her say anything so terrible," said Tomasa, looking sideways at Anita as she washed dishes. Anita reflected for a minute on all the talk heard everywhere about the "new revolutionary woman" and the "new revolutionary man." *My mother is far from being a role model for the "new revolutionary woman"*, she thought.

"Mamá has a university education, Tomasa, but has she ever worked? No! She mostly just flits around with her country club friends. Not that papá is exactly a model for the *"new man"* either. He does what he has always done—work, come home, read, play tennis or golf weekends at the club. But at least he thinks about things and discusses things with me—important things. But mamá . . . "

"Anita, you shouldn't be bad-mouthing your mother. Look at you. You've got everything a girl could possibly want, isn't that right?"

"Yes I have, but that doesn't make everything else right. What about you, Tomasa—and Gladis and Fernando? Not only will mamá and papá not let Mario and I volunteer to teach people to read and write, but they don't seem to care that there are three illiterate people right in our own house."

Tomasa dried her hands on her apron. "It would be great to be able to read and write, but I don't agree with you making your parents unhappy, calling them names and carrying on the way you and Mario are doing."

"Anyway Tomasa, if it ends up that I can't become a *brigadista*, I promise I'll spend the whole summer teaching you how to read and write—and Gladis and Fernando too, if they want." The door from the dining room swung open and Anita's mother entered telling Tomasa that she and Daniel were going out. Anita flushed, wondering if her mother had overheard any of the conversation.

"Anita, there's Marci's neighbour, *señora* Moore and her girls," said mamá. Anita looked up from the *Bohemia* magazine she was reading, following the direction of her mother's gaze. "I believe this is the first time I've seen her here at the club. You've met *señora* Moore, haven't you?" mamá asked.

"Yes, I have. Marci introduced me to her. She's a *gringa.*" Anita watched as Marjorie settled herself and her daughters in lounge chairs on the opposite side of the pool. "Marci told me she teaches English at the Medical School. She actually speaks Spanish quite well for a *gringa.*" When Marjorie happened to glance their way, she waved at them. Anita and mamá waved back. Anita returned to her magazine.

"Mamá, could we invite *señora* Moore and her family over to dinner? Marci says they're really nice."

"I hardly know *señora* Moore, Anita. We were introduced to her and her husband at a party once, but . . ."

"Wouldn't you like to make some new friends? *Señora* Moore seems really nice, mamá, and you'll love the girls. They're so lively!"

"Well . . . alright," mamá said, rising. "*De todas maneras, esta sería para mí una buena oportunidad de practicar conversación en inglés.* And it will give me an opportunity to practice conversation in English."

April 2, 1961

Dear Diary,

IT WORKED! The Ríos family came to dinner yesterday. When mamá and papá learned that Marjorie and the girls had joined the Literacy Campaign, mamá and papá started asking her and señor Ríos lots of questions. It was a really great discussion! Señor Ríos said that yes, there were risks involved, but the important thing was to "keep one's eyes on the big picture." He said the risks for any one brigadista or supervisor were small while the benefits for the whole country were huge. Then Marjorie said, "I think this literacy campaign will change Cuba's future in fantastic ways that we can't yet foresee, and I want my girls to be part of that." When she said that, mamá and papá looked at each other in a strange way. Then tonight at dinner, mamá and papá told Mario and I that they had talked to Marjorie about us, and that they would give their consent IF AND ONLY IF we consented to be part of Marjorie's group and AGREED TO COOPERATE WITH HER IN EVERY WAY. Mario and I said we would swear to that on a stack of Bibles and within two minutes our consent forms were signed. I'm pretty sure that mamá and papá never guessed that Mario and I asked Marjorie to be at the pool, and that our plan was to get mamá to invite her for dinner.

I sort of knew what made papá change his mind, but I just had to ask mamá what made her change hers. She told me that she came downstairs after our argument the other day to talk to Tomasa and overheard what I was telling Tomasa in the kitchen— about me feeling she was out-of-step and that she was not a good role model for me in these special times. She said she had felt ashamed. I am so happy! So Mario and I will be soon be off to Varadero for teacher training.

Faithfully yours,
Anita la cubana

The next big news about the literacy campaign was that almost seventy thousand young people, mostly teenagers, had volunteered so far, and that all high schools in Cuba would close early on April fifteenth. Each night, Anita put a big red X through the date on her calendar before going to bed. She pestered her teachers. "Can you tell us anything about teacher training? When will we leave for Varadero?"

"We don't know yet. Be patient," was always the reply. But how could she be patient?

April 14, 1961

Dear Diary,

It's been ages since I last opened your pages. I am very excited because tomorrow is the last day of school. Some kids leave for teacher training camp at Varadero Beach right away, but our district doesn't leave until sometime in May. When I leave, it will be the last time I see Marci, unless her family decides to come back to Cuba or I go to visit her in the United States. Lots of people are still leaving Cuba. Papá says it's because they are scared of the revolution, of what the future will bring. It seems so many doctors have left, that Cuba must hire doctors from other countries. Marci is giving me a whole bunch of stuff she loves but can't take with her because people leaving Cuba for good can only take one suitcase each. They can't sell their houses either. There's so much I just don't get. It's going to be awful saying goodbye to Marci when I leave for Varadero. When will I see her again?

Anita la cubana

INVASION!

A nita was jolted out of a dream by a terrific noise. She leaped out of bed and ran to her parent's bedroom. They were already out in the hallway with Mario, disheveled but wide awake.

"Was that a plane? It sounded like a plane flying very low."

"I expected to hear a crash," said Mario.

"*¡Dios mío!* Dear God, I hope nothing horrible is happening!" exclaimed mamá.

The sound of excited voices filtered through the closed shutters. Mamá wound open the slats of the nearest shutter and the voices became clear, all yelling the same thing: "What's happening? Is it an attack?" The questions were answered by distant sounds—a loud but dull *GRUMP GRUMP*, like explosions, then bursts of stuttering ack-ack-ack. Looking out the window through the slats, Anita saw everyone disappearing into their houses at a run, shouting "*¡Bombardeo! ¡Bombardeo!* An attack! Bombs are dropping!"

"Everyone downstairs quickly!" papá shouted.

Tomasa appeared from her room off the kitchen, her eyes wide with fear. They huddled together in a ground floor hallway where there were no windows, straining to listen. More explosive bursts, more staccato ack-ack-ack.

"That's definitely anti-aircraft fire," said papá.

The frightening sounds got no closer. Finally, there was silence. Mario started to stand up, but papá pulled him down, saying they should wait. After a long period of silence, they stood. Anita's legs felt stiff and shaky. They gathered around the radio in the living room.

"B-26 bombers disguised in the colours and insignia of the Cuban National Air Force made air strikes at dawn today on Cuban territory. Three airports were targeted: Campo Libertad in the suburb of Marianao in Havana, San Antonio de Los Baños, and Antonio Maceo International Airport in Santiago de Cuba. Several bombs were dropped. Anti-aircraft fire from the ground hit the invading planes, but the aircraft were able to fly away. At this time we can report there were no human casualties. Five Cuban aircraft were destroyed on the ground.

The country is in a state of national alert. Stay inside your homes, follow emergency preparedness procedures, and await further notice."

Regular radio programs were cancelled, replaced by classical music which followed the announcement. Papá turned the volume down and they all sat in stunned silence. Campo Libertad was a mere few miles from where they were sitting. San Antonio de Los Baños was just beyond the outskirts of the city. Questions whirled in Anita's head. *Would the planes return? Who is doing this to us?* Anita knew it was useless to ask questions her parents couldn't answer. But one question burned on her tongue.

"Why does whoever is dropping bombs hate us so much?"

Papa's answer was brief, the same answer that explained all the bad things happening since the dictator Batista had fled and the revolutionary government had taken power.

"There are people who want Cuba back. They want things the way they were before the revolution."

But who are "they"? Cuban rebels? The United States which had declared Cuba their enemy? Whoever "they" were, they dropped bombs. Anita's head ached.

The whole day was one big headache. Her parents hadn't paid any attention to emergency preparedness for anything—not household first aid, not hurricanes or tidal waves—never mind bombs dropping. They scurried around preparing for the scary, the unthinkable. Mario put together a first aid kit using his old Boy Scout instructions. Anita brought bedding downstairs and helped Tomasa make sandwiches and put other food and jars of water in baskets. *Some picnic!* Anita thought. Mamá and papá wrapped up some of their valuables and put them in a lock-box. Mamá was fiercely angry, and walked around the house much of the time without purpose, swearing at whoever was responsible for causing such distress. Papá's stress showed in his lips, stretched thin and bunched tight at the corners.

The radio and TV was on all day repeating the same news. The phone rang constantly with relatives and friends wanting to discuss the bombing, asking the same unanswerable questions. Marci wasn't allowed to come over. Anita wasn't allowed to go to Marci's. Anita and Mario played cards, then dominoes, then Monopoly. They read, they ate, then read some more, all the while their minds and ears tuned to the sky, like antennas . . . listening, listening . . .

"Go to bed, Anita. It's late," mamá said.

Go to bed and just lie there listening? Go to bed and remember the sound of a plane flying low over the rooftops to drop bombs near you, maybe on you, tonight or tomorrow. . . . "But mamá . . ."

"No buts Anita. Go to bed. There is nothing else we can do. Go to bed and try not to worry."

Mamá hugged Anita close, and papá kissed her forehead, cradling her head between his warm hands. Light shone under the closed door of Mario's room. Knocking, Anita called out, "*Buenas noches. Hasta mañana hermano*, Good night, brother. See you in the morning." *That's right. Be optimistic.*

Anita opened her diary, wrote the date — April 15, 1961— but felt too depressed to write anything. She told herself to close her eyes, to stop straining her ears to listen. *Try to remember that dream you were having before the plane woke you. What was it? Oh yes . . . Marjorie was introducing me and Mario to the people we would be teaching. Everyone was smiling and shaking hands.*

April 16, 1961
Dear Diary,

No planes. No more bombing. Papá brought the radio to his bedroom and left it on all night in case there were emergency alerts. Now we know ex-Cubans living in the United States flew the planes. There are rumours of an invasion. Everybody's scared. Marci and I talk on the phone every couple of hours. She is very upset because her parents actually hope there is an invasion, and that Cuba will surrender. I wish she could just come and live with us. Papá went to his office. Mamá is very nervous and doesn't know what to do with herself. Mario goes around cursing the damn gusanos. Yesterday was supposed to be the official launching day of the literacy campaign. There was supposed to be a special event but of course it couldn't happen. I couldn't sleep very well so I started reading Cimarrón, a story about a runaway slave.

Anita la cubana

April 17, 1961
Dear Diary,

I am writing this watching TV. What is happening is unbelievable! Ex-Cubans from the U.S. invaded Cuba at the Bay of Pigs near Playa

Girón. They landed on the beaches during the night. There is fighting, people being killed. I feel sick and scared. Mamá can't stop crying. A horrible thing is that the invaders destroyed some schools and took some teachers hostage. How scared they must be! I don't know if any kids were hurt, or worse. On the TV it showed a school with machine gun bullet holes in the walls and blackboards.

Anita la cubana

April 18, 1961

Dear Diary,

The fighting is still going on, but the news says many of the invaders have been captured. Papá says that Cuba will defeat the invaders. Many Cubans have been killed, soldiers and ordinary people. No one says how many. There are lots of bad thoughts running around in my head. Right now, I hate those ex-Cubans.

Anita la cubana

April 19, 1961

Dear Diary,

At last the invasion is over after three days of fighting! A lot of people died. The invaders are all ex-Cubans. On TV I saw them being marched away as prisoners. The news says fifteen hundred men invaded, 114 were killed, and the rest were captured. Papá says they were armed with U.S. weapons. Lots of Cubans died defending Cuba, at least 2000. The literacy campaign is not being cancelled, only delayed for a while. Mamá and papá are begging Mario and me not to go to teacher training in Varadero—not to be part of the campaign at all. I confess I feel nervous, Dear Diary. I keep thinking of the blackboard with bullet holes in it. What if there's another invasion? But then Mario and I talked about it, and both of us are determined to go. Mamá comes to my room and kisses me before she goes to bed, just like she did when I was little. War! Fighting! Killing! I hate it all!

Anita la cubana

THE ADVENTURE BEGINS

As soon as Anita opened her eyes, she jumped out of bed even though the clock on her bedside table showed it was only six o'clock. *Varadero, here I come!* She stuffed her small pillow and toiletries into her packed duffel bag. *I'm on my way*, she thought. *The adventure is really beginning.*

"Be careful, Anita. Look out for yourself," Tomasa whispered as she embraced her. When Tomasa told Mario to look after his sister, he just rolled his eyes. When it was time to leave, all eyes were moist except Mario's.

Banyan Tree Park was the appointed gathering place for student volunteers from Miramar. Hundreds of volunteers and their families and friends were streaming toward the park, pouring in from every direction. Anita walked ahead of her family. Only eight o'clock in the morning, and it was already hot, her neck sweaty under her lank hair. As they neared the park, the movement and sound was like a swarm of bees. Hundreds of young people and their families milled about, waiting for word to board the waiting transport trucks that would take the volunteers to Varadero to begin the crash course in teacher training. Anita pushed through the crowd toward the band shell where they had arranged to meet Marjorie and her girls. When Pam and Suzi spotted Anita approaching, they ran forward, each grabbing one of her hands. Marjorie introduced Anita and her family to Dani, an older girl who would also be part of Marjorie's group. Tall and slim, she carried a guitar slung across her back, had short, honey-coloured curls and cinnamon-coloured freckles closely dotting her face and arms. *¡Caramba! Is she ever pretty!* thought Anita.

"Nervous? Excited?" Dani asked, turning to Anita and Mario.

"A little." Anita said. "Maybe more excited than nervous. I can hardly wait to get started."

"And you, Mario?" said Dani. Mario was about to answer when a couple of his friends tackled him and carried him off a short distance.

"Boys!" said Dani. "Is Mario a good brother?"

"He's actually great!" said Anita. "Sort of macho, but then, my mother says practically all Cuban males are macho." Anita wondered why none of Dani's family had come to see her off, but felt that asking would be rude. Anita and Dani tried to talk, but Pam and Suzi chattered at them non-stop. Eventually an official began a speech from the bandstand. Even though there were loudspeakers, Anita could hardly understand anything because of the underlying buzz of so many voices.

"Did you understand what we're supposed to do, Dani?" she asked.

Before Dani could respond, Marjorie said, "Just stick with me, Anita. Don't get separated. Where's Mario?"

"He was here a minute ago," said Anita, craning her neck to look for him.

Dani rolled her eyes at Anita when someone else started another speech about how proud everyone should be of the student volunteers. A full head taller than Anita, Dani bent her head toward her conspiratorially.

"We already know we're terrific, don't we? So just let us get going, right?"

Anita giggled, admiring the older girl. When a band began to play the national anthem, people stopped babbling and sang. Then the words Anita was waiting for came bellowing over the loudspeaker.

"Volunteers and supervisors, proceed to the transport trucks."

Mario suddenly reappeared. Hugging mamá and papá, he promised to write, then disappeared into the mob of people heading toward the waiting trucks and buses. Observing mamá's and papá's anxious faces, Marjorie told them not to worry. "I'll be keeping track of him in Varadero," she assured them.

"Well, Anita, I guess you're on your own," said papá, "just in case you thought your big brother intended to stick by you."

"I'll be all right," said Anita. "Besides being with Marjorie, there are lots of kids going that I know. And now there's Dani," she said, smiling at her. She hoped Dani would sit with her on the transport.

Anita opened her arms wide and enjoyed a warm embrace with her parents. Foreheads touching, they stood for a long moment, a small pod of quiet in the noisy crowd. She pictured her parents sitting alone at the dinner table and thought how still her house would be now. "Just think about all the nice adult conversations you two can have at dinner while we're away," she said brightly. Both parents pretended to smile. Anita kissed them both, took her duffel bag from her father and headed off with Dani, Marjorie and the girls. *You promised yourself you wouldn't cry, so don't look back,* Anita told herself.

"Have your consent forms ready," she heard being repeated as she neared the trucks. Anita showed hers then climbed aboard the open back of one of the waiting trucks. The noise of the idling motors, everyone talking and parents yelling last-minute advice and goodbyes as the trucks pulled out was deafening.

Anita sat on her duffel bag next to Dani, crammed among dozens of teens. Ahead and behind, all she could see were trucks full of volunteers. The route took them east along the *Malecón.* Hundreds of people stood or sat on the wide sea wall, their backs to the ocean, waving as the trucks rolled past. Passing the billboard of the young teacher in the beret, Anita thought, *That's me now.* She wondered where Mario was in the convoy of trucks. *Will we be lodged anywhere close to each other during teacher training? Maybe Mario won't want to have anything to do with me in Varadero. He'll be making new friends. It's always so easy for him.*

Someone started singing *Elena La Cumbanchera,* and soon everyone was singing. Pam and Suzi sang loudly, their eyes shining. Banners and flags about the literacy campaign were on display everywhere. Leaving the wide *Malecón,* people still lined the streets, waving as the trucks of singing volunteers passed. Vehicles honked their horns. Anita waved till she couldn't wave anymore. Once Havana was behind them, the convoy of trucks barrelled east along the *Carretera Central,* the Central Highway. Anita's hair whipped about her face, and she had to squint against the brilliant Cuban sun. Eventually everyone quieted down and settled into the ride.

"It's the first time I've ever been away from home on my own," Anita told Dani.

"I'm glad to be getting away from home," said Dani. "I need to be away from my family for awhile."

"How come?" asked Anita.

"Some of my family is *gusano.* They've been putting a lot of pressure on me to leave Cuba and go to Florida with them. But I don't want to. Since I'm eighteen, I didn't need family consent to volunteer, so I signed up to get away from all the family discussions and wrangling. Saved by the campaign!"

"Look, Dani, we're the only ones still awake." Even Marjorie was dozing, Pam and Suzi slumped against her, their bodies swaying with the motion of the truck. Anita and Dani talked a while longer, until they too surrendered to drowsiness. Closing her eyes, Marci's face floated into Anita's mind. They both had cried a lot when saying goodbye yesterday.

"I'll write as soon as I get to my assignment," Anita had promised. They had exchanged keepsakes. She had given Marci a gold friendship ring, and Marci had given her a little heart-shaped silver locket on a chain. Inside the locket was a tiny picture of Marci's face. Brushing away some silent tears, Anita fingered the locket, wondering if she and Marci would ever see each other again. Her final thought before falling asleep was a feeling of pleasure that the pretty eighteen-year-old at her side had treated her as a peer, not a child.

Everyone was hot and bedraggled by the time they arrived at Varadero. The deep turquoise waters of the sea and the powdery white sand beach stretched before them. Everyone was wishing they could get into bathing suits and throw themselves headlong into the water, but they had to line up and wait to find out where they would be lodged. Mario showed up to tell them he was assigned to one of the big hotels where all the guest rooms had been turned into dormitories for boys.

"See you around ladies," Mario called out over his shoulder as he left.

"I don't think we'll be seeing much of Mario while we're here," Marjorie observed to no one in particular. Marjorie and her charges and three other girls were assigned to share a cabana beach house. Dominga, a girl Anita's own age, was from Guantánamo, a town on the far eastern shore of the island. Vanesa and Vera were identical twins from the city of Cameg̈uey.

"We're so lucky to get a beach house rather than having to be in one of the hotels!" Anita exclaimed, as they explored the rooms.

"OK gals, Pam and Suzi will stay with me in the downstairs bedroom," said Marjorie. "Figure out your sleeping arrangements, get your stuff organized and freshen up. We have to be ready to go to the cafeteria in the Kawama Hotel in half an hour for orientation."

Anita had hoped Dani would room with her, but neither of them wanted to seem as though they were snubbing anyone, so Dani was bunking in the other bedroom with the twins. Anita and Dominga stowed their stuff quickly, then went to see what the others were up to. What a laugh! Each twin had taped her name above the bed. "So you will know who you are waking up in the morning," they said, grinning identically. Just as the girls started chatting to get to know one another, Pam and Suzi came running up the stairs shouting, "*Apúrense, muchachas!* Hurry up! Mamá says it's time to go."

Hotel Kawama was one of the many hotels placed into service for the literacy campaign. There were no hotel guests, only swarms of young people. All the furnishings and large exotic plants in the airy, elegant lobby had been pushed to the perimeter to make room for the hordes of students pushing through to the cafeteria and dining rooms that now looked more like camp mess halls. Marjorie and the girls joined hundreds of volunteers and supervisors standing in long lines waiting their turn for food to be dished out by serving staff wearing long white aprons, their hair tucked into thick brown hairnets. Anita held her hands over her ears against the clang and clatter of dishes and cutlery and the din of a multitude of voices talking and laughing at once.

"Get used to it, *muchacha*," Dani said. "This is what it's going to be like living in an ant colony for the next while."

Anita ate and drank with gusto. After the tables were cleared, class locations, schedules and rules were explained over microphones. The room filled with groans. Breakfast at 7:30 am. No skipping classes. Everyone in their lodgings by 8 pm. No exceptions. No visiting after that. Lights out by 10 pm. Anita tried to listen, but couldn't stop yawning. Dani had to poke her once because she had actually fallen asleep. When free time was declared at last, everyone shouted, "*Vamos a la playa*! To the beach!"

Hours later, awake in bed after such a long and exciting day, Anita appreciated the stillness of the night. The constant shush, shush of the wavelets lapping the beach was the only sound except for Dominga's open-mouthed snuffling. *Classes start in the morning. I can hardly wait until we get our uniforms. Oh no! In uniforms, I'll never be able to tell the twins apart!*

The Year of Education,
May 6, 1961

Dearest mamá and papá,

We are lodged in a great cabana with three other girls. It's crowded with extra cots and all our stuff. There are more than 5000 kids in Varadero right now, and when we leave, thousands more will come. I'm learning so much about other parts of Cuba from all these kids. Most of them seem to be fifteen or sixteen but there are some older. And would you believe there is one girl here who is just ten? ¡Caramba! Some of the kids are from really remote villages and have never seen modern appliances. At first some thought the oven was a TV. Some kids even used the bidet like a toilet. ¡Dios mío! Actually, we are using our bidet to wash clothes in. All of Varadero is one huge training centre—75 large mansions, all the elegant hotels and their ballrooms, the cabarets and gambling rooms—all are being used to turn us into an army of literacy teachers. Would you believe even the former brothels are being used! (I'm blushing). 9 dining halls and 800 cooks are feeding us, but the food is only so-so—not like Tomasa's. I haven't seen Mario since I arrived, but I will soon. I have to end now—it's time to go to breakfast. I miss you, but not a lot. Just kidding. Love to Tomasa.

Lots of love from brigadista-in-training, Anita.

After breakfast, the large group that Anita was part of gathered in the huge lobby of Hotel Kawama. As they entered the makeshift classroom, each volunteer received a new workbook and a pen inscribed with the words *Brigada Conrado Benitez*. Anita and her housemates chose seats among the hundreds of metal folding chairs placed in long rows. Tropical heat streamed in the huge windows facing the beach, so soon workbooks were being used as fans while waiting for the instructors to arrive. Anita coiled her hair up off her neck and used the pen to hold it in place. Eventually a man and a woman appeared at the front of the room. The man spoke into a microphone.

"Hello everyone. We are your instructors. My name is René, and this is Leila. Our job is to teach you how to teach illiterate people. We hope you will not waste our time or your own because time is short and the task is big. Tomorrow we will begin using the actual teaching materials, but this morning we are going to talk about "trust". You cannot just walk into people's lives and start teaching literacy, no matter how much technique you learn. So this morning we'll discover together what you must first do so that your learners will be *willing* learners; so that they will be ready to put their trust in "you"—this young person who calls himself or herself a teacher. I want you to quickly arrange your chairs into groups of ten or so. Someone in each group please volunteer to take notes. You are to discuss the obstacles and problems you might expect to arise with the people you'll be teaching, whoever and wherever that may be—in a country *bohío*, in a home in town or in an improvised classroom in a community. You've got 30 minutes. Get to it."

Chairs were soon scraped noisily into position. "I'll take notes," volunteered Anita. For the next while, everyone forgot about the heat.

"Relating to illiterate adults will not be easy," an older boy started off. "First of all because we are young, and secondly, because they will probably be embarrassed about being illiterate." Someone else said many of the illiterates might think they couldn't learn because they were too old. *Just like Tomasa*, Anita thought, writing as fast as she could. Then a girl said if the illiterate people were poor, they might be embarrassed about strangers coming into their homes and seeing how poor they were. Everybody nodded in agreement. The discussion was energetic, and the ideas were still popping up when the instructors called time.

Anita's stomach did flip-flops when the instructor asked each note-taker to come up to the microphone and present their group's ideas. She hoped she would be able to read her own writing. When it was her turn, Marjorie gave her an encouraging look. Somehow, she managed to get through it, and as she returned to her chair, Marjorie mouthed the words, "Well done."

Some groups had gotten off-topic, so the room rocked with laughter at some of the things people had come up with. "What if there is no place to sleep?" "Is it forbidden to date a learner?" "Will it be OK if we don't bathe every day if there is no running water or if there is a shortage of water?" The instructors couldn't help but laugh too.

"Some questions may seem funny," Leila said, "but they all need answering. At lunch, you'll be told where to get your uniforms so return here dressed as *brigadistas*. We'll form into groups again and start to develop approaches and solutions to the problems you have identified this morning."

"Oh no! Look how long the lines are, Dani!" Anita stared, open-mouthed, at the enormous piles of uniforms stacked metres high against a wall. Shuffling forward slowly, the lines advanced toward long tables where people stood issuing uniforms and boots. "Make sure you get boots that fit," Marjorie cautioned her group. "You won't be very effective teachers if your mind is focused on painful blisters." Kids leaving balanced a pile of stuff in their arms and wore grins on their faces. At long last, Anita stood at the table before the stacks.

"What size?" said the man.

"Size nine," said Anita shyly. "No, size ten. I might grow," she added, blushing.

"Good thinking," said the man. He turned away and returned with two pair of heavy grey cotton pants and two military style grey shirts.

"Shoe size?" he asked.

"Seven and a half."

"No half sizes. Seven or eight?" he said.

Thinking of blisters, she opted for size eight even though they would make her feet look big or require her to wear two pairs of socks. The man returned with a pair of high-top black army-style boots, two pairs of khaki socks, an olive-green beret, a belt, a small backpack, a hammock and a wool blanket. Then, from a box, he took a metal medallion and two badges embroidered with the words, *Brigada Conrado Benitez,* and placed them on top of the pile. "Pin the medallion to the shirt, and sew the badges to the right epaulet of your shirts," he said. "You're all set, *señorita. Suerte,* Good luck. Next," he called out.

"There's so much to absorb! I feel like my head is spinning," Anita confessed to Marjorie one evening.

"I've been observing you, Anita. You have natural smarts, so you'll do just fine." Anita felt better knowing Marjorie had confidence in her, but still felt jumpy. The next time she saw Mario she told him about feeling nervous.

"Hey, where's the motor-mouth kid that convinced her parents that she was going to be the best *brigadista* going? And if someone gives you a hard time, tell them they'll have to deal with your big, tough brother," replied Mario.

"Oh sure! But what about you? Aren't you the least bit nervous?"

"A little, but knowing that we'll be getting together with teaching supervisors every week makes me feel a lot better."

"Isn't it great that we'll be together to help one another, Mario?" said Anita, offering him a bite of her popsicle.

"Actually I would rather be assigned as far away from my little sister as possible," he said, already raising his arms in self defense.

"Smart ass!" declared Anita, dropping the remains of her popsicle down the back of Mario's shirt.

The Year of Education
May 10, 1961

Dear mamá and papá,

When I last wrote you, I didn't know we would only be here only until May 15ᵗʰ—that's the day after Mothers Day. We have to leave to make room for the next group. Nobody knows yet where we'll be assigned or anything.

Classes are pretty intense. Our instructors tell us our success depends on us becoming part of our learners' lives "as equals". They tell us we must live as they do and be prepared to work alongside our learners when we are not teaching. If they cut cane, we cut cane. If they work in coffee plantations, so will we. If we stay on the property, we are to help the family with the garden, the children, the laundry, chopping wood—whatever. Then they will see that we are not putting ourselves above them, that they can trust us. We are even being taught how to dig latrines since there might not be one where we're assigned. Teaching time will depend on the family's work.

We have two books to use for teaching. One is a teacher's manual called WE WILL SUCCEED. It gives advice on how to teach the lessons and deal with problems. The other one is the learner's workbook. It's called LET'S LEARN TO READ AND WRITE. We have been working in small groups, taking turns being the teacher. We give each other a hard time, but it's fun. We all want to be good teachers and are getting quite excited. In fact, we are excited most of the time. Yesterday I bought a Santa Juana seed necklace just like the revolutionary fighters wore. Many of the brigadistas wear them all the time for luck.

Dani told me that before the revolution succeeded, black people couldn't be at Varadero Resort except as workers. Sharing space, talking, eating, studying and having fun with kids of every skin colour, I feel more mystified than ever about why some people are racist. I think a big experiment in integration is going on right here at Varadero.

Your loving daughter, brigadista Anita

P.S. I've seen Mario a few times. He's fine and looks very handsome in his uniform.

P.P.S. Everyone is being vaccinated against tetanus. My arm still hurts, but at least I didn't faint like some kids.

"Look at all the lanterns!" echoed voices around the room as the *brigadistas* entered the lobby for class.

"*¡Caramba!* They must be for us," said Anita. Arranged row upon row, the lanterns looked like a crowd of little people all wearing the same hat, quietly waiting for something to happen.

"The lanterns have been imported from China just for the campaign," instructor Leila explained. "It should be no surprise to you that there may be no electricity where many of you will be assigned. Some of you will have to give your classes when it's dark out, either before people go to work or after sundown when they get home. Either way, you'll need a lantern."

The lantern was seventeen or eighteen inches tall with a chrome carrying handle. A shiny chrome container held the fuel, and there was a pump to prime before lighting the wick. The glass chimney sat below a wide blue metal shade. Right at the top was a tent-shaped red cover. The instructors demonstrated how to light the lantern and take care of its parts, then everyone had to go through the drill. Everything had to be done just so, and it felt scary to Anita. A lot of kids were frustrated because they couldn't seem to get the lantern to light. Some thought it would blow up and didn't want to even touch it.

"*¡Brigadistas!*" called out the instructors. "Stop everything and listen up. Knowing how to handle this implement is important. You may be relying on it do the job you're being trained for. It's not dangerous if you do things correctly. Now calm down, take your time and learn how to do it."

When it was her turn, Anita approached the lantern gingerly. She took a deep breath, primed the pump and struck the match. Her hand was shaking, but only a little as she held the flame to the wick. *It lit! The glass didn't break. It didn't blow up! Hallelujah!*

Leila handed her a lantern. "Take good care of it, *señorita*. Treat it like a treasured friend," she said.

"Marjorie, do you already know where we'll be going? Tell us now if you do," begged Anita. The others echoed her question. Marjorie swore she didn't know. When assignment time arrived, the cafeteria was noisier than ever. The *brigadistas* just couldn't contain their excitement, so the supervisors and instructors had to shout to get everyone to quiet down. Table by table, groups were called up to a long row of tables set up at the front of the cafeteria. Each *brigadista* received a lettered and numbered cardboard hung on a cord that was to be slung about the neck on departure day. There were shouts of joy when friends found they were assigned to the same area. There were tears too as good friends and boyfriends and girlfriends realized they would be separated. Some kids clamoured to get assignments changed.

"It's our turn," said Marjorie.

Anita prayed as the woman's finger slid down the "Fs" searching for "Fonseca, Anita" on the long list. When the woman found it, she wrote BAINOA and a number on a placard. "Look for the truck and supervisor with that place name and number," she told Anita.

"Bainoa? Where's that?" Anita said, turning to Marjorie and Dani.

"It's a small town about fifty kilometres east of Havana," answered Marjorie. Anita stood looking at her card in disbelief. Only fifty kilometres! As they returned to their table trailing Marjorie, Dani told her more about Bainoa. "It's neither on the coast nor in the mountains, Anita. It's a dinky little nowhere and nothing town with no charm whatsoever," she said. Anita felt cheated. She turned to Marjorie, pleading. "Can't you get our assignment changed, Marjorie? Can't you say we are willing to go to some really remote area?"

"Girls, I know you're disappointed," said Marjorie, "but no more whining! It would be selfish to start complaining and asking for changes when organizers have such a huge job to do. We are teachers so we'll teach wherever we are needed. Even Bainoa will be an adventure," she assured them. Anita and Dani rolled their eyes.

The last day of instruction was all about the three literacy tests learners would have to take and pass before they could be counted as literate.

When it was time to be dismissed, the instructors shook everyone's hand and wished them luck as they left the big lobby that had served as their classroom. "Wish us luck too," the instructors said. "When you leave, another group of thousands will arrive. Soon our brains are going to be as mushy as rice pudding. You are lucky to have been the first group. *Suerte! Suerte!* Good luck, everyone."

That evening, an exciting rumour began to circulate: Fidel Castro himself would be in Varadero tomorrow to see the *brigadistas* off. The rumour was soon the only topic of conversation, even among those feeling upset about their assignments. At breakfast the next day, the rumour was confirmed. Workmen were already erecting a platform on the beach, and all the *brigadistas* and instructors were to gather there at 1pm.

"Have you ever seen Fidel in person?" *brigadistas* asked each other. "Will he look just like he does on TV?"

"I saw Fidel up close once," Anita told her housemates.

"Tell us about it," they demanded, crowding around her. Anita told them about the time she saw Fidel at a reception at the newspaper where her father worked.

"How close to him were you?" asked Dominga.

"Close enough to see the hairs of his beard," replied Anita.

The girls were awestruck. Everyone wondered what Cuba's leader would say to them on this historic occasion. After all, they would be the first brigade to set out across the country to teach literacy in The Year of Education.

Anita would be leaving at seven the next morning. She hadn't packed yet and her parents would be arriving any moment. She gulped breakfast and hurried back to the cabana, but no sooner had she started stuffing things into her duffel bag when Dominga shouted from downstairs, "Anita . . . your parents are at the campaign office."

Why didn't I pack when I had the time? Anita lamented as she ran to the campaign office.

As soon as Anita's mother laid eyes on her, she burst into tears. "My baby!" she blubbered.

"Some baby!" said her father. "Look how grown up she looks in that uniform!"

"Let's go find Mario," suggested Anita. "But mamá, you better take off your high heels. We'll be walking in sand." Hundreds of laughing, chattering *brigadistas* flowed by them, some greeting Anita as they passed. Anita returned their greetings gaily. Her mother suddenly stopped, a look of amazement on her face.

"What's wrong, mamá?"

"Nothing is wrong. I think I'm just beginning to grasp what you're a part of here. All these beautiful young people! It's unbelievable!"

Anita told her parents how disappointed she and Mario were to be going *just* to Bainoa; that they both had hoped for a more interesting, if not remote, location. Her father explained that Bainoa was located in a valley whose climate was notable for being the coolest in Cuba, and that the cold water from the natural springs in the region was used to make *Corona*, Cuba's best beer.

"Is that supposed to make me feel better, papá?" she said.

I will never forget this day as long as I live, Anita thought, sitting between her parents and Mario, surrounded by *brigadistas* and their families—an ocean of thousands that moved as restlessly as the ocean spread before them. Today, Mothers Day, was the last chance to be together before the *brigadistas* set off on their assignments. Waiting for Fidel to arrive and mount the stage, the *brigadistas* sang. As one song finished, someone would start another, the lyrics rippling through the throng until all had joined in. A new chant that someone had recently invented started up.

We're teachers
We're ready
Illiteracy we will fight
A million men and women
Will learn to read and write

Anita jumped to her feet with the rest, fist raised in the air, chanting with gusto. She heard her father say in a loud whisper, "Whatever happened to that quiet, reserved daughter of ours?"

"I think she's just perfect," Anita heard her mother say, and felt a rush of love.

The director of the training camp and several supervisors appeared on the platform, signalling everyone to sit down. Anita, like everyone else, strained forward in anticipation. When Fidel appeared in the familiar olive-green uniform and cap, a thunderous cheer went up.

People jumped to their feet and began to chant, *Fi-del, Fi-del, Fi-del.* It took the supervisors several minutes to get everyone to sit down again.

"As you teach," began Fidel, "you will also learn. You will probably learn much more than you teach. You can teach illiterate people what you have learned at school and here in Varadero, but they will be teaching you what they have learned from the hard life they have led. They will teach you why it was necessary to have a revolution in Cuba. From them, you will learn about the history of Cuba better than from any speech I could make, better than from any book you could read."

So restless just a few moments before, the crowd was now completely still.

"What you have volunteered to do will be tough," Fidel warned. "Most of you are sure to experience hardships, loneliness and physical risks."

Hardships, physical risks. . . . Anita purposely avoided looking at her parents, knowing how these words would affect them. But she felt thrilled. *Fidel is not treating us like children going off on a camping trip.*

". . . and it will be tough in another way," Fidel continued. "Your learners will be afraid of failure, so before you try to teach anything, you must first earn their trust and respect. I'm sure your instructors have drilled that into you. Make your learners like you. Be a sincere part of their lives. You are part of a brigade in an army of youth," Fidel concluded. "Your mission is to make Cuba a land free from illiteracy. I know you are capable of doing this job and I know that you will do it well."

Like everyone else, Anita leapt to her feet applauding, and again took up the *brigadista* chant:

We're teachers
We're ready
Illiteracy we will fight
A million men and women
Will learn to read and write
¡Venceremos! We will succeed!

At five o'clock, *brigadistas* and their families streamed toward the parking lots. The *brigadistas* had to rise early the next day, and lights out time was supposed to be earlier this night. From all directions, parents could be heard telling their kids, "Be careful! Be careful!"

"If I were young, I think I would want to be a *brigadista*. What about you, Daniel?" Anita couldn't believe her ears. *Maybe there is more to my mother under her makeup and fashionable clothes than I thought.*

"Pinch me, Anita," said Mario, laughing. "I must be dreaming. Our mother just said she'd like to be a *brigadista*."

Papá got the packages from the car that Anita and Mario had requested. "I also included boxes of chalk and a leather case for each of you containing stationery, envelopes, pens and stamps. I'm not leaving until you both promise to write once a week," mamá said. Anita and Mario looked at each other over their mother's head. "Don't start doing that stuff with your eyes. Just promise," demanded their mother.

"I won't promise to write once a week, but I promise to write," said Mario.

"Me too," added Anita.

Mamá sighed and embraced them both. Papá stuck some money in their shirt pockets, embraced them both then quickly got into the car. Anita wiped away tears with one hand while waving goodbye with the other until the green Studebaker disappeared from sight.

That night, fires lit the beach as groups gathered after lights out, talking, playing guitars and singing into the small hours. Marjorie didn't come looking for them, and the assigned watchdogs let them be. As Anita crawled into bed, she tried not to think about how soon she would have to get up.

Someone shaking her . . . Dani's voice. "Anita, wake up . . . "

"Go away!" said Anita, trying to pull the sheet over her head. "It's still dark!"

"No Anita, you've got to get up," insisted Dani, shaking her again. "We're all leaving for breakfast. If you miss breakfast you won't be eating for hours." Now all the girls were shaking her and dragging the blankets off. Anita sat upright, suddenly remembering. *Today we leave Varadero!*

"Wait for me. I'll be five minutes."

At the cafeteria Anita gulped her breakfast, then ran back to the cabana to finish packing. She heard the others return as she crammed her pajamas, toiletries bag and little pillow into her duffel bag. Lastly, she tied the lantern firmly to the strap then hung her assignment card around her neck. Then there was the last minute exchange of addresses with Dominga, Vanesa and Vera. When it was time to leave, they all hugged one another, promising to have a reunion when the campaign was over. Hoisting the bulky duffel bag to her shoulder, Anita called out, "*Suerte*, good luck everyone," one last time as she set out with Marjorie, Dani, Pamela and Suzi to their departure location.

"*Suerte, suerte*," the roommates answered in unison.

They had to jostle their way through crowds of *brigadistas* to find their numbered transport truck. Mario hadn't shown up yet. Fifteen minutes later, he still hadn't shown up.

"Wait here," Marjorie said. "I'm going to look for him."

Anita craned her neck and strained her eyes in every direction. No Mario. When Marjorie finally returned, she was scowling. "Mario has managed to get his assignment changed to Caimanera, a fishing village on the eastern tip of the island near Guantánamo—hundreds of kilometres from Bainoa."

"How did he manage to do that?" said Anita, her heart sinking.

"When I couldn't find him, I went to the administration office to see if they knew where he was. It seems Mario told them he had turned eighteen last week, and asked for an independent assignment. He assured them it was OK with me. They neglected to check and confirm with me, and now they are too swamped with problems. They simply left it up to me to straighten the mess out. I can't go chasing after him. I'm responsible for checking all these kids onto the truck, and the driver has orders to leave shortly. I'm disgusted! How could Mario lie like that and be so damn irresponsible! What will I tell your parents?"

"Let me look for him, Marjorie . . . Please," pleaded Anita.

"Ten minutes, Anita. No longer. We'll be pulling out soon."

Anita pushed through the crowd, searching along the many rows of trucks and buses, straining to locate Mario's face among the thousands. Just as she was beginning to think the vehicle he was on might have already pulled out, she spotted him. "Mario," she yelled as loud as she could. He turned and looked down at her with a grimace, then jumped off the truck.

"Some nice way to take off, and without even saying goodbye," she said.

"Little sister, it's independence day. Your big brother has no intention of being part of that protected little group of girls. I don't need a babysitter."

Anita looked at him, speechless, then turned abruptly and walked away, her eyes stinging. Everything was a jumble as she pushed through the crowd. Mario grabbed her by her belt. "I felt I had to do it this way, Anita. I had to agree to go along with the whole supervision thing so that mamá and papá would let us go at all. And I know Marjorie wouldn't have consented if I had asked her. Will you try to understand?"

Eyes swimming, Anita punched his arm—hard. As soon as Mario climbed back onto the truck the driver started the motor and pulled out. Anita waved a final *adiós*, then ran back to her transport, arriving out of breath.

"He's gone. He said he'd write mamá and papá as soon as he could."

BAINOA

The truck was only half-way to Bainoa when dark clouds began moving in from offshore. Soon they were driving through pouring rain and the truck had no cover. Those who had raincoats in their packs covered themselves and others near them as best they could. Anita sheltered under Dani's, but she and everyone else were thoroughly soaked by the time they reached the town. The truck came to a halt alongside the park in Bainoa's town square. Marjorie and the driver got out of the cab.

"Are you sure this is where we're supposed to be?" everyone was asking. "Wasn't there supposed to be a welcoming committee?"

"This is where I was told to come," the driver answered, shrugging. After waiting awhile, it was obvious that no one was coming to meet them, and it was still pouring. The driver suggested that everyone get off the truck and seek shelter under the overhanging roof of a restaurant across the street while he went looking for some official. Everyone got out, muttering, hugging themselves against the chill of their wet clothing, wondering what was going on. It seemed as if the village was deserted.

At last the truck reappeared. An unsmiling man got out and talked to Marjorie in a gruff voice. "The Mayor is away. I'm in charge of Public Works. No one told us that you were coming today so no arrangements have been made for you."

Marjorie told him very firmly that he couldn't just leave everyone out in the rain; that he'd have to arrange shelter for the group somewhere.

"The best I can do is open up an abandoned warehouse where you can spend the night, but you'll be sleeping on the floor," he said. "Follow me. It's not far." The whole troupe of *brigadistas* trailed along after the man through the empty streets to the warehouse, the truck following. The man unlocked a big padlock on huge double doors of a large windowless building.

"There's no electricity," he said to no one in particular, "but at least you'll be out of the rain. *Buenas tardes*, good evening." When he turned to go, Marjorie grabbed him by the sleeve.

"What about food and water for these kids?" she said.

"Everything is closed. There's nothing I can do," he said, and left without another word. Since nothing more could be done, Marjorie told everyone to get their stuff off the truck, insisting that the driver leave since he had to return to Varadero to pick up another group of *brigadistas*. She told everyone to get out their flashlights, then led the way into the forbidding building. The searching beams of light revealed an empty building, except for some old crates. "We'll have to sleep on the ground," Marjorie told the group. "No moaning and groaning please. I know this is a disappointing way to start, but obviously something went wrong—some misunderstanding. Tomorrow we'll get things straightened out. If you have to pee, use the great outdoors. Put on dry clothing, share any food, water and ground cover you have. And do your best to cheer each other up."

Huddled in her sleeping bag, Anita couldn't sleep. She lay rigid, cold and half-frightened by strange sounds. Mice maybe, or worse, rats.

"Dani, are you asleep?" Anita whispered so as not to wake up those asleep nearby.

"No," came the whispered answer. "I'm too cold, and I'm sure there are rats."

"When I write my parents, I'm not even going to mention anything about tonight," whispered Anita.

"Especially that we're sleeping with boys," giggled Dani.

"Wasn't that man mean? Maybe the people of Bainoa don't want us here." Huddling together for warmth, both girls eventually fell asleep.

The next day dawned bright, but the faces of the *brigadistas* were glum. Anita felt glum too. Everyone's uniform was rumpled and there was a lot of muttering about being dirty and dishevelled.

"OK, so this isn't exactly what we expected," said Marjorie, "but are you going to let one letdown get you down? There will be other bumps along the campaign road, maybe worse ones. Now, aren't you those same young people Fidel said he knew he could count on? *Pronto*, make yourselves presentable and get your things together as quickly as you can, then we'll see if that restaurant is open for breakfast."

As they marched down the still-empty street, the *brigadistas* cheered themselves up by singing.

We're teachers
We're ready
Illiteracy we will fight
A million men and women
Will learn to read and write

Though it was early, thankfully the restaurant was already open. As they trooped in—all twenty-four of them—the few customers there, all men, looked up with startled expressions.

"Good morning *compañeros*," Marjorie said cheerfully. "These young people are *brigadistas*, volunteer literacy teachers you have probably heard about. They'll be living in the Bainoa region for the duration of the Literacy Campaign." This introduction was met with stony silence, though a couple of men nodded in their direction.

"They're looking at us as if we were aliens that have dropped out of the sky," whispered Anita to Dani.

"I think that's what we actually look like," said Dani. "At least, that's what I feel like."

To everyone's amazement, not one of the men seemed to know a thing about the Year of Education and the National Literacy Campaign. Marjorie shook her head in disbelief, but said no more. The men returned to their food and conversations, ignoring the *brigadistas*. A rather sour-faced woman was both cooking and serving, so it took ages to serve everyone. Anita ate as though she hadn't had food for days. Breakfast over, Marjorie told the group they could explore the town while she hunted for the people who were supposed to be arranging things for them. "Stick together in groups and be back here in half an hour. Dani, Anita . . . look after Pam and Suzi."

Only the main street was paved and had sidewalks. The other streets were narrow dirt lanes with deep ditches on each side. "These streets look just like the ones in cowboy movies," Pamela observed. They stopped in front of a dilapidated building that had a sign hanging lopsidedly. BAINOA PRIMARY SCHOOL it announced in faded letters.

"It doesn't look as though the school's being used," said Anita. As they walked around, anyone they passed looked at them out of the corners of their eyes. A few women muttered *"Buenos días"*. Children stared at them from behind their mothers' skirts.

"I think we're in a time warp," said Anita, sighing.

"Ditto," agreed Dani.

Bainoa,
The Year of Education,
May 18, 1961

Dear Mario,

Mamá and papá will send this letter to you as soon as they know where to write you. I didn't dare tell them how things are here. Bainoa is so backward! The paved road to get here was finished only recently. The town is very plain and run down. At the very end of the main street there is a church that is opened only once a year when a priest comes to baptize any new babies. There is a school, but classes are held only once in a while when a teacher is sent from Havana. No one met us when we arrived. We were cold, wet and hungry and ended up sleeping in an old warehouse on the hard ground. Marjorie finally got everything straightened out the next day. Eventually we were taken to a schoolhouse that was built recently for a live-in teacher, but there's no teacher yet. This schoolhouse is in the middle of peanut plantations two kilometres from town. Don't ask me why! We are the first people to use it, and it will be our "home" while we're here.

There's a classroom, two smaller rooms, and a tiny kitchen. There are twenty-two brigadistas in our group, plus Marjorie and Suzi. The boys (there are nine) bunk in one of the smaller rooms, the girls have the classroom. The bathroom is an outhouse. There's a windmill in the yard and when it's pumping water, it makes a lot of noise. The first day in the schoolhouse, the officials still hadn't organized enough food for us, so we stole bananas from trees and scavenged the fields for peanuts. We still went to sleep hungry. Even though food is now being delivered to us, meals aren't very good because none of us, including Marjorie, knows how to cook. We were given a whole side of pork, but what do you do with that? The windmill never pumps enough water for all of us, so we have to carry buckets of water from a well about half a kilometre from the schoolhouse. We haven't started teaching yet, but that's all being organized. That's why I had time to write this long letter. I miss you, even though I haven't forgiven you yet. WRITE SOON AND TELL YOUR SISTER EVERYTHING.

Love, Anita

ASSIGNMENT

A nita had been waiting impatiently for this day: the day when she would meet the people she'd be teaching. She couldn't remember ever being so nervous. Her hands were clumsy tying her bootlaces and she could hardly swallow her breakfast of bread and coffee.

"Ready, Anita?" called Marjorie. "The Jeep is here."

Anita straightened her beret, and put on what she hoped was a brave face as she jumped into the back seat with Marjorie. The air shimmered with heat waves even though it was still early in the morning. The Jeep followed an asphalt surface until it ended, then bounced along a red dirt road with deep ruts. There were no other motor vehicles on the road, but there was much coming and going of people in horse-drawn carts and on horseback. The going was slow.

Anita looked closely at the *campesinos* they were passing. The faces of both the men and women were thin, deeply lined and leathery looking from exposure to the relentless sun. The men wore palmetto hats woven from fresh palm leaves, the brims often pushed back off their forehead. The women wore almost shapeless cotton dresses, were barefoot or wore simple sandals. Everyone nodded as the Jeep passed, and Anita smiled back. Shy children craned their necks to look back at them. Occasionally the Jeep passed an oxcart loaded with fruit or palm fronds used for thatching roofs. The ox-cart drivers raised their whips in salutation and called out *"Muy buenos días"*. The oxen, their thickly lashed brown eyes wet and huge in their enormous white faces, plodded along, the cowbells on their harness clanging with each step.

"Marjorie, tell me again about the family I'll be teaching."

"Alright. The Perez family consists of mother, father, one child— a baby boy, only five months old—and the mother's younger sister, Zenaida. Clara, the wife, is young—only nineteen. Ramón, her husband, is much older. He says around fifty but doesn't know for sure. He works on a peanut plantation and raises a few pigs which he butchers and sells. All three adults are illiterate."

"What's Zenaida like?"

"She's not much older than you, Anita. I was told that she's a bit sulky."

As the Jeep bumped along the roadway, skidding along the deep ruts carved into the earth by cart wheels, Anita thought back to the days following their rainy day arrival. Their first job had been going door to door with ladies of the Federation of Cuban Women to interview and register people who were illiterate. Most of the country dwellings were simple one or two room *bohíos*, dismal dirt-floor huts set in hardened earth clearings. Such a sameness to all the people! Most of them were short and thin with suspicious faces and bad teeth. Their kids ran about naked or almost naked playing in the dirt, their bodies streaked with grime. Even the dogs were runty and dirty. And every place had a pig or two being fattened up. Wherever they went, there was the stink of animals.

When the people were asked if they had been to school, if they knew how to read and write, most answered no to both questions. Some said they had been pulled out of school to work, to help put food on the family table. Again Anita was reminded of Tomasa. A few refused to register in the campaign, and nothing would make them change their minds. But most gladly allowed their thumb to be inked on the pad and pressed onto the registration form to indicate their consent. "Maybe there's some hope for us yet," they said, allowing themselves thin-lipped smiles. All expressed amazement when told the young *brigadistas* would be their teachers.

"Does the Perez family want a teacher, Marjorie? Do they really want to learn?"

"Well, they didn't say no when they were interviewed during the census and registration process. They did consent."

Anita's heart thumped when the driver said, "Here we are, *señora Moore*." He wheeled the Jeep off the dirt road onto a path so narrow they had to duck to avoid being scraped by branches. The Jeep emerged into a large clearing. Chickens squawked and scattered before the Jeep's wheels and a tethered goat began to bleat. A neatly thatched *bohío* stood to one side, and a small structure at the rear. From an open, thatch-roofed shed came the snorting and snuffling of pigs and the stink of the pigpen. Nausea rose in Anita's throat and she began gagging. Marjorie was trying not to gag.

"You'll get used to it," said Marjorie quietly as they got out of the Jeep. "Breathe through your mouth. The smell will affect you less."

As they advanced across the clearing. Anita felt eyes marking their progress.

"Muy buenos días," called out a man who straightened up from his task of tying bundles of thatch. He stood stiff and awkward, but not unwelcoming. As Marjorie and Anita approached the man, a woman appeared in the doorway, a baby in her arms. She neither smiled nor raised a hand in greeting. *Where is the young girl, the wife's sister? What was her name?*

"Buenos días, señor Perez. My name is Marjorie Moore Ríos. I'm one of the literacy campaign supervisors for Bainoa region. This is *brigadista* Anita Fonseca, your literacy teacher. Anita, meet *señor* Ramón Perez."

Ramón touched earth-stained fingers to his straw hat. He looked similar to many of the *campesinos* Anita had just seen on the road—a face thin and lined, a scrawny deeply-tanned neck atop a stringy body. He wasn't much taller than she was. She noticed one eyebrow was nicked by a scar.

"Mucho gusto. Glad to know you," he replied, using the formal grammar that signifies respect. He had a surprisingly deep and pleasant voice. Anita responded likewise as they shook hands. Again silence. Turning slightly, Ramón quietly called his wife to come and meet the young teacher. Eyes downcast, the young woman came to her husband's side.

"Mi esposa, my wife, Clara," said Ramón simply.

"Mucho gusto. Glad to meet you," Clara said, her voice barely audible.

"Mucho gusto," replied Marjorie and Anita in unison.

No smile accompanied or followed Clara's greeting. Anita couldn't believe Clara was only nineteen. She was so petite that the baby looked large in her arms. She wore a sleeveless dress, showing thin but muscular arms. Her coppery skin stretched tight over high cheekbones above hollow cheeks and her hair was abundant, long and perfectly straight—so dark it seemed almost black. *Could Clara be a descendant of Cuba's aboriginal people?* Anita wondered.

"And where is Zenaida?" asked Marjorie.

Ramón called out, "Zenaida, come meet the *maestra,* the teacher."

No reply. Only the buzzing of flies. A slight breeze rose, wafting the nauseating stink of the pigpen into Anita's nostrils. She swallowed and swallowed, breathing through her mouth, willing herself not to gag or worse, vomit.

"Zenaida, come out. Now!" commanded Ramón, his voice sharp.

Oh, oh! Maybe trouble between these two, guessed Anita.

"*Voy, voy.* I'm coming, I'm coming," finally responded an irritated voice. Zenaida emerged from the *bohío*, taking her time strolling toward the group. She was petite and pretty, copper-skinned like her sister, with a single black braid hanging down the middle of her back. As she drew close, Anita looked into dark eyes that were decidedly unfriendly. Zenaida resembled her sister, except the contours of her face were less angular.

"Zenaida, I'm Marjorie Moore, and this is Anita Fonseca, your volunteer literacy teacher. Will you help her get acquainted with everything when she arrives to start teaching?" asked Marjorie.

"If I have to," was the answer.

Ramón scowled. Everything Anita had been looking forward to evaporated with those insolent words. Feeling awkward, Anita turned to Clara.

"What's the baby's name?"

"Nataniel," responded Clara, adding nothing more. When the baby heard his name, he smiled and gurgled.

¡Caramba! Finally someone who knows how to smile.

"They aren't very enthusiastic about my coming to teach, Marjorie," said Anita, as they drove off. "How can I teach them if they don't want me? Especially Zenaida! She was downright rude!"

"Remember what you were taught at Varadero, Anita. First you must fit into their lives, help them in any way you can and work at getting them to like and trust you. Eventually they will let down their guard, and you can begin to teach. Now, lighten up. You have already scored points with Ramón by telling him you wanted him to show you how to feed the pigs and other animals. Good thinking, girl!"

One good thing . . . At least there is an outhouse, sighed Anita.

Brigadistas whose assignments were too far away from the schoolhouse had gone to live with their learner families. Those who returned to the schoolhouse every evening had to get to and from their assignments on their own, either on foot or on horses provided by the *campesinos.* Of course, they had to know how to ride. Anita didn't, so she would be walking to the Perez *bohío* since they lived less than three kilometres from the schoolhouse.

Spirits were running high at the schoolhouse as the *brigadistas* ate breakfast on the day teaching assignments began. Anita and Dani set out together taking shortcuts along earthen paths between planted fields to get to the road. They passed *bohíos* where barefoot children played in clearings, chasing chickens or rolling metal hoops with a stick. Clotheslines sagged with colourless clothing. People outside doing chores stopped what they were doing to wave and call out *buenos días*. Passing these places, Anita was reminded of her mother's comments about the life of poor peasants.

Crops of many shades of green stretched as far as the girls could see. Sugar cane fields ready to be harvested were like oceans of gigantic grass. Any breeze bent the enormous leafy stalks before it like waves upon the sea. Hawks glided above, their sharp eyes scanning the ground for small mammals. Turkey-necked buzzards circled slowly, searching for the remains of dead animals. Egrets sat atop the backs of the hump-shouldered zebu oxen grazing in the fields, the snowy-white birds searching the oxen's hide for blood-swollen ticks.

At the turnoff where Dani would continue in a different direction to go to her assignment, they paused.

"Nervous?" Dani asked Anita.

"Sort of," Anita admitted.

"Me too. I'll be waiting for you right here in the evening as we arranged . . . or you wait for me if you get here first," said Dani. They hugged and parted. Anita ran the rest of the way.

Clara was weeding the vegetable garden when Anita arrived. Nataniel lay on a blanket nearby in some shade.

"What can I do to help you, Clara?"

Clara shrugged, so Anita started helping weed the garden. She had never worked in a garden before. Fearful of pulling out something wrong, she had to ask Clara quite often what things were. Clara's responses were brief, and she avoided meeting Anita's eyes. When Nataniel began to whimper, Anita picked him up and played with him. It wasn't until they went inside for lunch that she saw Zenaida who sat at a wooden table cleaning grit from rice kernels spread on a cloth. Anita smiled in greeting, but Zenaida didn't even look up.

Mindful of not being rude, Anita looked around the *bohío*. It consisted of a main room and two small bedrooms. The few pieces of furniture and shelving were simple and unvarnished. The walls were made of the usual palm wood, but the door to the *bohío* was very unusual—not made of bound bamboo stalks as Anita had seen on television, but fashioned from thick layers of huge tropical leaves sewn together with some kind of fibre and stiffened with thin bamboo stalks lashed on both sides. The door hung on hinges of knotted thatch.

"I've never seen a door like that, Clara. It's really beautiful."

"Ramón made it. He built the *bohío*," Clara said with some pride.

After a simple lunch of boiled rice and fried eggs, Anita mostly helped by tending to Nataniel so Clara could do other things. Changing Nataniel's diaper, which was just a piece of cloth cut from a worn sheet, Anita gagged. The diaper was full of caca. Clara smiled at her for the first time.

"Don't mind me, Clara. I'll get used to it."

Anita did the best she could helping Zenaida with other chores, but Zenaida was touchy and grouchy. When Clara told Zenaida to show Anita how to do something or where to find something, she scowled. Anita tried her best to be friendly, but Zenaida wasn't having any of it.

Before leaving to return to the schoolhouse that first day, Anita showed Clara and Zenaida the little sign each *brigadista* had been given that said *A LITERACY TEACHER IS TEACHING HERE*. When she attached it to the outside of the door, Clara seemed pleased, but Zenaida just walked back into the *bohío* without a word.

And so went that first day and the following days. Anita did the best she could, helping with one thing or another. Her admiration for Clara grew as she witnessed how the young mother looked after her baby, cooked, cleaned, tended the garden, helped feed the animals and clean their pens, sew new clothes and mend others, and complete a dozen other tasks—and do everything without complaint. Her attempts to befriend Zenaida, though, were not rewarded. The older girl remained aloof and insolent. Returning to the schoolhouse in the evenings, Anita was always relieved when her flashlight picked out Dani's tall figure waiting for her at the crossroads.

"How's the pig maiden?" Dani would tease her.

"Still getting used to the beautiful aroma. I don't think I'll ever get all the pig shit off my boots! And how are all the men in your life?" she asked Dani. Dani's assignment was a family of six: a husband and wife and four grown sons.

"Still treating me like a queen," said Dani. "When the men arrive from the fields, they always strip to the waist and wash up before coming inside to class so they won't offend me with their sweaty bodies. The sons are good-looking, and except for the youngest son who is really stubborn, the whole family is eager to learn."

"My family still isn't ready," said Anita. "Well, Ramón probably is, but Clara still doesn't really look at me or speak to me very often, and Zenaida just avoids me as much as possible."

"Don't worry, Anita. They'll come around."

Bainoa,
The Year of Education,
May 29, 1961

Dear mamá and papá,

It's already dark by the time all the brigadistas arrive back at the schoolhouse after a day spent with our learner families. Even though we're all really tired, we exchange stories until we run out of steam or Marjorie insists we go to bed. Some nights, I hear one girl or another crying. Sometimes I see Marjorie sitting on the side of a cot talking to a homesick or stressed girl. I wonder if any of the boys feel homesick. I think there's been less crying the last couple of nights. Either that, or I'm falling asleep quicker. I haven't started classes with my family yet, but I'm hoping to soon. Ramón gets a kick out of teasing me, especially about things I don't know how to do, which is almost everything— feeding the pigs and chickens, collecting the eggs, chopping wood. He wants to teach me to ride the horse, a mare called Bufi, but I'm too scared. When will you come to visit?

Anita la cubana

One evening, just as Anita was leaving to return to the schoolhouse, Clara said simply, "Tomorrow we will go to the river to do laundry."

When Anita arrived in the morning, the bundled laundry was on the stoop. Clara gave Anita a cup of warmed goat's milk, then they started out for the river, each carrying a large bundle. Clara also carried Nataniel riding tucked into a sling across her back. Walking single-file along a well-trodden path to the river, Anita could hear scurrying sounds in the underbrush on either side of the path. Fearful of encountering snakes or a hairy spider, she struggled to keep up with the others. As usual, Zenaida was barefoot. Anita would have liked to go barefoot because her feet always felt so hot in the boots. The thought of getting the hookworm parasite they had been told about in Varadero—how it enters the body from the earth through the tiniest sore or scratch—compelled her to keep her boots on.

When they arrived at the river, an older woman was already there, bent over, soaping a heap of clothing. Clara greeted her, and made brief introductions. Rosa was a neighbour. Anita hadn't known anyone else lived nearby. "So this is the *maestra* . . . Too bad I already know how to read and write," she said, her eyes twinkling.

After Clara lay Nataniel down on a blanket with a few wooden toys, she led Anita to the water's edge. "You can work over there," she said, pointing to a group of flat rocks a short way out in the stream. She handed Anita a bar of yellow soap. "Wring the clothes as dry as you can so they won't be so heavy to carry back."

Anita removed her boots and socks and rolled up her trousers. Before wading out to the rocks, she glanced at the others. Clara had kicked off her worn sandals and hitched up her skirt by gathering up the hem and tucking it into her waistband. She had waded to a spot away from the bank where the water moved more swiftly, and was already absorbed in wetting and soaping Nataniel's diapers. Zenaida had gone to a spot just upstream, and was also hard at work. Anita picked up the bundle of laundry and put a foot into the water. Cold, icy cold! Heading toward the rocks, she winced from the pain of sharp-edged stones digging into the soles of her city-girl feet.

"Go fast," said Clara. "It will hurt less." Anita realized this was the first personal thing that Clara had ever said to her.

Just do as they do, Anita told herself once she was on the rocks. Watching the others from under lowered lids, she wet and soaped each item, then laid them out on the rocks to soak and bleach in the sun. Then, one by one, she slapped the clothes, the towels and sheets against the rock, rubbing stubborn spots between her fisted knuckles until the clothes were as clean as she could get them. Ramón's trousers were stiff with heavy red soil that wouldn't wash out completely. She was thankful Clara hadn't given her Nataniel's dirty diapers to wash.

As Clara and Rosa laboured, they chatted and laughed. Clara was even animated. *It's just with me that she's so shy,* Anita realized. Even Zenaida laughed now and then. Anita knew they were watching her to see how the city girl would do. Every once in a while Rosa would call out, "*Maestra,* watch out for killer piranhas!" or, "You're doing such a good job, next time I'll give you my laundry to do too." She wondered how they managed to talk and laugh when this was such hard work. Soap and rub, slap, slap, slap, rinse and wring, wring, wring. Even after using all her strength to wring the clothing and bed sheets as dry as she could, they were still heavy. It wasn't long before Anita was soaked and exhausted. Her neck, back and arms were aching and her hands were stiff, numbed by the cold stream whose waters sprang forth from distant hills.

Thoughts of Gladis, the family laundress in Havana, came into Anita's mind. Small and chubby, skin the colour of the seedpods of the *almendro* tree, she was not young, but not yet old. She pictured Gladis coming and going on silent feet, padding through the house, gathering all the dirty laundry from all the laundry hampers. Twice a week, Gladis washed the dozens of pieces of clothing of a family accustomed to using an item only once. Each item was washed by hand in outdoor laundry tubs, hung to dry, ironed and folded, then quietly delivered back to the drawers, shelves and closets of her employers. Anita remembered a particular day when she had bounced down the steps to the side patio where the laundry sinks and clotheslines were located. Gladis' arms were elbow-deep in suds.

"I need my tennis outfit right away, Gladis. I'm being picked up in an hour."

"Yes, mistress," said Gladis.

"My new pajamas too, Gladis. I'm going to sleep over at my friend Marci's."

"Yes mistress."

The clothing lay fresh on her bed within the hour. Gladis had ironed them dry.

"Anita. . . . Anita. . . . Come and have something to eat." *How long had Clara been calling her?*

Anita stood up stiffly, still thinking about Gladis. Searing pain shot through her muscles. She couldn't remember whether or not she had thanked Gladis properly that day. Despite being cold and numb, Anita felt flushed with shame. As she walked toward the women, she forgot to walk fast, wincing with each step. She wished she could tell Gladis about today, about understanding now what hard work it is to wash clothes by hand. *I'll never be so thoughtless and demanding about my clothing again,* she promised herself. Looking up, she became aware of the three women pointing at her and laughing.

"It's her first time," defended Clara.

Anita looked down at herself. She was as wet as the laundry she had washed, and felt even more wrung out. She must look a funny sight!

June 4, 1961

Dear Diary,

I can't seem to keep my promise to write regularly. By the time I climb into my cot at night I can barely keep my eyes open, and tonight my body is aching from washing clothes at the river today. No matter what, before going to sleep I never forget to cross off the day on my calendar. I am writing this outside by flashlight on the schoolhouse steps. The fireflies have turned on their lights, and Dani is sitting behind me playing guitar and singing Guantanamera, Pamela on one side, Suzi on the other. They adore her. Everybody does. Today I felt I had connected with "my family", so before I left this evening, I said it was time to start classes. Zenaida made a face. Clara said nothing. Ramón said, "You're the teacher". I was relieved because I thought there might be some resistance. So the first class will be tomorrow as soon as Ramón arrives home from work. I just hope I can remember how to light the lantern.

Anita la cubana

All day long, Anita thought of nothing else but the first lesson as she helped with chores. While Clara and Zenaida rested during the afternoon *siesta*, Anita rehearsed the lesson in her mind. Every so often she would think, *please, please let the first lesson go well!* Feeling hot, she dipped the gourd calabash dipper into the rain barrel and drank deeply, then refreshed herself with a quick wash. Her uniform was alright, but her boots. . . . They were dull and dusty, the soles caked with bits of muck and animal dung.

She thought of her father's special shoeshine box containing many flat cans of different colour shoe polishes, even a bottle of whitener for summer shoes. There were folded clean rags for applying the various shoe creams, a mahogany-backed hand brush for buffing the dried polish, and long strips of soft flannel cloth for bringing up the final sheen. She pictured her father, one foot placed on the raised foot-piece of the wooden shoebox, snapping the cloth as he polished the toes of his black leather shoes until they gleamed. The only shoes Ramón had were worn work boots and frayed rope sandals which he repaired himself.

Anita knew it was unusual that her father shined his own shoes. It was customary for Cuban men to get their shoes shined frequently, so the streets of Havana were full of bootblacks, young and old. Some men had their shoes shined daily, reading the daily paper while sitting on tall ornate chairs in the street or standing, smoking a cigar with a foot up on the bootblack's shoeshine box. Her father had purchased a shoeshine kit soon after the revolution. "It's time we learned to shine our own shoes," he told the family that day. "Soon all the bootblacks will have better jobs."

Anita bunched up some leaves and tried to remove mud caked on her boots.

"Here, use this."

Anita jumped. She hadn't heard Zenaida approach. Zenaida was holding out a crude brush with stiff bristles. She turned and left as soon as Anita took the brush, before she could even say thank you. As Anita brushed off the mud and dung, she thought that maybe Zenaida didn't actually hate her after all.

Clara had been evading her eyes all day, and had spoken even less than usual. Anita figured it was just nervousness about the first lesson that would follow an early supper. They were nearly finished the meal when Clara suddenly put down her fork, and blurted, "*Maestra* Anita, I will not take the class."

"Why, Clara? Don't you feel well?"

"I feel well," said Clara. "I just don't want to take the classes. I have no need of them."

Anita was dumbfounded. The lovely picture in her head of her teaching the family sitting around the table learning happily together disappeared just like dirty dishwater heaved out the door, swallowed by the hot earth.

LANTERN

Anita looked at Ramón and Zenaida for clues to Clara's words, but Ramón looked as surprised as she felt. Zenaida just looked away. *She must know. Maybe that's why she was being nice to me. Should I try to convince Clara? Should I remind her she signed up to learn by placing her thumb mark on the consent form?* Then she recalled Marjorie telling her to use her wits when problems came up. A voice inside her head said, *Don't push. Be patient.*

"That's alright, Clara. You can join in anytime," is all she said, trying not to let her voice betray her disappointment.

Anita had brought the lantern with her and now placed it in the middle of the roughly built wood table that served as kitchen counter, dining room table, diaper change table, laundry folding table and sewing table. The room was dimly-lit by a primitive lamp made from a blackened can of kerosene, a small wick dangling from the narrow neck. It sat on the one piece of painted furniture in the small room, a tall cupboard with shelves and drawers that held dishes, pots and pans, cutlery, and groceries. The kerosene smoked badly and the burning wick produced a weak yellowish light. Standing before Ramón and Zenaida, she primed the pump and struck the match. *Don't fail me lantern.* Light flared, strong enough to illuminate the table and Ramón's and Zenaida's expectant faces. She heard Clara utter a small gasp of surprise as the light leaped toward the corner where she was sitting rocking Nataniel to sleep.

"From now on, this table will be our special classroom," Anita began, "and these are your lesson workbooks." She held one up to show them the cover with the picture of a huge crowd of people, Cubans of all ages and skin colour. A man in the foreground held a Cuban flag high above people's heads. As she had been taught to do at Varadero, Anita pointed to the one word at the top printed in large red capital letters. "This word says ¡VENCEREMOS! We Will Succeed! And by the end of this year, I'm sure you will have succeeded in learning to read and write.

Ramón looked a little sceptical, and Zenaida sat expressionless, slumped in her chair.

"Don't you believe me, Zenaida? It's true." *At least, I hope it is*, her inner voice whispered. When Zenaida just shrugged in response, Ramón frowned at her. Following the advice of her teachers at Varadero—Don't give orders—she began the first lesson as she had been taught.

"Let's begin, shall we? We'll start with the letter *A*, the first letter of the alphabet."

By the end of the lesson there was a good feeling in the room. She could feel it, even though Zenaida had pretended to be bored. Anita was surprised when Zenaida asked if she could draw in her workbook.

"Of course, as long as you only use the margins."

Zenaida showed Anita a drawing of the lantern she had already done, obviously pleased when Anita told her it was really good.

The Year of Education
June 5, 1961

Dear mamá and papá,

I feel incredibly excited and disappointed at the same time. Excited because I taught my first lesson tonight, and I think it went well, but disappointed because Clara refused to take the lesson. Even so, I could sense that she was paying attention to everything from where she sat in the shadows. Zenaida is not exactly unwilling, but she's not enthusiastic either. Ramón's face glistened with sweat and he chews his tongue as he struggles to make the letters. He said afterwards that doing the lesson was more tiring than hours of harvesting peanuts or cutting sugar cane.

I read the first theme to them called "The Revolution" and we talked about that awhile. I asked them what words they thought were the most important, or which words they remembered. I wrote those words on the table (our "blackboard") with the coloured chalk you gave me mamá. I pronounced the words and asked them to copy them in their workbooks. Then I wrote a series of common words—things they could see around them that had the sound "ah" in them—like mesa and linterna, and their own names. We repeated the words, pointing to the objects. Then they copied those words into their workbooks, and underlined all the "ah" sounds. It felt strange to see their heads bent low over their notebooks, struggling to reproduce the shapes of letters that I learned in grade one. Ramón needed encouragement in the actual copying stuff because he said his hands were too big to hold the pencil.

There is one serious problem—Ramón has to squint to see the words. He may need glasses. As I was leaving, Ramón shook my hand and said gracias, maestra, thank you, teacher. I love being called "maestra" and can hardly wait till the first seminar to share all this with the others.

Anita la cubana

★

"As my father would say, Dani, 'Another beautiful day and no relief in sight!'" As the days dawned hotter and the air on the plains of Bainoa grew steamier, Anita missed being able to go to the beach, missed the sea breezes, missed the smell of salty sea air. Even though she was looking forward to the first seminar where all the *brigadistas* and supervisors in the Bainoa region would review classes so far, she wasn't looking forward to the walk to town under the blazing Cuban sun.

Trooping along under a sky like blue glass, Dani began improvising a song.

We are walking, walking, on our way
We are walking, walking, hear me say
Muscles like iron
Muscles like lead
Muscles harder than a donkey's head.

Other *brigadistas* took up the words, adding made up verses.

We are walking, walking, on our way
We are walking, walking, hear me say
Muscles like coco
Hard as your head
Muscles harder than last week's bread.

Royal palms dotted the flat agricultural land they were walking through. Their pale grey trunks were unbelievably tall and thin. Since she was little, Anita had always wondered how such skinny trees managed to stay upright. On the ground beneath the palms lay fallen *pencas*, the dried-out palm fronds that were used to thatch roofs. Great clusters of royal palm fruit, the *palmiche*, hung from the umbrella of leaves at the very top of the palms. Anita marvelled at the agility and strength of the *campesinos* who climbed the skinny trunks to harvest the *palmiche*.

The meeting place for the seminar was the park in the town square. Supervisors allowed all the arriving groups time to mingle before calling them together. The Bainoa campaign director addressed the large group.

"These seminars will serve several purposes. We want to know how you are doing generally; how you are feeling emotionally and physically. Most importantly, we want to know how you are getting along specifically with teaching. I'm sure you have encountered problems, right?"

The response was a buzz of voices.

"By sharing—not hiding—your problems, we can help solve or overcome them," she continued. "Also, we will be tracking the progress of each of your students. Those of you who haven't started a detailed progress journal should start tomorrow." The supervisors directed the *brigadistas* to break into discussion groups, and for the next hour each group shared problems and stories with a supervisor.

What funny stories came up in Anita's group! Trying to understand toothless learners, not all of them that old either; being frightened by strange sounds while going to the outhouse at night; having to learn to do a hundred things they had never done before—like changing caca diapers. Many admitted to having fallen out of their hammocks a few times. Anita was amazed at how similar problems were—learners so shy they hadn't yet opened their mouths, homesickness, lanterns that wouldn't light, feeling uncomfortable about not being able to shower every day, the general backwardness of everything. When Anita reported that Ramón had eyesight problems, others said some of their learners did also. Everyone complained about the food! Some even said they never wanted to see a dish of rice and beans again. Not ever!

When they reassembled, the director announced that the ladies of Bainoa had prepared a picnic lunch for everyone. "Free time until lunch is ready," she said, "but before you disperse, come up here to see if you have mail and leave letters you want sent. One more important thing . . . Anyone who has anything physically the matter—diarrhoea, rashes, allergies, headache—anything at all—please report up here so we can arrange for medical treatment. This is important so you don't get really sick and have to be sent home."

June 8, 1961

Dearest daughter,

How goes the campaign? I think of it as a kind of frenzy sweeping the country because everywhere you turn, there is something new happening that is all about mass education. I have started a campaign scrapbook for you, but I will tell you a few of the things I have heard and read about lately. I know you will enjoy telling your brigadista friends about them. I guess the most controversial is the program to rehabilitate prostitutes by teaching them literacy and instructing them in other occupations. Mostly they are being taught to be taxi and truck drivers. Instruction takes place during the day, right in the brothels, and the girls return to their work after 5pm. The rumour is that all brothels will be closed down as soon as the prostitutes have other options. I never thought I would be talking to you about prostitution, but it's just another part of what you are involved in—educating people to give them a better future. Yesterday there was an article in the newspaper about 17,000 country girls who will be brought to Havana over time for literacy classes and vocational training. They will be lodged in the International Hotel. How exciting that must be for those girls who have probably never been more than a few kilometres from their homes!

Another program is for domestic servants. An article in Bohemia magazine says that 70% of Cuban women work as domestic servants. For those who want to make a change, night schools have been established all over Havana and other cities offering free courses to be trained as secretaries, drivers, bank tellers and child care workers. I imagine that servants with some education will not want to be servants anymore. This campaign is going to affect everyone, not just those who become literate. I have to tell myself over and over not to fret, not to be selfish. But I am so spoiled, Anita. I admit it. Imagine me doing the housework and the laundry!

Your father is fine, working very hard at the newspaper. He told me to tell you that every day he sees fewer and fewer beggars and homeless people when he goes to work. We know how much that used to upset you. We want to meet the Perez family soon. Send us a map in your next letter. Tomasa sends you a big hug. Keep your letters coming, no matter how brief.

Much love, Mamá

The Year of Education
June 11, 1961

Dear mamá,

I just got your letter today and I loved it. I read it to Marjorie and my friends. Please don't get upset about what I'm going to ask you. I don't have the full confidence of my learner family yet, at least, not Clara and Zenaida. In fact, Clara still refuses to take classes. So when you come to visit, don't expect to meet the Perez family yet. I think they would be too shy and overwhelmed right now. When will you come? Can Marci come with you? I never take off the locket she gave me. Love to you and papá,

Anita

P.S. Please bring toilet paper.

DANGER STRIKES

After the novelty of the first few weeks had passed, the schoolhouse group usually went to bed soon after supper, exhausted by the volunteer agricultural work they sometimes did and the effort of teaching. At night, the schoolhouse and surrounding countryside lay in deep silence, lit only by stars and moonlight. Occasionally a donkey brayed in the distance, and the windmill creaked when the wind rose. The only constant sound other than the breathing and snuffling of sleeping people was the chirping of crickets inside and outside the schoolhouse. So the night Anita heard the pounding of horses' hooves, she thought she was dreaming. As the sound grew louder, joined by shouting voices, she realized it wasn't a dream and sat up, alarmed. Around her, others were waking and sitting up.

"*¿Qué pasa?* What's going on?" *brigadistas* called out in the dark. Some kids ran to the windows to try to see what was happening. Rifle shots rang out and kids started screaming.

"Everyone, get away from the windows!" yelled Marjorie. "They must be rebels. Get down on the floor, pull your cot mattresses over you and stay down."

The riders circled around and around the schoolhouse, shouting and firing their rifles into the air. Anita tried to make out what the rebels were shouting, but the shooting and the pounding hooves of the whinnying horses were too jumbled with the voices to hear anything clearly. Many girls began to cry. Marjorie was crawling about, doing her best to calm the frightened group. The boys had crawled in from their dorm, squeezing in where they could. Anita held her hands over her ears to try to blot out the terrifying sounds. *Would they shoot through the windows? Would they enter the schoolhouse? Would they set the building afire? Did they intend to kidnap or kill anybody?*

How long did everyone lie trembling as the mounted men circled the schoolhouse shouting and shooting? Five minutes? Fifteen minutes? An hour? Anita had no idea. The noise outside suddenly stopped, and a menacing voice shouted, "Leave this place while you can." A window shattered, and something bulky came hurtling through, landing with a thud. Those nearest the object shrieked and squirmed away from it. Anita found herself screaming too. Gradually the screaming stopped as Marjorie managed to make everyone be quiet. They could hear the sound of horses galloping off, then nothing. Even the crickets had stopped chirping.

"Stay where you are," Marjorie said in a low voice. "It's possible some are still out there." No one moved. No one spoke. When it seemed sure the rebels were gone, everyone began to talk at once.

"What did they throw in?"

Someone beamed their flashlight on the object. Everyone gasped at the sight revealed. Those nearest shrieked and kicked themselves further away from it, knocking into those behind them. A donkey's severed head, the blood still red and clotting, lay in their midst. Its eyes were open and glassy. A girl fainted. Many began retching. Suzi vomited. A note was tied to one ear. Anita felt she would faint too if she didn't do something. She crawled near the grisly head and removed the note, revolted when her fingers touched the ear. She crawled over to where Marjorie was attending to the girl who had fainted.

"Read it. Read it," everyone demanded. Anita looked at Marjorie, who nodded and told someone to turn on the lights.

Anita's voice trembled as she read:

WE WILL HAVE YOUR HEADS TOO IF YOU DON'T LEAVE BAINOA AND GO HOME!

Marjorie took the note, folded it and placed it in her pajama pocket. "We'll discuss this later. Right now, everyone get your boots on. Be careful not to step on glass. First, let's get this gross thing out of here."

She told those nearest the donkey head to throw it out the door. "You, you and you," she said pointing, "shake the glass off the mattresses carefully and sweep it up thoroughly. Once the glass is swept up, clean the blood off the floor. Dani, clean up Suzi's vomit. When that's all done, you boys go to your dormitory and bring your mattresses and sleeping bags in here."

When everything was cleaned up as best they could, Marjorie went from person to person, checking on everyone, soothing and consoling them. Some had been cut by the flying glass, but none seriously. She dressed wounds using the First Aid Kit. Getting the frightened group calmed down took a long time.

"Are you alright Anita?"

"I'm afraid to go to sleep. It makes me think of what happened to Conrado Benitez."

"It's unlikely they will return tonight," said Marjorie, "and Dani and I will be keeping watch. Try not to worry."

Dani, always ready to lighten things up whispered in Anita's ear, "Hey, here we are sleeping with the boys again!"

Gradually there was less and less talking and whispering as people fell asleep. Marjorie had lit a candle, and sat on a mattress, her back against a wall, her arms around Pamela and Suzi who were asleep huddled close to their mother and Dani. Anita was still awake when roosters began crowing at dawn. Marjorie put Dani in charge and said no one was allowed to leave the schoolhouse except to go to the outhouse in groups of four.

The Year of Education
July 2, 1961

Dear Mario,

I have never been so scared in my life! For two nights in a row, gusano rebels galloped around our schoolhouse shouting and shooting into the air, yelling that we should all go back to where we came from, OR ELSE! The second night was even wilder and scarier than the first, because they kicked the door down and one of the rebels stood in the doorway and yelled horrible things at us. Before they left the second night, they set the outhouse on fire. Marjorie went to the campaign headquarters in Aguacate after the first night, but it wasn't until the day after the second night that two militiamen were assigned to guard the schoolhouse for the rest of the campaign. Marjorie said that extra military will be stationed in the region to try and round up the rebels. Everyone feels safer now that the guards are here. The guards take turns sleeping during the day, and at night they sit on the roof with rifles.

One of the brigadistas in our group went home, but the rest are staying, though we're all scared. Some of the kids still have trouble falling asleep (me too), and some are having nightmares. Remember how we were so sure that stuff like this wouldn't happen to us? I'm not going to tell mamá and papá about this. Promise me you won't tell them either. I'm sure they would insist on taking me back to Havana. Because of the danger, the brigadistas who walk to and from their assignments (like me) will be moving to our learners' homes if that's OK with the learners. My learner family has agreed.

Write me more often – PLEASE.

Love, Anita

FITTING IN

Anita stood in the clearing waving goodbye to Marjorie until the Jeep disappeared. She hoisted her duffel bag to her shoulder, but was reluctant to turn around, reluctant to confront Zenaida's resentful look knowing that Zenaida hated the idea of sharing her bedroom with her. Once the hammock was hung, it would take up almost all the available space in the small room. Of course the hammock could be taken down during the day, but still. . . . As Anita approached the *bohío*, Zenaida turned and went inside, leaving Clara on the stoop.

"Well, here I am. I hope it's really OK with everybody that I have come to live with you," Anita said, smiling feebly.

"No te preocúpas. Don't worry," replied Clara in her quiet way. "Go in and settle your things in the bedroom."

"What about Zenaida? She's still upset, isn't she?"

"She'll get over it."

This first day as a live-in *brigadista* was spent no differently than any other day. Anita helped with chores, harvested beans from the vines and split some wood, something she was secretly proud of having learned how to do, and of having developed the muscles to do it. At first she had been terrified of swinging the axe, but Ramón was a good teacher. Now she loved seeing the chunks of wood fly off the cutting block. Ramón told her the nick in his eyebrow was the result of a small chunk hitting his head.

"Ramón, will you put in the hooks to hang my hammock?" she asked after supper.

"Show me where."

"Zenaida, help me decide," she asked. "What would be best?"

Zenaida shrugged a shoulder. She hadn't directed a glance or a word Anita's way all day.

"I think hanging it on the opposite side of the room from Zenaida's bed would be best."

Ramón glowered at Zenaida, but said nothing.

The reading that evening was titled, *HEALTHY PEOPLE,*

HEALTHY COUNTRY. It was about setting up medical clinics throughout the countryside, about building more hospitals, training more doctors and nurses, about public health being a right of the people. As part of the lesson, Anita encouraged them to talk about the reading.

"What happens here if there is an emergency? The only telephone is in Bainoa."

"Since there has never been a hospital or clinic in Bainoa region, we rely on ourselves and the local *curanderos*, the natural healers who live in the area," Ramón said. Anita thought of her family's regular check-ups with their family doctor in his posh office.

"Won't it be good to have a medical clinic nearby?" Anita asked. They nodded, but with little enthusiasm. *They probably don't believe there'll ever be a clinic and doctors to serve them.*

The grammar and vocabulary of the lesson was based on the sound "*ch*". She wrote down twelve words that contained that sound, then went over these words many times until they could recognize and read whichever one she pointed to. Then she read sentences with those words in it, and wrote them down. "Now copy the sentences into your workbooks". Ramón could now do fill-in-the-blanks exercises quite quickly, but he still had trouble with dictation. Zenaida did it all easily, but was always sulky. Clara still sat in the corner. A small *lagartija*, a lizard, running up the wall caught Anita's attention. She recalled a childhood memory—she and Mario catching these creatures and letting them bite their ear lobes and dangle like living earrings. She realized she missed her brother terribly.

As the lesson was ending, Anita wondered what would happen now that she was staying. *Would everyone just go to bed since Ramón got up very early to leave for the fields?* When the lesson ended, Ramón thanked her formally, as he always did, then went outside. Clara began washing the supper dishes and Anita was drying them and putting them away when Ramón called out, "The fire is going."

A bonfire! What a surprise! Clara squeezed fresh lemonade and they toasted plantain chips over the fire. Ramón told jokes and Anita answered questions about her family. Mosquitoes whined behind their ears, but the smoke helped keep them away. Anita figured the bonfire and treats had been planned especially to make her feel welcome on this, her first night with them. Zenaida continued to sulk, sitting as far away from Anita as she could. *What's her problem?* Anita wondered for the thousandth time.

Anita waited until everyone else had gone to bed before she used the outhouse, washed up and brushed her teeth. She extinguished the lantern, tip-toed into the dark bedroom and undressed quietly. A rustling in the thatch of the roof made her stiffen. She knew many kinds of *bichos* could be living in the thatch—scorpions, mice, even snakes. She told herself to remember to shake out her boots before putting them on in the morning. Holding her breath, she climbed into the hammock. The ropes squeaked. Zenaida turned over.

"Sorry Zenaida."

No answer, but she could feel the waves of Zenaida's resentment. The darkness was complete, behind her eyes and all around, inside and outside the *bohío*. Anita held her hand out in front of her face, but couldn't see it. She remembered trying to imagine being in a hammock in a dark room like this when she was in Varadero.

> *Caimanera,*
> *July 9, 1961*
>
> *Dear sister,*
>
> *I know you wanted adventure, but those two scary nights were way too much adventure! I promise not to tell mamá and papá, but you must promise to be extra careful. Those counter-revolutionaries are nasty! About my learner family—it's very big and very noisy. The father Eliades is a really big strong guy, a fisherman. His wife, Corazón, is a plain, tall, bony woman who is always talking and laughing. There are four kids—I call them the Bible boys because they all have Bible names—Moses, Jacob, Solomon and Joshua. Then there's the grandfather, abuelo Carmelo. He seems ancient. Eliades had some schooling when he was young, but seems to have forgotten everything. Everyone else in this little hamlet of 100 people or so is illiterate, except for two people, the storekeeper and the boss of the fish boats.*
>
> *Eliades gets up at four every morning except Sunday to be out on the sea by dawn. He's part of a state fishing cooperative, and they fish for tuna and marlin. He comes home by mid-afternoon and goes straight to bed for a couple of hours. He's the only one in the family who is quiet, though he has a wicked sense of humour. Corazón is like her name—all heart. She's always doing everything for everybody and*

little for herself, but is always in good spirits. She makes up songs to go with her tasks and makes us laugh all the time. Today after supper she sang—We ate the soup, we ate the fishes, now it's time to do the dishes.

The boys are ages 12, 10, 9 and 7. They are very boisterous, except for Joshua, the youngest, who is crippled by polio. His legs are withered and useless. Eliades has made him a special wagon, and his brothers take him everywhere and play with him a lot. I hope they will be able to get a wheelchair for him someday. The bigger boys are always plotting practical jokes. The other day, they put a fish under my blanket. Abuelo may be old, but he's still quite active. He tends to the kitchen garden and cleans the fish—there's fish for dinner every day. What a challenge! You know how much I dislike fish!

This family is black, Anita. Not mulatto, but African black. I feel funny mentioning it. Why should it matter? At first I felt a real strangeness living with black people—like being the white rice in the black beans—but it doesn't feel at all strange now. This campaign is really bringing the races together. It's good.

I teach the boys in the morning and the adults at night. The quickest learner is Joshua. Actually, I found I couldn't use the teaching book for the boys. They just don't relate to it, and just getting them to be still is a problem. So I make up lessons using whatever is around me—the house, the sea, boats, fish, the mangrove swamp, animals, the village, the activities of the people, and especially the games the boys love to play. I'm not sure abuelo Carmelo will be able to remember what he learns. I asked him how old he is, but he doesn't know. He's all twisted like the mangrove trees, his face is as wrinkled as a prune and he has no teeth.

I feel good here, in spite of the noise, the pranks, the mosquitoes, and eating fish every day. I don't seem to miss hanging out or going to movies. I do miss my Deportes magazines. I've asked papá to mail them to me. Of course, there's months to go, so I may go crazy yet! The four Bible boys alone could drive anyone crazy!

Love, Mario

P.S. I've decided to drop the "little sister" routine. Happy?

There were few places to escape the relentless July sun beating down on the flat plain of Bainoa. No breeze blew. It was only slightly less hot in the shade. Animals stood or lay motionless, skin twitching, ears and tails flicking to shoo away the flies always tormenting them. Clara threw water on the ground near the *bohío* to settle the dust. The deep rumbling of thunder by mid-afternoon announced the daily tropical downpour was about to begin. Relief was short-lived. Soon after the rain stopped , it was hotter and more humid than ever.

At first Anita stayed outdoors wherever she happened to be when it started raining, happy to let the rain drench her. But when she found it took too long for her uniform and boots to dry, she ran for cover as soon as the thunderclouds began rolling and grumbling. She would have liked to strip and bathe in the downpour, but knew that Clara and Zenaida would be scandalized. At the end of each day, she sponge-bathed with cool water collected in a rain barrel. Real privacy wasn't possible, so she bathed quickly on the backside of the *bohío* where there was no window opening. She forced herself to stop wondering whether she was clean-smelling all the time, but often thought about the long showers she took at home. The best escape from the naked sun was the river. How good it felt getting wet doing the laundry now!

Despite the heat, lessons continued every night around the lantern-lit table. Clara still sat off in the corner, and Zenaida's attitude toward learning wasn't improving. Anita had decided to try being more friendly toward Zenaida, so had purchased a set of coloured pencils for her in town. She chose a time when no one else was nearby to give them to her.

"Your drawings are so good, Zenaida. Would you like to know how to write the names of the things you draw? If you leave some space, I'll write the name under each drawing, and you could copy the words."

"What's the use of my learning how to read and write anyway?" said Zenaida.

"What's the use?" Anita echoed, surprised by the question. "There's so much you'll be able to learn and do once you know how to read and write."

"All I do and ever will do is housework, laundry, feed animals and look after my sister's child. And soon there'll be another, or haven't you noticed that Clara is pregnant? And when I get married someday, I'll be doing more of the same for the rest of my life, my feet nailed to the floor of some *bohío*. So why do I need to know how to read and write? You're a rich city girl. You'll be leaving. I'm stuck here."

Zenaida's expression dared Anita to disagree. For a moment, Anita felt confused. *Why would anyone want to remain illiterate? And would it be disloyal to Clara if I encourage Zenaida to think about herself differently, to be more independent?*

"Learning to read and write can unstick you, Zenaida. After I leave you can continue to learn in the new school being built in town. If you read and write, get more education, then you can get work that you do like, where you like. You don't have to do domestic work if you don't want to. That's what this campaign is all about—changing things, giving people options. I know it just seems like a speech, Zenaida, but give yourself a chance, and give me a chance to help you."

Zenaida was already shaking her head. Thinking fast, Anita jumped in with an idea just as Zenaida was opening her mouth to respond.

"I'll make you a bet, Zenaida. Let me teach you to read and write, and I bet you that by the time you are twenty you will have a paying job, and it won't be domestic work. If I win, you have to buy me a meal in a nice restaurant with money you've earned. If I lose, you will be my guest in Havana for a week. I'll even ask my good-looking brother to take you to the movies. What do you say?"

"I say you're crazy!"

"But do we have a bet?"

"OK, we have a bet, but I still think you're crazy!"

"Let's shake on it then," said Anita.

Anita decided to take advantage of this moment. Marjorie had twice tried to convince Clara to study, but Clara had lowered her eyes and shook her head both times.

"Zenaida, why won't Clara take classes?"

"Because she thinks the same as me. She says she doesn't need to read and write to be the peasant wife of a *campesino*."

"Then why *have* you been doing the lessons, Zenaida?"

Zenaida's answer was her usual shrug.

You're not fooling me girl. It's because you think knowing how to read and write is better than not knowing how, that's why.

July 20, 1961

Dear Diary,

    I couldn't get to sleep last night, it was so hot. So I lit the lantern and finished reading Anne Frank: The Diary of a Young Girl. On the book's back *cover, it says all the notebooks in which Anne wrote her diary were found scattered on the floor, thrown around when the Nazi soldiers searched the hiding place for money and valuables. The notebooks were rescued by friends and kept safe until the end of the war and given to Anne's father, the only one in the family who survived. The Diary turned out to be very valuable because Anne's voice comes to us telling her amazing story. She was thirteen when she began keeping a diary, and even though she couldn't leave the hiding place and be with friends, she still wrote about many things any normal teenager would write about. She wrote about a big crush she had on a boy also in hiding in the same place, and she's funny and wicked when she describes her honest feelings about her sister and some of the others in hiding that bug her. I wish I were inspired like Anne to be faithful about keeping up my Diary, especially about describing my work as a brigadista and the campaign. I wonder if Anne would have become a writer if she had survived the holocaust.*

Faithfully yours,
Anita la cubana

The nights were so hot and humid that Anita was glad to hear the rooster crow and welcomed the light of dawn so she could get up. The hammock was fine for sleeping, but not for lying in wide awake for hours in the dark. One night, in addition to the heat, no one got much sleep because Nataniel was sick and cried most of the night.

"I can't go to do laundry today," Clara said. "I want to keep Nataniel here so he can sleep. But I need diapers. Nataniel had diarrhoea last night." Nataniel, ordinarily so bubbly, lay listless on Clara's bed while they ate breakfast. While Clara and Zenaida got the bundles of laundry ready, Anita went and sat near Nataniel. She tried to make him smile, but he didn't respond. His face was flushed. She felt his face and body. His skin was very hot. Not sweaty summer hot—dry hot.

"Clara, I think Nataniel has a high fever." Clara came and felt the child.

"He is feverish," she agreed. "I will give him some baby aspirin. The laundry is bundled. Lunch will be ready when you and Zenaida return."

"Did you finish the book you were reading the other night?" said Zenaida over her shoulder as they followed the path to the river.

"Yes. It had a sad ending."

"What is the book about?" asked Zenaida.

"It's the diary of a young Jewish girl named Anne Frank whose family and another Jewish family hid for two years to try to escape being sent to a Nazi concentration camp. Their secret hiding place was discovered though."

"I can't imagine reading a whole book," said Zenaida.

"One day you'll be reading books, Zenaida. I'm sure of it. Maybe you'll read the book about Anne Frank."

"And maybe trees will talk." But the smile playing at the corners of Zenaida's mouth told Anita the girl was more hopeful than she let on.

By the time they reached the river, both girls were perspiring. Anita felt her scalp prickling with sweat.

"Zenaida, let's go swimming *desnuda*—naked as newborn babes!"

"*¿Estás loca?*" Zenaida said, looking at Anita as though she had gone crazy.

"Why not? No one is around, and it will feel so good. Besides, it will be fun. C'mon."

"No," Zenaida repeated. "It's . . . it's not proper to be naked outside."

"Well, proper or not, I'm so hot, I'm going in naked."

Anita stripped quickly and waded into the summer-warmed water. Among the flat rocks where she washed clothes, the river deepened into a pool of slow-moving water. Anita flopped onto her back and floated.

"It's fantastic!" she shouted. "C'mon in Zenaida."

No answer. Anita lifted her head to see what Zenaida was doing and was surprised to see that she was pulling her dress over her head. *She's actually going to come in.* As soon as Zenaida got close, Anita kicked hard, splashing her. Shrieking, Zenaida splashed back, then ducked herself completely. They floated blissfully, their eyes closed against the blazing sun. It was the very first time Anita had seen Zenaida enjoying herself. When they emerged from the water Zenaida begged Anita not to tell Clara and Ramón about being naked. "I know they would be very angry," she said.

"I promise, but let's do the laundry *desnuda*," said Anita. "It will be so much cooler, right?" Zenaida refused, completely scandalized, and was soon dressed again. Anita gathered the dirty laundry and proceeded back out to the rocks wearing only panties and bra. Chatting as they washed, they reminisced about how clumsy and slow Anita had been the first time she had done laundry.

"Listen . . ." said Zenaida, motioning Anita to be quiet.

"Sounds like someone yelling," said Anita.

"Hurry," said Zenaida. "Get your clothes on."

A CLOSE CALL

Leaving the laundry scattered on the rocks, they splashed to the riverbank, ignoring the sharp stones. Now they could hear that it was Clara yelling, "Zenaida . . . Anita . . ." Anita struggled to get into her uniform.

"Hurry, Anita," Zenaida urged. Anita had only gotten her pants on when Clara emerged from the path running, carrying Nataniel in her arms. Her face was flushed and anxious. Anita's heart flip-flopped. Nataniel lay completely limp in Clara's arms. *Was he dead?* Clara slumped to the ground, out of breath, sobbing.

No, he was breathing— but shallowly, oh so shallowly.

Between sobs, Clara explained. "I gave him some baby aspirin, then went outside to do some chores, but I left the baby aspirin on the table near the bed. When I came back in I went to check on him. The package was on the bed and he was limp, hardly breathing, like this." Clara began to moan. "I don't know what to do. I don't know what to do. What shall we do?"

Zenaida knelt beside her sister and began pinching Nataniel's cheeks, but Nataniel did not respond.

"How many aspirins did he swallow, Clara?" asked Anita.

"I don't know how many were in the box, but I think he swallowed all there were," she said, sobbing. "What shall we do?"

What could they do? Anita wondered. *There's no phone to call a doctor. No hospital nearby. No transportation. Should Zenaida go for their neighbour, Rosa? Would Rosa know what to do? Is there even time for that?*

"Clara, I don't know what you're supposed to do for aspirin poisoning, but I know that the sooner you can get any poison out of the body, the better. You must make Nataniel vomit. If he doesn't vomit, then you must take Nataniel to Bainoa on the mule to get help."

Clara turned Nataniel on his side and stuck her finger in his mouth and pressed down on his little tongue. Nataniel gagged, but didn't vomit.

"Try again, Clara."

This time Nataniel vomited, milky vomit streaked with the pink of baby aspirin. Anita wet her sock and squeezed river water into Nataniel's mouth. He coughed and sputtered, but swallowed a bit. She repeated this several times. "Now make him vomit again, Clara." When there seemed to be nothing left to bring up, Anita gave the child more water, then lifted him from Clara's arms and took him to the river's edge. She cooled his face and head and chest, then wrapped him in her uniform shirt. Nataniel's breathing seemed more normal and a few minutes later, he began to cry.

"That's a good sign, I think," said Anita. As soon as Nataniel began to cry, Clara began to cry again, but this time they were tears of relief.

"Anita, you saved him! He was poisoned, and you saved his life."

"See if he'll take milk from your breast, Clara. Now he needs liquid." As Clara nursed Nataniel, Anita and Zenaida gathered and bundled the wet laundry.

"How did you know what to do?" Zenaida asked.

"In school . . . I took a First Aid course last year."

Lacing up her boots, Anita saw Clara staring at her. Of course! She had only managed to get her pants on, but not her shirt. She didn't offer any explanation, and Clara didn't ask for any. By the time they arrived at the *bohío*, Nataniel was sleeping peacefully, his breathing regular. When they entered the bedroom to lay him on the bed, all their eyes flew to the little box of baby aspirin on the bed. A couple of tiny pink tablets remained on the bed cover. Anita picked up the box. One end was soggy where Nataniel had sucked and chewed on it. She remembered baby aspirin—how sweet the tablets were. *That's why he wanted more*, she thought. She read the information on the back of the box, then put it in her pocket. Once Clara was satisfied that Nataniel was sleeping normally, they sat down to eat, though Clara was still too upset to eat much.

"Clara, I want to show you something," said Anita, taking the little aspirin box from her pocket. Clara looked at it with eyes still red and swollen.

"See these words printed in thick black letters. They say: **Caution: Keep this medication out of sight and reach of children. Severe poisoning can include coma, seizures and death.** Then, further down, it says: **If a child swallows even a few pills, get emergency treatment as soon as possible. If possible, induce vomiting.** Clara, in an emergency, knowing how to read, knowing what to do, may save a life." Anita didn't want to rub it in, so she went outside to hang the washed laundry to dry. The unwashed would have to wait until tomorrow. But before she could do anything, she had to sit down on the stoop and wait until she stopped trembling.

By late afternoon, Nataniel was laughing and playing as if nothing had happened. That evening, Ramón, snuggling his little boy, thanked Anita with all his heart for rescuing Nataniel. Later, as the parents stood together rocking Nataniel to sleep for the night in his hammock, Anita prepared for the evening lesson as usual. Zenaida sat down with her workbook, grinning as she doodled.

"What are you grinning about?" Anita asked.

"A couple of things," Zenaida replied. "Mostly, thinking of you walking home in your brassiere."

"Yeah, that must have seemed pretty funny. Anything else? You look like the cat that swallowed the canary."

"You'll see," answered Zenaida.

When the lantern was lit, Anita called Ramón to come for class. To her surprise, Clara came and sat down at the table too. "I am ready to learn," she said simply. "For Nataniel . . . and for the baby coming. I have been thinking. . . . I want to be able to read them stories, as well as save their lives if I ever have to."

To get caught up with the others, Clara agreed to an extra class during the day while Nataniel napped. Every evening the three family members bent their heads to the task of further unravelling the mystery of reading and writing. Sometimes Ramón would arrive home from work so exhausted, Anita would have to wake him up for the lesson. Once, after Anita woke him up, he began complaining bitterly about his hard life.

"Sometimes I feel like a donkey on a treadmill," he said, "and just like a donkey in harness, I can't get off. When I first heard about the literacy campaign, I thought, what's the use, what difference would learning how to read and write make at my age?"

"What made you change your mind?" asked Anita.

"Some of my *compañeros* convinced me that it might be possible for us to get better jobs and wages if we knew how to read and write. I started thinking that maybe this donkey *could* get off the treadmill and have a better life, so when the campaign people came around I stuck my finger on the ink pad and made my mark. But tonight I feel just like a tired old sway-backed donkey."

"What kind of job would you like to have, if you could?" Anita asked.

"I'd like to be the foreman in charge at the plantation. Then I would organize things so work was really fair to everyone."

Touched by Ramón's wish, Anita had an idea. She wrote the words *RAMÓN PEREZ PLANTATION FOREMAN* on the table, and told him what the words said. She handed Ramón the chalk. "Copy the words underneath," she instructed him. The table was easier to write on with chalk now because Anita had asked Ramón to sand the table smooth. While he copied the words, she cut out a square of paper." Now print those words on this piece of paper," she said, and asked Clara to get a pin from her sewing box. "Maybe one day this will come true," Anita said, pinning the pretend badge with the words *PLANTATION FOREMAN* to Ramón's shirt. Clara looked at Ramón as if he already were the foreman. *The books we are using are good,* thought Anita, *but taking advantage of opportunities really works.*

Opening **LET'S LEARN TO READ AND WRITE**, she said, "OK Mr. Plantation Foreman and family, tonight let's talk and write about Cuba's new Fishing and Agriculture Co-ops. Listen while I read this paragraph . . ."

Afterwards, while they did a fill-in-the-blanks exercise, Anita observed them quietly and concluded the lessons were going well. Ramón was sweating less in his efforts, and Zenaida's surly attitude had disappeared. A quick learner from the start, she was progressing rapidly now. In fact, Anita was worried that Zenaida might get bored with the pace. As for Clara, Anita felt pretty sure she would catch up in no time.

The Year of Education
July 23, 1961

Dear Mario,

Your newsy letter arrived along with letters from mamá and papá and Marci. I am trying to answer everyone so they can be ready to take for mailing at the next Sunday seminar. Your family sounds great, even though they are noisy and mischievous pranksters. I could use a little of that chatter—my family here is quite quiet and reserved. It took a long time, but Zenaida has finally warmed up to me. Thank goodness! I bet if you were the brigadista here, she would have warmed up to you the very first day!

Marci's last letter made me feel very sad. Her parents are really splurging on her quinceañera, and she says she's just not into it, but is pretending to be for their sake. I will have to be careful what I write—her mother is such a snoop. Do you know Marci's parents wouldn't let Marci come to see me with mamá and papá? They didn't want her socializing with brigadistas, and they're really mad at Marjorie. Mamá mentioned a surprise in her last letter. Do you know anything about that?

Lots and lots of love,
Anita

"Soon you will be ready to take a test," Anita informed her learners one night as they closed their workbooks. Anita saw panic in their eyes. She explained about the three tests that literacy students everywhere would be required to take.

"The first test will show that you have arrived at a certain level of understanding. I promise you will not be asked to do anything you haven't already been taught. The second test will show that you know how to read and write at a higher level than level one. And the final test will show that you are definitely able to read and write anything in the **LET'S LEARN TO READ AND WRITE** study book."

The panic in their eyes was not receding.

"Let me show you something," said Anita. She went to the bedroom and came back with a little triangular flag made of paper attached to a wooden dowel. "The writing on this flag says *Territorio Libre de Analfabetismo*." Anita stuck the flag into the thatch of the ceiling above their heads. "When you all have passed the final test, we will take this flag and place it outside above the door for the world to see that literate people live in this house. Except for Nataniel, of course."

The panic in their eyes was now replaced by looks of disbelief. Clara took Ramón's hand. "Will this be true?" she asked, her voice tremulous. Ramón turned to Anita, "Can I do this, *maestra*? Do you think this donkey's head of mine will be able to do those three tests?"

The memory of the grisly donkey's head flashed before Anita's eyes, but she pushed the image away and answered reassuringly, "I'm positive the three of you can and will do it," — *even if I have to kill myself getting you there.*

July 29, 1961

Dear Diary

Today is Marci's quinceañera. Should I be there with my friend? Havana is so close, but seems a million miles away. I hope Marci enjoys this day. I would like to be able to see her all dressed up and beautiful, even for just one moment. I will have to be satisfied with the pictures papá said he would take.

Anita la cubana

At the Sunday seminar, *brigadistas* were told how to administer the first of the three tests. In the days that followed, Anita completed the first section of the literacy lessons with her learners. "You're ready to go on to the second part of the study book," Anita said as casually as possible one evening, "so tomorrow evening we'll do that first test I told you about."

They received this news in silence, but Anita sensed their tension. The following day, Anita, Clara, Nataniel and Zenaida went to the stream to cool off as they did every day now. They took with them cold boiled *malanga*, toasted plantain chips, goat's milk cheese and green-skinned juice oranges. They ate in the shade of the great *ceiba* tree, its massive prickly trunk the colour of elephant skin. Anita was reading Mario's last letter aloud, but saw that Clara was not paying attention.

"Clara."

Clara looked up, her eyes refocusing.

"Don't worry about the test, Clara. I know you can do it. Only Nataniel won't pass the test." Clara's angular face relaxed, but only a little.

★

Cuban Diary: Reflections on the 1961 Cuban Literacy Campaign.
Credit—Joanne C. Elvy

★

Cuban *bohío*, a typical country dwelling.
Credit—Hilda's Cuban Postcards Museum

★
Brigadista holding
ALFABETICEMOS (Let's
Learn to Read and Write),
and *¡VENCEREMOS!*
the teaching manual and
lesson guide

★
How young some
brigadistas were!

★
Brigadista with *mochila* (backpack)

★ A helping hand

★ *Brigadistas* holding teaching manuals, lesson books and kerosene lanterns

★ 49% of the *brigadistas* were male

★

Woman *campesina* doing her lessons

★

Note the seed necklaces worn by many of the *brigadistas*

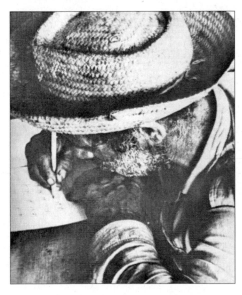

★

Many elderly people learned to
read and write

★

Outdoor class

★

Lucky to have a blackboard

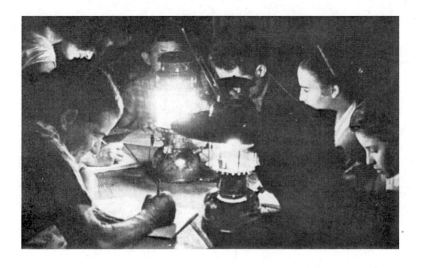

★

Lighting the way to learning

★

December 22, 1961, celebrating the success of the campaign

★

Flags proclaiming *¡Vencimos!* We Won!
(the battle to overcome illiteracy)

★

Fidel Castro at the victory celebration, December 22, 1961

★

Cuba, Territory Free From Illiteracy!

Habana junio 7 de 1961

Dr Fidel Castro
Ciudad
Compañero Fidel:
Mis deseos son se encuentre bien,
Compañero Fidel Castro me siento muy contento aprendí a leer y escribir para defenderme mejor, grasias a la revolución Sosialista de los humildes puedo decir.
Patria o Muerte
¡Venceremos!
Año de la Educación.
Ricardo Perez

★

One of the thousands of letters written
by newly-literate people to Fidel Castro.
There are 707,000 such letters in the
Museo Nacional de la Campaña de Alfabetización
(National Museum of the Literacy Campaign)
Address: Calle 29-East, #8610
between 86 and 102, Ciudad Libertad, Marianao, Havana, Cuba
Telephone: (537) 260-8054

FIRST

The lantern was lit in readiness and her learners sat waiting to take the test. Ramón had even bathed and dressed in clean clothing. Nataniel was asleep in his hammock. The *ribbit-ribbit* croaking of frogs filled the night beyond the *bohío*.

Keeping her voice as calm as she could, Anita said, "Let's begin. Turn to a fresh page in your workbook and write your full name, the names of the others in the family and their age." Three heads bent over the lined page, and each began to write. When they finished, she said, "Now write a full sentence naming the place where you live." Ramón's fingers gripped the pencil so tightly, the tips of his fingers blanched. Zenaida lay down her pencil. *Oh no! Don't quit Zenaida*, but glancing at the page she saw that Zenaida had completed the task and was just waiting.

Ramón chewed his tongue vigorously as he concentrated. He now was able to write in large cursive script that slanted up the page. When he finally lay down his pencil, he rubbed his eyes. "I feel like I just picked five bushels of peanuts". He and Zenaida sneaked sideways looks at Clara. Her hand moved slowly but steadily. When she raised her head, husband and sister relaxed.

"Now," said Anita, "let's read."

She had written out three short paragraphs from the lesson book in large letters—subjects they had already read and talked about. One was about farming, one about workers' rights, and one about equality. All three paragraphs were short and simple. "Ramón, will you go first? Read these three lines about farming, and then I will ask you a couple of questions about what you have read."

"Wait please," said Ramón, rising to fill a cup from the pot of boiled water. He drained one cupful, and then another. Ramón read the paragraph laboriously, but correctly. Anita beamed at him, and he exhaled hugely. His answers to her questions showed he hadn't just sounded out words; he had understood what he had read.

"Who would like to go next?" asked Anita.

"I will," said Zenaida. Ramón and Clara listened with pride as she read the paragraph about being equal, her voice clear and even. When she answered the questions without hesitation, her eyes never left Anita's. When Anita said, "Zenaida, that was well done," Zenaida turned and hugged Clara. It was the first time Anita had ever seen her show affection for her sister. Clara then read about workers' rights, stumbling a few times, her arms tightly crossed over her chest. Then she answered Anita's questions. When Anita said, "*¡Brava!* Clara," the tension drained from Clara's face and body.

The final part of the test was dictation of one of the paragraphs. Anita knew there would be spelling mistakes, but supervisors had instructed the *brigadistas* to overlook spelling errors. They had been told that if the words were written and recognizable, that would be good enough.

When the test was completed, Ramón, Clara and Zenaida sat expectantly.

"Do you want to go to bed and I will let you know the results tomorrow, or do you want to wait while I look them over?" Anita asked.

"*Maestra*, I would never be able to sleep," said Ramón. "I will wait." The others said they would wait too. So they sat while Anita examined their tests. Ramón's and Clara's writing was clumsy and uneven. Clara had made more spelling and other minor mistakes, but both had been able to complete the test satisfactorily. Zenaida's handwriting was small but legible, and she had made only a few minor errors. Anita didn't mark mistakes. She wrote across the top of each page in large letters, *APROBADO, PASSED*, drew a red crayon star in the upper corner and handed the workbooks back.

"*¡Felicidades!* You all passed the first test. Congratulations!" Anita wanted to jump up and down or run around whooping, but restrained herself. All three sat staring at their test papers.

"What's the matter? Aren't you happy? Aren't you proud of yourselves, especially you Clara?" said Anita.

Ramón looked around at the others, open-mouthed. "Yes *maestra*, we are proud, and happy. It is just so hard to believe. We have passed a test. We are really reading and writing. We are showing that we are not just ignorant *campesinos*. And who would have thought that a mere child would be capable of doing this for us! We must have a drink of good Cuban rum to celebrate! But maybe I shouldn't offer you rum. After all, you are still a child and your parents might disapprove . . . even be angry if they knew."

"Well, I don't know for sure, but I think they would understand," replied Anita. "It's such a special occasion! But *muy poquito*, just a wee bit for me, Ramón."

¡Salud! ¡Salud! To your health! they toasted in unison, clinking their cups together. The noisy celebration woke Nataniel up crying, which made them laugh and toast again to Nataniel's health.

★

"Would you like to see a cockfight, Anita?" said Ramón. "I'm going to one today."

Anita knew cockfights were popular, but never thought she'd ever go to one. Her father said cockfighting was a blood sport, like bullfighting. He said it should be banned, in Cuba and everywhere. Her mother had said just thinking about it made her nauseous. *But it's nice of Ramón to want to show me*, Anita thought, and she didn't want to seem girly and squeamish.

"Will Clara and Zenaida be coming too?" she asked hopefully.

"No. They went once and hated it," replied Ramón.

Anita could hear excited shouting even before she and Ramón reached the yard of the *campesino* where the cockfight was being held. Ramón looped Bufi's reins to the fence post, and hurried toward the noisy group of people gathered in a circle in the clearing. "Make room for us, *compañeros*," said Ramón, elbowing his way into the circle.

The first cockfight was about to begin. The crowd of onlookers consisted mainly of excited men and boys. Everyone stood around a crude, shallow pit about a foot deep and ten feet across. Two men holding hooded roosters stood facing each other inside the pit. A man whom the people called El Gallero, the cockfight master, walked around the inside of the pit collecting money as people bet on one or the other fighting cock. The man was square-built, dressed like a cowboy. As El Gallero made the rounds, he never stopped talking.

"Are you here for a picnic, *compañeros*? No, you're here to watch a combat. Place your bets, *compañeros*. Place your bets."

"Those are not just any roosters, Anita," explained Ramón. "They are gamecocks, specially bred and trained to be fighters. You can't tell now because they are hooded, but the comb and wattle of all gamecocks are cut off so they can't be slashed in combat. But look at their legs." Anita looked closely at the gamecock nearest her. A curved steel spike was taped tightly to each leg where its natural spurs would be.

"Last chance to place your bets, bellowed El Gallero. A fight to the death between two great combatants. Is your favourite *El Diablo*, The Devil, or *El Fierabràs*, The Spitfire? Place your bets. Last chance to place your bets."

A frenzy of last minute betting took place, with hands reaching out to press *peso* bills into the money-man's hands. Anita wondered how El Gallero kept track of it all. Ramón called out to the money-man, anxious to place a bet. When El Gallero stopped to take Ramón's money, he looked straight at Anita, his eyebrows raised. "What about you, little lady? Will you place a bet, too?" There was something menacing about El Gallero. Anita shook her head and looked down to escape his mocking eyes.

"Let the cockfight begin," El Gallero finally announced. "*Caballeros,* gentlemen," he said to the men holding the gamecocks, "place the combatants in the middle of the pit, beak to beak. When I count to three, remove the hoods and leave the pit immediately. The bird that remains standing will be declared the winner."

At the count of three, the competitors swiftly removed the hoods from the cocks and leaped out of the pit. Immediately the spectators surged forward and began to yell, urging their favourite cock to kill the other. Anita covered her ears. The gamecocks moved around each other for a few seconds, like animals sniffing each other out, then there was a blur of bodies and a flurry of feathers as the gamecocks jumped at each other feet first, slashing with their steel spurs. Before Anita could tell what was happening, the crowd broke into cheers. One of the gamecocks strutted around in the pit while the other lay dead, grotesquely twisted and bloodied, its neck gashed by the knife-sharp steel spur of its opponent. Plum and black-coloured feathers lay scattered in the dirt. The winning cock's owner walked around the pit holding the bird aloft, exhibiting his fighter with pride. The loser, a grizzled *campesino,* limped into the pit to retrieve his dead bird. Anita watched him shuffle out of the yard, dangling the creature by its feet, leaving a trail of blood in the dust. El Gallero made the rounds again, distributing winnings to the winners, including Ramón.

They stayed for a few more cockfights, but Anita kept her head turned away during the deadly action. Soon the smell of blood was in the air, making Anita gag. She turned away so Ramón wouldn't see, but he was enjoying the spectacle so much, he didn't take notice. *What is it that fascinates and excites the people so?* she wondered.

Ramón was jubilant as he counted the money he won. As they rode home he kept talking about cockfighting, but Anita hardly listened.

"That man they call El Gallero . . . He gave me the creeps Ramón."

The Year of Education,
Caimanera,
August 1, 1961

Dear Anita,

Quite a few learners in my region were not able to pass the first test. I am picked up every day in a Jeep to go to nearby Guantánamo to do extra teaching from 5pm until 7pm. When I return, I grab something to eat and teach my learner family until 9pm. I received a letter from mamá. Do you already know they are planning a trip to be with you on your birthday? An amazing thing happened recently. During the night I woke up to a strange sound, like a wind chime of hundreds of dangling bamboo sticks (kind of poetic for a jock, don't you think?). I got up and looked outside and there were black and red crabs everywhere. It was the annual migration to the inland hills. That's where the crabs lay their eggs, then return to the sea. People sleeping outdoors in hammocks because of the heat woke up with crabs crawling all around them! Over the next few days, the roads became slimy with dead crabs run over by trucks and tractors. What a mess!

What Mario wrote next made Anita groan aloud.

"What?" demanded Zenaida.

Tears welled up in Anita's eyes. "A *brigadista* died—an asthma attack. A doctor arrived too late. She was my age, Zenaida." The two girls gazed at each other in dismay. Anita heard her father's words echoing again in her head. *Life among the poor in the countryside is no picnic.*

"I think you have an admirer," whispered Dani, nudging Anita.

"What are you talking about?" Anita whispered back.

"Claudio," whispered Dani. "Haven't you noticed he's always sitting somewhere near you at seminar meetings?" Anita looked around, then quickly faced front again. Claudio was right behind them.

"Maybe it's you he's admiring."

Dani harrumphed. "It's definitely not me, my dear. I've been noticing him watching you for some time now. You really haven't noticed, have you *boba*, you silly girl?" Marjorie turned around and shushed them. Dani winked at Anita. Blushing to the roots of her hair, Anita stared straight ahead, fanning herself with a notebook.

The director updated everyone. Anita felt lucky. Her learners had passed the first test, but not everybody had the same good news to share. The director made an effort to cheer them up.

"Think of yourselves in your schools. Not everybody learns at the same pace. Unlike you, most of your learners don't have time to study. Some of them are so tired from their day's work, they can hardly stay awake to concentrate. We are not blaming your teaching. We know you're all doing your best. To reach Cuba's literacy goal before year's end, we'll just have to work a little harder."

Anita felt glum. All the *brigadistas* looked glum.

"Here's some advice," said the director. "As a student, isn't it so that you want to do well for a teacher whom you really like?" The *brigadistas* buzzed in agreement. "Then my advice is this: Work harder on your personal relationships in any way you can, but always in a proper way. Remember, as teachers, you represent the country.

"It's almost lunchtime, but first, there are a couple of important announcements—one good, one bad. First the good news. One hundred and seventy seven thousand men, women and children registered in the campaign have been tested by optometrists and fitted out with prescription eyeglasses free of charge. This will make their learning so much easier."

Anita giggled. "What's so funny?" Dani asked.

"Ramón is one of the people who needed glasses. The first time he put them on he immediately began joking about being scared now that he could see what his wife really looked like. Clara chased him around pretending to beat him with a wooden spoon. It was really funny."

". . . and the bad news. Counter-revolutionary bandits have made threats about kidnapping *brigadistas*. Another donkey head was thrown into Bainoa's campaign headquarters last night."

Anita's giggles dried up. Would she ever forget the horsemen galloping around the schoolhouse, the shots fired in the air, the horses whinnying, the sound of shattering glass, the sight of the bloody donkey head, the ugly threats, the outhouse on fire, the goosebumps of shivery fear?

"From now on, you will see more civilian militia and maybe even regular military presence in this area," continued the director. "We have been fortunate not to experience any further direct attacks since the ones early on at the schoolhouse, but we cannot take chances. Be extra aware, extra careful. Report anything suspicious to the supervisor of your group. If you are living in the countryside with your learners, report anything suspicious to your learner family and they will get the information to us somehow. Now, the roast pig barbecue will be ready soon. Enjoy! Group dismissed."

Dani seemed undisturbed by news about counter-revolutionaries. Her mind was on playing matchmaker, so she picked up the conversation where she had left off. "I think you and Claudio would like each other," she said quietly. "Try to get a conversation going with him at the B.B.Q. It won't be hard. And don't try to pretend you're not interested, *señorita*."

"And just how exactly do you get a conversation going?" asked Anita.

"Spill pop on him. Squirt ketchup at him. Do anything that will get his attention. Or if you like, I'll tell him that you want to talk to him."

"No, don't do that!" blurted Anita. "I'll think of something—really I will." After Dani threatened for the third time to go tell Claudio that Anita wanted to talk to him, Anita forced herself to walk toward where he was standing with friends. She didn't have the slightest idea what she would do or say when she reached the spot, but she needn't have fretted. When Claudio noticed her approaching, he separated from the group and said simply, "Hi Anita."

As they stood talking, comparing their learner families and their teaching challenges, Anita studied Claudio. He had fantastic eyelashes, longer than most girls. His smooth skin was the colour of pecans. When he smiled a distinctive space between his upper front teeth was revealed. All in all, she concluded that Claudio was a handsome mulatto boy. But the best thing about him was his natural sense of humour. She hadn't laughed so hard in ages.

When Ramón arrived to take her back, Anita extended her hand. "See you next week, Claudio." The hand that pressed hers held on just a little longer than she expected. Anita turned to look back as Bufi trotted off, and felt pleased when she saw Claudio still standing where they had parted, watching her ride away.

August 5, 1961

Dear Diary,

I had a nice time with one of the brigadistas named Claudio today. He's so nice, really simpático. I'd like to get to know him better but I'll only get to see him for a short time each Sunday. I received a letter from Mario today. I think he'd like Claudio.

Anita la cubana

Ramón was transferred from work on the peanut plantation to clearing brush for the planting of more sugar cane.

"Ramón, could I go with you tomorrow to volunteer to help with clearing if it's OK with Clara?"

"It's very hard work, Anita. Are you sure you want to tackle it?"

"I'm sure," said Anita, striking a pose that made her biceps bulge.

In the dark before dawn, Anita dressed quickly, stuffing her hair under a palmetto hat. Ramón gave her a kerchief to tie around her neck to help keep seeds and chaff from getting under her shirt collar. As Ramón placed his machete into its leather sheath and tied it to the saddle, she put the sandwiches of goat's milk cheese Clara had made them and a cantina of fresh water into the saddlebag.

"Which fields are we going to?" Anita asked, hoisting herself up on Bufi behind Ramón.

"Near Santa Cruz del Norte, close to the coast," Ramón replied. "It will take us over an hour riding double."

Anita had not seen much of the countryside so was glad to see they were heading in a direction away from Bainoa. They rode through mist floating about in low places. As day broke, the sun popped above the horizon. Cresting a hill, the countryside spread in a gold-green panorama before them. Was there any place in the world more beautiful? Anita started to sing softly.

Cuba, que linda es Cuba
Quien la defiende la quiere más.
Cuba, how lovely is Cuba
Those who defend her do love her best.

Ramón joined in, their voices ringing out in the stillness of the early morning.

"Ramón, were you born and raised around here?"

"No, I was born and raised on a sugar plantation in Camegüey province, and never knew anything else. When my first wife died, I wanted to get away from there. The plantation owner did nothing to help my wife in her illness—she had tuberculosis—so I quit and came here to work on the peanut plantations. It's donkey work too, but I was able to save some money and build my *bohío*. That was seven years ago."

"What about Clara?" Anita probed. She had been thinking how little she actually knew about her learners. She once tried asking Clara some personal questions, but Clara had said, "Let the past be," so Anita had never asked again.

"Clara's story, and Zenaida's, is very sad," said Ramón. "The family was small to begin with, and through death from accidents and illnesses over the years, they have been left orphaned and with no relatives. I met Clara harvesting *maní*, peanuts. As you see us, that's all the family she has."

Orphans! Now I understand the sadness that Clara carries around with her, and maybe why Zenaida acts so strange at times. A wave of homesickness swept over Anita.

When they arrived at the fields, they dismounted along with dozens of *campesinos* arriving to work. Zebu oxen, their impressive folds of wattles sagging heavily from their necks, stood motionless in harness waiting to pull the first cartloads of cleared brush to burning piles. While Ramón tied Bufi up with the other horses and gave her water, Anita wandered over to watch some of the men sharpening their machetes with long files.

"Will you show me how to use a machete, Ramón?"

"I thought you'd help load cut brush, Anita. I'll have to ask the foreman. He may not want to spare the time." Ramón led Anita to meet the foreman.

"The *brigadista* here wants to learn how to handle a machete, *compañero*. What do you say?"

"Well, well, well. Another little lady who wants to do a man's job," the foreman said good-naturedly. "That's my wife over there," he said pointing with his chin, "so I can't very well say no, can I? You go to work, my good man, and I'll see if the little gal can handle it."

Some men are so macho! thought Anita. She made up her mind right then not to give up easily, no matter how hard it was. The foreman handed her a machete and work gloves and led her a short distance away from *macheteros* who were already cutting brush, moving swiftly with practiced strokes. The land was a tangle of tough weeds, brambles and young saplings. The foreman showed her how to grasp the machete and the technique of cutting each type of growth. Anita's first attempts were pathetic. The weeds and long grasses just bounced back, and it took several blows of the machete to cut through even a thin stalk. Sometimes the machete just bounced off thicker stalks. Anita expected the foreman to laugh or suggest she give up, but he didn't. He corrected her swing, and told her to keep trying. When things started going better he didn't make a big deal of it. "Just keep your distance from others in case the machete flies out of your hand," he said. "That can happen with beginners, and you wouldn't want to hurt anyone, would you?" He cautioned her to stop and rest frequently and drink plenty of water. "Thanks for volunteering *señorita,*" he added over his shoulder as he walked away.

Anita worked as best she could. She soon had to remove the kerchief from her neck and tie it around her forehead to keep sweat from stinging her eyes. It wasn't long before her back and shoulders were aching, but she was determined to show she could do the work. Sometimes a nearby *machetero* would catch her eye and flash an encouraging smile without missing a swing of his machete. When she began to feel dizzy, and noticed that her swings were getting weak, she decided to call it quits. The sun was still low in the morning sky, but she had cleared a fair area and felt good. She found the foreman and asked him to put her on another job.

"I was watching you, young lady. Not bad for the first time. Not bad at all. Now, get something to eat, then help load brush into the carts."

Anita managed to hang in until the end of the workday. Her clothing was full of chaff, soaked with sweat and smelly. Ramón's too. They picked burrs and sticky seeds off each other's clothing and poured water over their heads to cool off. Ramon gave Bufi water before mounting to leave for home. A large group of mounted *campesinos* and two boy *brigadistas* Anita had seen at gatherings but didn't really know by name all left together. Daylight was fading as they rode along talking, bidding each other goodbye as riders peeled off to follow side roads to their homes.

Anita was so exhausted she began nodding off, rocking to Bufi's motion, too tired to mind the smell of Ramón's sweaty shirt as she rested her head against his back. In her half sleep she sensed Bufi slowing down and felt Ramón withdrawing his machete from its leather sheath. Just as she was about to ask what was happening, why they were slowing down, Ramón reined Bufi in sharply. Wide-awake now, she saw what the trouble was. Three mounted men about twenty metres ahead were blocking the way. They wore kerchiefs masking their faces, and all were pointing rifles right at them. Anita's mouth went dry and her heart began to thud wildly.

NARROW ESCAPE

"Hand over the *brigadistas*," one of the masked men demanded. "Scrunch down behind me, Anita," Ramón told her.

Making herself as small as she could, Anita looked around and behind. There were fewer people than when they had started out. Including Ramón, she counted nine *campesinos* and the two *brigadistas*. *Twelve people, counting me, but what can I do?*

"I said, hand over the *brigadistas*," the man called out again.

"Let us pass and we will do you no harm," Ramón answered.

"Fools! It is we who can do the harm. Don't you see we are armed? Now hand over those *muchachos*, including the little *señorita* hiding behind you."

Ramón twisted slightly in the saddle, and spoke just loud enough for the others to hear. "*Compañeros*, we cannot give in. You know what those men will do to these kids. We must rush them to take them by surprise, and if we have to, we will show them what the sharp blade of a machete feels like. All agreed?"

"*De acuerdo*, Ramón. We are with you," came the replies.

"Hang on as tight as you can, Anita," Ramón said softly. Digging his heels hard into Bufi's flanks, Ramón growled, "*¡Vámanos hombres!* Let's go!"

The horses lunged forward and the next few moments passed in a burst of horsepower, shouting and rifle shots. The *campesinos* sped toward the rebels brandishing their machetes and shouting loudly. The horses whinnied, and their pounding hooves kicked up dirt and stones. Anita clung to Ramón, the side of her face pressed tightly against his back. One of the attackers crowded his horse against Bufi, and tried to pull Anita onto his horse by grabbing her around the waist. Anita tightened her hold around Ramón's waist and pulled away from her attacker with all her strength. Pain coursed through her leg squeezed between the two horses. The attacker grabbed hold of Anita's arm, attempting to drag her off Bufi. Anita was losing her grip on Ramón when a flash of silver passed in front of her as Ramón brought his machete down, slashing the attacker's arm that held the reins. Bellowing with pain, the attacker released Anita and spurred his horse toward the woods, calling the other two men to follow. Before disappearing into the trees, the leader reined in his horse and turned around to shout, "You won't get off so easily next time, *hijos del diablo*, you sons of the devil!"

In a cloud of dust, the *campesinos* reined their horses into a tight ball circling the mounted *brigadistas*. The horses skittered about, wild with excitement, their eyes still rolling. The men held them on tight reins until they calmed down. *Please, oh please don't let anyone be shot or wounded* Anita prayed as she looked around, counting. All eleven were in their saddles, all sitting upright.

"Are you hurt, Ramón? Is anyone hurt?"

"No, Anita. They fired shots in the air to frighten us. When we didn't stop, they tried to surround you and the *muchachos*, but we were able to drive them off with our machetes. Obviously they did not want to kill anyone, so when their plan failed, they took off. They probably didn't expect us to attack, and we outnumbered them. *Pobrecita*, you are still trembling, poor girl."

She and the *muchachos* were safe because the men had been so brave. The *muchachos* had been brave too. But Ramón . . . he had been heroic! All rode keeping close together while taking the boys to their places. Under cover of the fading light, Anita let the tears fall as she recovered from her narrow escape. Shudders ran through her body as she thought about what might have happened if things had gone differently.

When they arrived home, Ramón was agitated, and began pacing back and forth as he told Clara about the attack. Finally he paused in his pacing, and stood before Anita.

"Anita, I can do little to protect you if the rebels are so aggressive now. We are simple *campesinos* with no defense. What is a machete against rifles?" Ramón began reasoning with Anita, determined that she arrange to be reassigned to a less isolated place where there were more people and better protection by militia.

"What could we do if rebels came here? How could I protect you, protect my family? Our only neighbour is Rosa, an elderly widow living alone. What could she do?" Pacing around, he stopped in front of his wife. "Why are you so silent, Clara? Don't you agree the responsibility for Anita's safety is too great for her to remain here?"

"It is a great worry. If Anita feels she should leave . . ." she replied, her voice trailing off.

Anita realized that Clara didn't want her to leave. *But I should leave so as not to put myself and the family in danger. I have no right to do that. And what about my own family? Their worries have come to pass.* Anita knew she should agree that it would be best if she returned home or had her assignment changed to a safer place. Why not just say so? But she couldn't bring herself to say it. She had invested so much in the effort to be a good teacher, a good *brigadista*. She felt her stubborn streak rising like some physical thing. She knew she wasn't being reasonable, but she just didn't want to give in or give up.

"If I were to leave, how would you continue to study and learn?" said Anita. "They probably wouldn't assign another *brigadista* to live with you. What about becoming a foreman at the plantation someday? What about Clara's dream of reading to Nataniel someday? What about Zenaida's future?"

Ramón's arms hung heavily by his sides. He looked at Clara and his little son. "If my family were hurt, if you were hurt, or worse, how could I live with myself? We were plain lucky this time, Anita. Next time . . . I don't want to even think about a next time." Glancing around, Anita was startled to find Zenaida's eyes fixed on her, silently beseeching her not to leave.

"Ramón, I had to deceive my parents to become a *brigadista*." She pointed to the miniature literacy flag she had stuck in the thatch above their heads a month ago. "I promised myself that that this household would become a territory free from illiteracy; that we would place that flag outside the door of this *bohío* together. What happened was scary, really scary . . ." She paused, folding her arms across her chest. "I'm not quitting, Ramón. I won't leave unless you and Clara tell me to my face, or the campaign director makes me."

Later, lying awake in her hammock, Anita's mind was still racing. In the end, Ramón had agreed to her staying, but only if *señora* Marjorie and the Bainoa campaign director allowed it. If she was allowed to remain, Ramón would request a rifle from the local people's militia headquarters, and get instruction in its use. He would carry the rifle when taking her to and from Bainoa for the Sunday seminars. They had decided it would be safer to have classes in the early morning before Ramón left for work so that everyone could be more alert to the approach of intruders at night. Anita promised to never leave the *bohío* clearing. Zenaida was to keep watch when Anita was bathing. They had even discussed creating a hiding place she could run to somewhere away from the *bohío*. Almost asleep, Anita thought of one more thing. She got up and stood outside Clara and Ramón's bedroom.

"Ramón . . . Ramón . . ." she whispered.

"¿Qué quieres? What now, Anita?"

"Promise me you won't talk about what happened today when my parents come for my birthday." At first, Ramón said he could not promise that, but Anita persisted. Finally, with a great sigh, he agreed. As she climbed back into the hammock, she realized how much her whole body hurt, especially her arm and leg. Probably she would have big bruises.

"Anita . . . ?"

"What Zenaida?"

"I hope they let you stay."

"I'm glad you want me to stay."

August 17, 1961

Dear Diary,

Hooray! I was allowed to stay on with the Perez family, but I had to beg and plead with the director and Marjorie and promise never to leave the bohío except on Sundays when Ramón takes me to and from the seminars in Bainoa. Ramón has a rifle now and has been shown how to use it. My bruises are fading. I'm hoping they will be gone by the time my folks arrive for my birthday.

Anita la cubana

DAY OF DAYS

The morning of her birthday, Zenaida tumbled Anita out of her hammock, shouting "*¡Feliz cumpleaños!* Happy Birthday sweet fifteen!"

Despite Clara's protests that there was still too much to do before Anita's parents arrived, Anita insisted on teaching right after an early breakfast. Anita had tried to keep the family from fussing, but it was impossible. Every day when Ramón got home he worked, cleaning the pig pen and chicken coop, refreshing old thatch on the roof of the *bohío*, finishing the outdoor bathing shed that he was building.

Despite her big belly and swollen ankles, Clara was like a whirlwind. She made a new apron from an old bed sheet, sewed a little shirt for Nataniel, washed and ironed the family's good clothing with the most antique-looking iron Anita had ever seen. Clara had insisted that Zenaida scrub the few pieces of furniture. The dirt floor was swept and received a fresh sprinkling of lime to control insects. Even Bufi and the mule were washed and brushed after Anita had removed all the burrs from their tails and manes.

Clara had wrung the necks of two chickens. Anita still wasn't able to watch the killing, but she did pluck the feathers after and hold the naked, bumpy-skinned chicken corpses over flames to sear off the pinfeathers. The air still reeked of burnt flesh and feathers. Ramón had slaughtered a piglet, something else she couldn't bear to watch. Pigs seemed to know something terrible was about to happen to them and tried to squirm away. Their terrified squeals sounded so human.

When Anita went to check Clara's workbook, Clara covered the page with her hands. "*Maestra*, I could not concentrate on the lesson today so there must be many mistakes. I can't stop thinking of all that I must still do. Please excuse me from the rest of the lesson." Giving in, Anita declared the lesson over.

While the family lay down for a brief *siesta* in the afternoon, Anita sat outside waiting, straining to hear the approach of the Studebaker. Would they never arrive! Aroma of the suckling pig roasting on a spit over a charcoal fire filled the air. The fire hissed and flared as fat dripped onto the flames. The progress notebook lay open on her lap. She was always behind, but couldn't seem to keep her mind on it today. A movement in the nearby flower bush distracted her. A *zunzún*, a tiny bee hummingbird, the smallest of all its kind, whirred in and out of the red trumpets of hibiscus flowers. Anita thought the *zunzún* looked like a tiny iridescent helicopter.

"Anita! Anita!" Her mother's voice. She had been so captivated by the *zunzún*, she hadn't heard the car until it pulled into the clearing. Her mother was leaning out the window waving and calling. Anita's flight toward her parents almost equalled the flight of the *zunzún*. Even her usually reserved father couldn't contain his emotion, jumping out of the car and folding her in his arms. And what a surprise! Tomasa emerged from the back seat, her round arms open wide to embrace her. After much hugging, Anita said, "Come and meet my learner family," and led them toward the *bohío*. Anita could feel her mother taking in the whole scene, the primitive buildings, the hardened dirt clearing, the poverty and shabbiness of it all. Anita realized she couldn't identify when she had stopped seeing things as her mother and father must see them at this moment.

Ramón and Clara had heard the car, and stood on the stoop, waiting. Worried that they would be dazzled by the car and by her parents' city clothing, Anita was glad that her mother was wearing slacks, a simple blouse, and flat sandals. Her father wore a traditional loose *guayabera* shirt over tan slacks.

Ramón and Clara stood stiffly, seized by shyness. Ramón wiped his hands on his clean pants before shaking hands. During the introductions, Anita noticed Clara staring at her mother's long crimson fingernails. After shaking hands, Clara hid the ragged nails of her blunt fingers by curling her fingers up tightly. Zenaida was inside with Nataniel and wouldn't come out until Anita went in and dragged her out. It was Tomasa who made everyone relax, going into raptures about the sight and aroma of the roasting piglet. "We had to come to the countryside to find some honest-to-goodness Cuban food!" she exclaimed.

Papá helped Ramón carry the kitchen table outside where they sat on homemade benches drinking fresh coconut water flavoured with lime juice and cane sugar.

"Well," said papá, "our daughter tells us in her letters that she is very proud of you . . . that you are all learning well. Does this mean she is a good teacher?"

"Papá, don't put them on the spot. What can they say in front of me?"

"We can say the truth, *maestra*," said Ramón. "When we consented to participate in the literacy campaign and agreed to let a teacher come to our poor house, we could not even sign our names on the consent paper. Our thumbs were dipped in ink, and we signed by making a mark with our purple thumbs. Now when I go to the store to get supplies, I sign my name for the bill. Anita has taught me how to count and write numbers, so now I can tally my own harvest of peanuts. My wife learns quickly and writes even better than I do—these hands of mine are so rough and clumsy. And Clara's sister here . . . I am proud to say she is quicker than either of us. *Señor y señora* Fonseca, you should be very proud of your daughter."

Anita felt a flush creeping down from her scalp to the open vee of her shirt. Even her ears felt hot! And this was the first she knew about Ramón's practical use of numbers.

"Tomasa has a special surprise for you, Anita," said mamá. "But first, let's get all the things you asked us to bring out of the trunk." As the trunk was emptied, everything that Anita had requested appeared amid gasps of excitement and pleasure. The blackboard was a good-sized one; there was lots of chalk and even an eraser brush. Clara held the stew pot to her body as though it were a priceless jewel. Nataniel's curls were fluffed with a little blue hairbrush. Ramón examined every moving part of the Swiss army knife before replacing it in its holster and attaching it to his belt. Anita made Zenaida close her eyes, then held up the dress mamá had chosen for her. When told to open her eyes, Zenaida was speechless as a sky blue tight-waisted dress with a scoop neck and a flared skirt was placed in her arms.

"Go, Zenaida," Clara spoke softly and affectionately. "Go put it on."

"These too," said mamá, pulling red leather sandals out of a box. When Zenaida appeared in the doorway a few minutes later, papá made her blush, telling her she was the most beautiful young woman on the whole island of Cuba.

"Marci asked me to give you this," said mamá, taking a cream-coloured envelope from her purse. Anita withdrew a birthday card with sweet birthday wishes and a close up photograph of Anita and Marci hugging each other when they were nine. On the back of the photo, Marci had written:

1955, Anita and Marci, Best Friends then, now, and forever.

Anita fingered her locket as she always did when thinking of Marci. She replaced the card and photo in the envelope, her eyes swimming with held-back tears. After everything had been admired twice over, Tomasa asked, "Don't you want to know what my surprise is, *señorita* Anita?" Anita looked about, but there seemed to be nothing else.

"What is it, Tomasa?"

She watched with curiosity as Tomasa placed the blackboard on the table and removed a piece of chalk from the box. *Is she going to draw me a picture?* Anita wondered. Slowly and carefully, Tomasa began to write on the blackboard. Anita couldn't believe her eyes as the words appeared. *Feliz quinceañera, señorita Anita. Tu gran amiga*, Tomasa. Happy fifteenth birthday, Miss Anita. Your special friend, Tomasa.

"Tomasa, this is a fantastic surprise! But how?"

"*Señora* Mirta teaches me and Gladis every day for one hour before we start our work. We started soon after you left. It was *señora* Mirta's idea." Anita hugged Tomasa, chiding her, "You see, Tomasa. You aren't too old to learn new tricks." Turning to her mother, she could only say, "*Madre*, you are an amazing woman!"

There is one more surprise," said her mother. "Tell her what it is, Daniel."

"I am teaching Fernando," papá said simply. "At first he was very reluctant, but he allowed himself to be convinced."

As the afternoon drifted into evening, they sat around the fire. They were so full of roast pork, roast chicken, rice, yucca, fried plantain and a dessert of freshly-sliced mangoes, they were almost too full to continue talking. *What a day this has been*! reflected Anita, her legs stretched out. She looked at her scuffed, dusty boots, and smiled to herself thinking of the silk or taffeta dress and satin party pumps she'd be wearing if she had been in Havana this day. She caught her mother staring at her. *Are mamá and papá at all upset that they are here rather than celebrating my quinceañera in Havana as they had hoped*? She rose and kneeled close to her mother.

"For me, this has been the best birthday, mamá. Are you sorry to be here rather than at the country club?"

"I won't lie, daughter. I would have liked to celebrate your *quinceañera* with family and friends in Havana. But being here with you and your learner family is special in its own way. Truly."

The conversation advanced lazily from one thing to another as evening approached. Papá asked if they had heard about a *brigadista* who had died when the tractor he was driving tipped over, crushing him.

"How terrible! The worst thing that has happened to anyone in our Bainoa group is a boy who got bitten on the shoulder by a horse," said Anita.

"We know that's not true, Anita," papá said, his voice now serious. "We know you didn't want to alarm us, but we know about the rebel ambush that you and other *brigadistas* narrowly escaped recently. When it was reported to the local authorities, they notified us to assure us you were safe and unhurt. Marjorie called us too. She talked us out of rushing here to take you home. But we do intend to take you home with us when we leave tomorrow."

Ramón and Anita exchanged looks.

"*Señor y señora* Fonseca, we have been told that the army and military police are now stationed throughout the Bainoa region. People say the rebels will be afraid now, but that doesn't mean there's nothing to worry about. Clara and I are doing all we can to protect Anita, but if you decide Anita must leave here, we would understand. . . ."

"Mamá, papá," Anita interrupted, "don't even think about it. I'm not leaving. I have official permission to stay, so let's change the subject." Before her parents could object, Anita turned to her learner family and announced firmly, "Tomorrow morning in class we will learn to write the names of your gifts and describe them."

Papá threw up his hands, his face registering a mixture of frustration and pride. "You see what my wife and I must endure from this spunky and very stubborn girl? OK Anita, we'll drop the subject—for now. The group sat in awkward silence until Anita's mother spoke.

"Aren't you wondering about your birthday gift, Anita?"

"I thought the blackboard and chalk was my gift."

Papá went to the car, and withdrew a brightly wrapped box from under the front seat. Anita tore off the wrapping and withdrew a camera and several rolls of film. Anita wasted no time in inserting a roll and taking pictures of her two families, though Clara protested because of her big belly. Papá took a picture of Anita with the Perez family. As if by some signal, Ramón, Clara and Zenaida rose, excused themselves and disappeared into the *bohío*. Anita's mother took advantage of the moment. "They are very nice people, Anita . . . but these conditions . . ." Anita hoped the others hadn't noticed the expression of disapproval on her mother's face as she crossed the yard coming from the outhouse earlier.

Papá cut in before Anita could say anything. "Mirta, you said you wouldn't."

"Anita, close your eyes," called Zenaida from the doorway. Grateful for the interruption, Anita shut her eyes and soon felt things being placed on her lap. "You can open your eyes now," Zenaida said. Somehow, Ramón had found time to make her a hinged palmwood box with her name carved into the lid. It was perfect for storing letters and photographs. Clara had made a pillow cover with her name embroidered on it surrounded by embroidered flowers and birds. Zenaida gave her a framed coloured drawing on cloth of Anita teaching by lantern light, the literacy flag in the background. Anita, speechless, hugged each of them hard.

"*¡Ay¡ ¡Ay¡ ¡Ay¡* She's breaking my bones!" goofed Ramón.

"Hugging you these days is like hugging a watermelon," she teased Clara.

Zenaida returned her hug with affection.

Just before her parents left for Bainoa where they would spend the night in the small hotel there, Anita leaned through the car window to talk to her mother. "I think you are still upset, mamá," she said quietly.

"I didn't mean to spoil anything . . ." began mamá. "It's just . . . well, we're so frightened for you, and everything is so . . . primitive." Then her mother squeezed Anita's hand. "Never mind, Anita. Today was a never-to-be-forgotten day for all of us. You are doing something wonderful for these people, and your father and I are really proud of you and Mario."

"*Yo también.* Me too," echoed Tomasa from the back seat.

"Good," said papá. "We have a mutual admiration society. But tomorrow we will talk again about you coming home."

August 27, 1961

Dear Diary,

Celebrated my fifteenth birthday today—a different kind of

quinceañera. It wasn't traditional, but it was great! My parents and Tomasa were here. Definitely not going back to Havana with them! Too tired to write more.

Anita la cubana

"Anita, I have never heard you so talkative!" exclaimed her mother the next day as they drove to the schoolhouse to see Marjorie. "And I notice you have changed in other ways too," she said, nudging her daughter while looking sideways at Anita's chest in a meaningful way. Anita knew what her mother meant. Her breasts had grown making the buttons of her shirt pull apart under the strain. She glanced at her father, who pretended not to hear. *Lucky I took a bigger size uniform*, she thought. She nudged her mother back, and changed the subject.

"Tell me all about Marci's *quinceañera*," she said.

Her mother began describing the highlights—Marci's dress, her hairdo, the decorations, the food, the orchestra—but Anita found she wasn't really listening. Everything connected with Havana seemed so unreal now. A year ago she might have been impressed with what she was hearing, but now . . .

". . . there were at least two hundred guests . . ."

The guests, Anita knew, would all have been white people. Anyone of colour would have been parking cars, serving food and drinks or cleaning up the mess. The Country Club was still like Varadero was *antes,* before the revolution, when guests were white and the help was black. Her thoughts turned to the lesson she had taught on the theme of racial discrimination. The reading had started off with a quote by the much-loved Cuban writer, José Martí: *Mankind is more than white, more than mixed blood, more than black. Just say person, and already you have stated all the rights to which a man and a woman is entitled.*

Anita interrupted her mother to tell them about that lesson, and quoted Martí's words to her parents. "Do you know what Ramón said about that quote? He said, 'If my father were here, he would laugh his head off at those pretty words. My father worked hard all his life, and died with no education, no rights, no nothing.' Ramón says that sometimes it seems that his life is only a little better than his father's."

"Based on Cuba's history, I can imagine that it is hard for Ramón to imagine that a poor *campesino* like himself would be treated by everyone as an equal," papá said.

"I told Ramón about a bet that I have with Zenaida—that in a few years she will be working in some place or educating herself in some way that he and Clara never would have dreamed possible."

"What did Ramón have to say about that?" papá asked.

"He said he'd believe it when he saw it. Zenaida told me she prays every night that I win our bet."

"That shows that Zenaida has hopes for herself. She is beginning to see herself as a child of the Revolution. That's a good thing."

Child of the Revolution. . . . She had first heard that expression when her father said that about Conrado Benitez. Anita thought about how different her life was since she started teaching and how good she felt doing something really meaningful.

"You know what?" she said. "I'd say that I'm now a child of the Revolution too. And that's why I can't and won't return home before finishing my assignment."

Havana
August 29, 1961

Dear Anita,

It sounds like you had a wonderful birthday celebration. Your mother brought over the letter you sent back with her. I have kept all your letters and postcards, and will take them with me to Florida to read again and again when I'm really missing you and missing Cuba. Your mother told me all about where you live, about your campesino family, what they are like and what you're doing—which I mostly knew already. I imagine that your mother told you all about my party. It was a pretty snazzy affair. I received so many wonderful gifts, but I'll have to leave almost all of them behind when we leave. I can't say I didn't enjoy the party, but I really did miss you being there, even if I did say that day in the Big Tree Park that I was glad you wouldn't be there. I often wonder if I would have made a good brigadista. I'll never know.

We know when we'll be leaving on the big bird for Florida—on September 15th. I dread the day. I feel so angry with my parents for taking me away. They say I'll feel different when I'm settled in and have friends and everything. Maybe they're right, but that doesn't mean I won't miss you horribly. And do you know what my parents and their friends say? They say this government won't last, that Fidel Castro will be overthrown soon by the counter-revolutionaries, and *that all the people who have left will come back and Cuba will be just like it used to be. It's all kind of confusing, isn't it? When I dare my father to say you're not doing a good thing, he doesn't answer. He actually does worry about you—especially about the danger from those counter-revolutionaries who are doing such horrible things. I worry too. I wear your friendship ring all the time. Are you still wearing the locket?*

Take special care of yourself, dear best friend. Love and hugs, Marci

Anita closed her hand around the little locket she never took off.

The Year of Education
Caimanera,
September 3, 1961

Hi Anita,

Mamá and papá just told me in their last letter about you and Ramón and the others being ambushed. The thought of it makes my blood boil! I understand why you didn't want to go home, but I think you should. After all, I only have one sister, and you can't be replaced. I've heard that most of the active counter-revolutionary groups have been caught, but that doesn't mean you shouldn't take precautions.

It's great that mamá and papá are teaching, isn't it? At last they're getting into the swing of things. They're coming to see me soon. I have stopped shaving so now Eliades calls me El Barbudo, the bearded one. Mamá and papá will probably hate the beard, but now that I'm teaching in two places, I don't have time to shave. I'd like to write more often, Anita, but I honestly can't make the time. Be extra careful. That's an order.

Love, Mario

P.S. I owe you a birthday present.

"Owwwch, Nataniel! Stop pulling my ears." Riding on Anita's shoulders as they walked the path back to the *bohío* from the river, Nataniel just kept right on. "*¡Sueltame, diablito!* Let go, you little devil!" said Anita, tickling him.

Zenaida walked ahead balancing a basket full of wet clothing on her head. Anita had been keeping her promise to never leave the clearing of the *bohío*, so it fell to Zenaida to do most of the laundry as Clara's belly grew bigger. Today the pile of laundry was very large, so Zenaida had gone to see if their neighbour Rosa could help, but she wasn't home. Anita had insisted on helping. Both girls had assured Clara they would be extra watchful and careful. Clara said she would come to the river as soon as she got up after a rest. When Clara still hadn't arrived by the time they finished the laundry, they had started back.

Anita began singing Nataniel's favourite song about the cockroach that couldn't walk anymore because it had lost its most important leg. "*La cucaracha, la cucaracha.*" Nataniel repeated those words in baby talk over and over as Anita sang.

"My arms are tired. Let's trade bundles," Zenaida said, waiting for Anita to catch up. They exchanged burdens, Anita now leading. Both girls sang the silly song over and over again to amuse the child. Ahead, where the path opened to the dirt road, Anita noticed a shadow elongated across the pathway. She stopped and motioned Zenaida to stop.

"What?" said Zenaida.

Anita put her finger to her lips. "Someone's there, on the road," she whispered, pointing.

Nataniel kept shouting for more *cucaracha, cucaracha*. "I think it's Clara hiding . . . intending to scare us," whispered Anita. "Let's scare her instead." They proceeded along the remaining few metres of path as quietly as they could. A few steps from the road, Anita sped up and jumped out shouting "BOO!"

NIGHTMARE

As soon as Anita emerged from the path onto the road, two men grabbed her. The basket of laundry went flying, scattering the wet laundry in the dirt. The men, all but their eyes masked with neckerchiefs, dragged Anita backwards as she writhed and screamed. Zenaida put the now-wailing Nataniel down on the ground and followed at a run, screaming at the men. When she caught up, she grabbed hold of one of the men and began kicking his legs and dragging on his arm. The man let go of Anita, grabbed Zenaida with both hands and sent her sprawling onto her back.

"*¡Lárguete! muchacha, o te doy aún peor.* Scram kid, or you'll get even worse," he hissed.

"Run, Zenaida, run! Go for help," screamed Anita, as the men continued dragging her away. *How could I have been so stupid! They must have some kind of vehicle hidden close by, so I must get free!* She writhed, dug in her heels and struggled with all her might, but couldn't get loose, so she bit the hand of one of her captors as hard as she could.

"Bitch!" yelled the man. "We should have gagged her right away!" He yanked a dirty handkerchief from his pants pocket and forced it into Anita's mouth, then they pulled her off the road into the trees and tied her hands behind her back. Anita could still hear Nataniel bawling and Zenaida screaming for help. Two horses were tethered to a tree. Through her panic, something told Anita to get a good look at her captors. Both were white men, one much brawnier than the other. Both wore the clothes of ordinary *campesinos*—nothing distinctive. Battered straw hats covered their hair and foreheads. Both had dark eyes, but with the hats and kerchief masks covering most of their faces, she couldn't make out any distinguishing features. Then they blindfolded her.

Terrified, Anita resisted as hard as she could as the men forced her up onto a horse. One of the men mounted behind her, grasping her tightly around the waist. She heard the second man mount his horse and flick the reins to urge the horse into motion. Desperate, Anita tried to throw herself off the horse, but the man's grip around her waist tightened, making her gasp.

Kidnapped! Her heart raced and she trembled uncontrollably. The gag in her mouth was nauseating. Anita remembered how she and Mario had made fun of their parents' fears of kidnapping; how they had accused them of exaggerating. The two attacks on the schoolhouse and the attempt to kidnap her and the other *brigadistas* had shown that her parents' concerns had been justified. But when security had been greatly increased in the whole Bainoa region and stiffer guidelines put in place for all the *brigadistas*, the whole worry about kidnapping had faded.

Are they going to kill me, put a rope put around my neck and hang me like Conrado? Will they torture me first? Oh God, will they rape me? Growing more terrified by the second, Anita leaned as far forward as she could and threw her upper body and head back with as much force as possible.

"Bitch!" the man snarled again as Anita's head cracked against his face.

Good! I hope I broke his nose. Her own head hurt plenty from the impact, but she didn't care. Her mind leapt to her parents, knowing the agony they would soon be feeling when they learned about this. Anita thought of the panic back at the *bohío*. Then thoughts of Mario, Claudio, Marjorie, Dani . . . of all the others who would soon hear that she had been kidnapped. She tried to spit out the rag gagging her mouth, but couldn't. Her jaws were already aching. *Try to keep calm. Someone may see me. Someone's got to see me!*

It wasn't long before the horsemen reined in the horses. Branches scraped Anita's face. They weren't on the road. She struggled again as the men dragged her down off the horse, but was helpless against the two. When the men began prodding her forward, she made herself go limp, compelling them to drag her. She was forced up onto something hard, forced to lie face down. They bound her feet. Stuff was being placed on top of her. What? The smell and scratchiness told her it was hay. She was being completely covered with hay. She felt she would suffocate. Then whatever she was on started moving. The plodding clip clop of hooves sounded loud through the floor boards. She was on a horse-drawn cart. Occasionally there was the sharp crack of a whip as the driver urged the horse to trot. Tensing her body, Anita tried to control the way she flopped about as the cartwheels bumped along the rutted road. Her breasts hurt. There would be bruises.

"*Buenos días,*" someone called out.

"Buenos días," came a reply.

Anita tried to heave her body; tried to make noise with her bound legs; tried to make grunting noises.

The cart rolled on. *No one can see me or hear me. Where are they taking me? No one will know where to look for me.* The full weight of her situation took all the fight out of her. Sobs rose in her throat. The gag in her mouth almost strangled her and her skin itched violently from the harshness of the hay. She should have gone back to Havana with her parents. Insisting on staying had been foolish. Why had she acted so stupidly . . . thinking the shadow was Clara? Helpless, terrified, Anita let the bouncing cart punish her body.

When the cart stopped, Anita heard the driver get off. She went rigid, listening. Footsteps. The hay was lifted off. She inhaled deeply through her nose. Hands untied the ropes around her ankles but not her wrists. Blindfolded and gagged Anita lie still, waiting.

"So, young lady, I hope the trip wasn't too unpleasant."

That voice . . . Where had she heard that voice?

"I'm going to lead you someplace. I advise you not to put up a struggle. If you cooperate, you won't get hurt." The man dragged her off the cart and pulled her to her feet. Gripping one arm, he steered her along. The ground was rough. Anita stumbled frequently. Except for snapping sounds underfoot, it was very quiet. Anita sniffed the air. No animal smells. It felt like being in the woods.

"Stop," the man ordered.

A door on squeaking hinges was opened. The man pushed Anita forward into a room, into darkness beyond the dark of the blindfold. Hands forced her down on a chair, untied and retied her wrists behind the chair and bound her feet together. Then—*oh thank goodness!*—the nauseating gag was pulled from her mouth. Anita stopped herself from saying thank you. How wonderful it felt to be able to swallow normally, though her jaws ached.

"If you scream, girlie, this rag will go back in your mouth and stay there. Do you understand?"

Anita nodded. "Will you take off the blindfold?" she asked. "I promise not to do anything stupid." The answer was a blunt no.

"Someone will give you food, and take you outside to do your business, but in here, you will always be tied up. An armed guard will be right outside the door at all times. Until we get what we want, this is where you'll be, girlie. Let's hope for your sake that the people we contact meet our demands."

A few footsteps, the sound of the door closing, and the click of a padlock.

Anita tried moving, but the chair almost tipped over. She had to pee, bad. *How long can I hold it?* Anita tried to figure out what her surroundings were by listening, by feeling with her skin, by tasting the air. *It's dank in here and there's an earthy smell. The ground is bumpy, probably dirt.* She tilted her head in different positions, but couldn't detect any light through the blindfold. She concluded she was being held in some sort of shed with a dirt floor, no windows. Or maybe any windows were covered up. A mess of questions with no answers troubled her head. *Who has kidnapped me? Where am I? What do they intend to do with me? Who will bring me food? Will they give me a toothbrush? Will they let me walk around at all or ever take off the blindfold? Where will I sleep?* One thought troubled her more than any other. *Would any of the men lay their hands on her?*

Already the cold dampness of the room and the forced stillness was creeping into her body. She began to shiver. She tried to keep thoughts of what might be in store for her out of her head, but couldn't. *How long have I been here? Fifteen minutes? An hour?* Now Anita had to pee really badly. And she was feeling creepy, like there were things in the dark—things like real *cucarachas,* the big kind with their long, waving antennae. She had itches she couldn't scratch. She wanted to scream but didn't, remembering how awful the dirty rag had felt in her mouth. At times she wanted to cry, but what good would that do? She wriggled her hands to try to free them, but only rubbed her wrists raw. She did her best to think about rescue. *But who would rescue her, and how?*

The door opened.

"I have to pee!" she blurted. "Right now!"

Hands untied her wrists from behind the chair, retied them behind her back, then untied her legs. "Stand up, and I'll lead you." A woman's voice. *Thank goodness for that!* The woman led her outside. A man's voice, not the same man as before, said, "Don't try anything funny girlie. I'm right outside this door."

Will he be watching while I pee? The woman led her some distance, then said, "You'll have to let me help you with this, and started undoing Anita's pants.

"This is so humiliating! Can't you untie me so I can do this myself?"

"No, I can't."

Back in the chair, the woman tied Anita's feet again. Some kind of sandwich was placed in her bound hands. Anita didn't feel like eating, but forced herself. When she finished eating, the woman called the guard to help move the chair back against the wall. "That way, she can rest her head against the wall to sleep."

"Can you get me a toothbrush . . . and a blanket? I'm very cold. And will you let me wash?"

"I'll be back later," was all the woman said.

"What's your name?" asked Anita, but the woman didn't answer. The door closed and was locked. Anita leaned her head against the wall. They hadn't had to drag the chair far, so the space was probably small. She still hadn't heard any sounds that might give her some idea of where she was. *But I must be near a house for them to bring me food. It feels like the middle of nowhere. The woman seems nice enough. Maybe I can find out more from her.*

The door opened and closed . . . *Maybe it's the woman bringing me a blanket?* No one spoke, but Anita felt someone standing in front of her. Despite being dreadfully cold, pinpricks of sweat erupted all over her body, and her flesh crawled. She sensed some movement, then she felt hot breath on her face. All she could do was turn her face away. Dare she scream?

"I'll bite," she said.

"Don't scream or I'll gag you." The guard's voice.

Hands slipped inside her shirt, moving over her breasts, squeezing them. She heard and felt the man's breathing inches from her face. Seconds later he removed his hands, the door opened and closed and she was alone again. So humiliating! Hot tears wet the rag covering her eyes and streaked down her face. What next? She forced herself to take some deep breaths. Exhausted, she closed her eyes and dozed.

"So, the *teacher* is having a little nap."

How sarcastically he says "teacher"! Anita didn't move. *Let him think I'm still asleep.*

"She will be in pain if we don't let her walk around now and then."

The woman's voice. "And with Aurelio right outside, I think we can let her sleep at night without being tied up. What harm could be done? She's just a child."

The sound of a hard slap and the woman's gasp of pain made Anita jump, tipping the chair over on its side and her with it. Pain shot through her shoulder as she landed.

"Did you hit her? Why did you hit her? She was only being decent." Anger flooded Anita's body. "What kind of creep are you, anyway?" She and the chair were set upright. A rough hand took hold of her chin, squeezed it painfully and shook her head violently back and forth before letting go.

"You'd better watch your tongue girlie and mind your own business or there's more and worse where that came from. If people respond properly to our demands, you'll be sleeping in your own bed soon enough. Meanwhile, things will stay just exactly as they are. And you," he said—Anita guessed he was talking to the woman, his voice edged with menace—"you'll do just as you're told." With that, the door opened and slammed closed.

"Are you alright?" the woman asked.

"My jaw and neck hurt. And I wet my pants a little. What about you? Are you alright?"

"Don't worry about me," the woman replied. "I'll take you to the woods again now, and then you'll eat. I brought some hot food."

"Will I have to sleep tied up like this?"

"*Sí, señorita. Así es.* I'm afraid so."

They went through the routine of untying her and re-tying her, leading her outside to "do her business" in the woods, retying, and eating. The woman fed her—boiled rice, some tough meat. The woman had brought a toothbrush and water, but refused to untie Anita's hands. Anita attempted to brush her teeth, but it was too awkward and she soon gave up. Before leaving, the woman tied Anita's wrists behind the chair, then began wrapping a heavy wool blanket around Anita, chair and all.

Should I tell her the guard felt me up? Anita decided not to, fearing she would be gagged again for blabbing.

"I am pinning it firmly so it won't slip off."

"You are very kind. Thank you," said Anita, hoping the blanket might also protect her from the guards probing hands. Maybe the woman understood. When the woman left, the sound of the door closing and the sound of the padlock clicking firmly into place were almost more than Anita could bear. She felt so alone.

Anita had learned a few things, important things. When the chair tipped, the blindfold had slipped up slightly, enabling her to see a bit out the bottom. What she saw shocked her. The man's boots—she had recognized those particular boots. The kidnapper and boss man was El Gallero, the man who ran the cockfights. That's why his voice had seemed familiar. When he had stood in front of her at the cockfight, kind of mocking her, she had looked down to avoid his eyes and noticed his distinctive boots—black leather with embossed patterns, silver studs around the top, pointed toes and perforated silver toe caps. And he wore his jeans tucked in. She remembered that too. And she also knew the name of the guard who had felt her up—Aurelio. *Maybe he's one of the two who dragged me off; the one I bit. Or maybe he's the one who held me on the horse. I don't think so, though, because that guy would be really mean to me because I head-butted him. This guy isn't mean—just creepy. If he puts his hands on me again, I'll have to tell. And I think the woman must be El Gallero's wife.*

Anita was furious thinking of the way El Gallero had treated the woman. But *I must be careful not let them know that I know anything about them. I mustn't slip up or it could be bad for me.* Alone, cold despite the blanket, facing a night tied up in the dark, Anita was again struck by the terrible situation she was in.

Crying as noiselessly as she could, she made a mental note: *Captive, end of day one.*

Anita had felt sure she wouldn't be able to sleep, and so was surprised when she woke up. Awake, she could think of nothing else except hoping the woman would come soon. Her mouth was dry and foul-tasting, her lips crusted. She felt stiff and horrible all over. She needed water. She had to pee. She wanted to talk. Anita thought of talking to herself, but was afraid to. *How much longer will I be held like this? What are the kidnappers demanding? Something about the campaign probably.* She thought about the conversation her class had about gusanos, about why counter-revolutionaries killed Conrado Benitez. She thought about the sneering way El Gallero said the word "teacher". *He must hate the brigadistas. He must hate the whole literacy campaign. And so I guess he must hate la revolución. What else could he demand using me? Maybe he is demanding money from my parents.* This thought alarmed Anita. She didn't know how much money her family had. They lived well, but she knew they weren't rich—at least, not rich like Marci's family.

Conrado's terrible end was always in her thoughts. That she was still alive was enough to give Anita some hope that Conrado's fate would not be hers. She worked hard convincing herself that she might be rescued. Maybe even today. But the hours passed as before, except the guard was a different man. He didn't tie the ropes quite as tight as Aurelio, but tight enough that she couldn't get loose. The woman came and went as she had done yesterday, bringing food and taking her outside to do her business. Outside, Anita begged the woman to let her remain just a little longer so she could breathe fresh air.

"I can't. The guard will notice and tell my husband," she said.

So El Gallero is her husband. What will they do with this woman when I'm rescued? From reading detective novels, Anita knew the wife would be considered an accomplice, even though she was forced to do everything against her will.

How slowly time seemed to be passing! Anita did multiplication tables in her head. She recalled important names, dates and events in the history of Cuba. She experimented with rocking the chair from side to side—just enough so she didn't tip. The rocking soothed her somehow. She began longing for a bath, for any kind of wash. She thought of the river, how good it had felt floating in the warm water pooled among the rocks. She thought of cool sponge baths from the barrel of rainwater outside the *bohío*. She thought of her room at home, of her comfy bed, of reading in bed. She wished she could click her heels together three times, like Dorothy in the Wizard of Oz, and be transported to Havana.

She thought constantly of all the people who would be sick with worry about her. Over and over she reproached herself for having let down her guard walking back along the path, for singing *la cucaracha*—for having been so generally foolish. Often her throat constricted painfully with the urge to cry, especially when the woman wrapped her in the rough wool blanket once more and left her for the night.

And so day two of being a captive came and went.

★

"Guard! *¡Ayúdame! ¡Ayúdame*! Help!" Anita screamed. She couldn't help herself, even though it meant she might be gagged again.

The guard burst in. "*¿Qué pasa?* What the hell's the matter?" The voice was Aurelio's.

"There's an animal in here. Something ran over my feet and I can hear it moving around—maybe a rat."

"I'll have to go and get a flashlight and a *machete*," Aurelio said.

"Don't close the door. Please don't close the door."

When Aurelio came back, she could hear him walking slowly about the shed. She heard something whack. Aurelio swore and then there was another whack, this time quite close. Anita screamed again.

"*No grites. Ya la maté.* Stop yelling. It's dead."

"Was it a rat?"

"Yes."

"A big one?"

"Just an ordinary rat. There are crumbs of food on the ground near you. That's probably what attracted it. I will tell Marlena to sweep up any spilled food after you eat."

"Please don't close the door. I promise not to scream again. It's too scary being alone in the dark with the door closed."

"I'll have to check with the boss first."

"Are you taking the dead rat away?"

"Yes."

"And don't dare touch me again, or I'll tell."

"Just you take it easy now, girlie."

But Anita couldn't take it easy. There might be more than one rat. She strained to hear scuffling noises. Her head ached. Everything was hurting. She couldn't remember what day it was. Footsteps.

"The boss says I can leave the door open a little during the day, but I have to lock it at night. Any noise from you and the boss said to close the door and keep it closed. Understand, girlie?"

"Thank you," Anita whispered. She had learned something else. *The woman's name is Marlena, and she and her husband live close by.*

The remainder of day three dragged by, the hours of forced stillness making her numb. With the door open a crack, she was grateful for the fresh air that entered, for the distraction of hearing Aurelio move around from time to time, hearing the scratch of matches when he lit his cigarettes. Even the smell of cigarette smoke that wafted in was a relief from the dank smell when the door was shut. She was tempted to try to talk to Aurelio, but held her tongue, fearful that he would shut the door—or worse, gag her.

Sometimes she thought about Claudio, imagining conversations with him about how they would write each other when the campaign was over and make plans to visit each other. She imagined writing her brother long letters, telling him about being kidnapped as though it were just an exciting story. She thought about the Perez family. When she was free again and her kidnappers locked up tight in jail, her learners would take the second test. Anita hoped they were studying a little no matter how worried they were about her.

As El Gallero's wife came and went, Anita didn't let on that she knew her name. Anita was very thirsty, but didn't drink as much water as she wanted so she wouldn't have to worry so much about holding her pee. And thankfully, she could hear Marlena sweeping the dirt floor before she left for the night. The shed had gotten colder with the door open all day, but it had been worth it, knowing Aurelio was there, feeling the outside world. But when the door was shut, when she heard the click of the padlock, Anita felt as though she were alone on earth. Then, all at once and for no reason, a wonderful feeling came over Anita, a feeling that came from the inside out, warming her to her fingertips. *My parents are not far away. Maybe in town. Maybe at the schoolhouse. But they are near. I feel it.*

Despite the chill dank air and her stiff and aching body, Anita felt she could sleep without fear even though she was still captive at the end of day three.

When Marlena came to do the morning routine, Anita knew something was wrong, very wrong. Marlena was clumsy, fumbling as she untied the ropes. Her voice sounded clenched in her throat. She made Anita hurry back to the shed after their trip outside.

"What's the matter?" Anita finally asked, scared to hear the answer.

Marlena didn't answer, and remained silent while Anita ate some bread dunked in lukewarm coffee. "Wrap the blanket around me again before you go," Anita said. "I can't stop shivering."

Maybe El Gallero's patience was running out. Anita couldn't avoid thinking about what would happen to her if El Gallero did not get what he was asking for—his "demands", whatever they were. *He won't just let me go. But would he actually kill me?* The possibility that she might end up dead flashed about in her head today like a June bug's crazy flight, zigzagging and colliding with anything in its blind path. She felt nauseous. At times she was able to remind herself that her intuition told her she would be rescued, that she would emerge from this nightmare. But today, she didn't seem able to hold that thought for long. She fought against rising panic as the hours passed. Her head throbbed. She wished the blanket was pinned up tighter. Would she ever get warm!

Approaching footsteps refocused her thoughts. El Gallero entered speaking, his voice angry. "Things aren't looking so good for you, girlie. People have had plenty of time to meet our demands, but nothing has happened. Now I'm forced to consider what to do with you," he said, his voice edged with menace.

"Will you tell me what the demands are? Maybe I can help."

At first, El Gallero didn't reply.

"The demands are simple," he said, finally. We want all the *brigadistas* and supervisors in the Bainoa region to clear out; to go back where they came from. The Bainoa campaign must end. This madness of teaching common labourers who are not fit to do anything better than swing a machete in the cane fields or harvest peanuts has to stop. And teaching the bastard children of slaves that they are my equals? Oh no, girlie! All that has to end!" El Gallero's voice shook with the passion of his words. "The administration was informed that they have until tomorrow 5pm.," he continued, his voice more controlled. "So girlie, I suggest you start praying that they get moving real fast." Anita heard him turn to leave.

"Wait . . . Maybe they need proof that I'm . . . that I'm still alive. I could write a note."

"Nice try, girlie. But that blindfold stays on. If you do get out of here, we wouldn't want you identifying anyone, would we? Like I said, pray."

Time and El Gallero's patience *were* running out.

How do you stay calm when you can't do anything to help yourself, when you're pinned down, trapped, afraid for your life and the darkness gathered all around seems to be pushing you forward to something . . . to what . . . ?

Anita made herself think of all the things she would do once she was rescued. First she pictured herself as she was now—filthy, her eyelids sore and crusted with dried secretions from dirt and tears she couldn't wipe away, her clothes rumpled, soiled, smelling bad, her hair a tangled mess. Then she pictured herself soaking in the luxury of a hot bath, the water fragrant, getting thoroughly clean. After that she made a few resolutions, promises she would keep when she was free. *Number One: I promise not to be mouthy to my mother and to try to develop a better relationship with her. Number two: I promise to look after my things at home more responsibly. Number three: I promise to write a letter to Marci in Florida every week.* At the thought of her friend, she felt a desperate need to touch the locket at her throat, the fingers of her bound hands curling and uncurling behind her back.

Eventually she felt steady enough to think about more than El Gallero's threats. *If the demands have not been met it's because there is a plan,* she reasoned. *People in charge of the campaign wouldn't just abandon everything—just leave me. No . . . they do know where I am and there is a plan to rescue me. Whatever the plan is, it will happen soon. It has to happen soon.* Convinced of this, Anita stopped shivering and the headache behind her eyes didn't throb quite so much.

As Marlena led her outside that evening, Anita pleaded with her in a low voice.

"I can tell you don't like doing this—that you are doing this against your will. Help me, please. Help me escape."

Marlena's reply was brief and chilling. "I can't. He would kill me."

"Do you think he will kill me if things don't go his way?" Anita asked.

Marlena didn't answer. *I guess that means she knows he will.* Her legs felt like jelly returning to the shed. When Marlena left for the night, she hesitated before closing and padlocking the door.

"*Hasta mañana, señorita.* See you tomorrow."

Maybe not, thought Anita. *Maybe by tomorrow I'll be out of here.* But again Anita made a mental note: *Captive, end of day four.*

Anita tried not to think of El Gallero in his house wondering what to do with her if his demands weren't met. She didn't want to sleep, and anyway, she was so tense she figured sleep would be impossible. But as the night wore on she was having trouble keeping her eyes open . . .

. . . Conrado stopped to rest. Shrugging off his heavy backpack he squatted with his back against a tree. He had been hiking quickly up the hilly paths through the mountains, anxious to reach the village before dark. After a week away visiting his family, he was returning to his work as a maestro voluntario, a volunteer teacher in a pilot literacy program. He could hardly wait to get back to the children, to the little schoolhouse he had helped build. The forest on all sides was dense and dark, a jungle of trees and vines. Clearing the sweat from his face and neck with his handkerchief, he tipped his cantina and took a long drink. Just as he rose to his feet to continue on his way, a threatening voice broke the stillness.

"Going somewhere, negrito, black boy?"

Startled, Conrado swung around in the direction of the voice. A man he had never seen before stood a few metres away, pointing a rifle at him. Crunching noises informed him of others closing in. Conrado looked around. He was surrounded by men, and they all had rifles. Escape was impossible. Despite the late afternoon heat that had stifled even the songs of birds, the chill of fear swept over Conrado. The man approached him, his pockmarked face twisted into a sneer, his eyes registering hatred. Never had Conrado seen such eyes, so light in colour they seemed transparent. Facing these eyes, Conrado had to lower his own against their cruel expression. There was no mercy there.

The warnings the campesino farm labourers had given him last night and again this morning flashed into his head now. "While you were away, a gang of counter-revolutionary rebels has been active in the area. They tried to ambush two literacy teachers near Sancti Spiritus, but the teachers were lucky and got away. It could be dangerous for you to hike through the mountains now."

"Why would the rebels attack literacy teachers?" Conrado asked.

"Chico, they have many reasons, but the truth is, the rebels hate everything la revolución is doing throughout the country, including the literacy programs," said one. "And they hate that we now must be paid decent wages," said another. "Stay," they said. "Wait until the gang has been rounded up." But Conrado had been eager to leave. Now he wished he had listened to them.

"Empty your backpack, negrito," the cruel-eyed man ordered.

"It's just personal stuff," protested Conrado.

"Do as I say," the man said, boxing the side of Conrado's head with the rifle butt. Conrado saw stars, but didn't cry out. The man shook the back-

pack, emptying the contents on the ground. Last night Conrado had shown the campesinos the gifts he was bringing the children. "These toys, colouring books and crayons will be the first those kids have ever seen." Now the toys lay tumbled about on the ground. The man kicked at them, scattering them into the bush. The man picked up two books.

"And these?" he said.

"Books I plan to study," Conrado answered. The textbooks had made his backpack heavy, but he didn't care. All he ever wanted to do was study, learn more. Remembering his many years as a shoeshine boy and bread seller, happy that those days were behind him, he had sung as he climbed the trail. The new revolutionary government had offered him a chance to become a literacy teacher, to be something, and he had grabbed the opportunity. Someday he hoped to teach in a public school.

"Imagine that!" the man said, turning to his men, holding the books up for them to see. "Anatomía. Matemática. What big ideas the negrito has!" Jutting his face within inches of Conrado's, he tore pages from the books, first from one, then the other, sneering at Conrado with curled lips and those terrible eyes. He threw what remained of the books into the bush, followed by a thick gob of spit. Then he forced Conrado to his knees and told him he was on trial.

"Trial? For what? What have I done?" Conrado asked.

"For being a nigger who doesn't know his place," the man said. "You're on trial for being a trouble-maker, for following that cursed Fidel Castro, the biggest trouble-maker of them all—he and his whole damn revolution— thinking his revolution can take property away from men like us and give it to trash like you." As he spoke, the man's face turned red with anger, making his eyes seem paler still, terrifying Conrado even more. The man jerked his head toward Conrado. The gang of men closed in.

"All I'm doing is teaching little kids to read and write . . ." Conrado tried to say, but the men wouldn't let him finish, wouldn't let him say anything. Each time he tried to say something they beat him with the butts of their rifles and kicked him until he couldn't talk, until he lay silent, curled up on the ground, his ears ringing from the blows to his head.

"We are your judges and your jury, boy."

Turning to his men, the leader of the rebel gang said, "If we let this nigger live, he and others like him will be teaching your sons and daughters someday. Are we going to allow that? You've heard the charges against this trouble-maker. Now let him hear your verdict."

With eyes almost swollen shut, Conrado saw the men turn down their thumbs and one by one he heard each say:

"Guilty."

"Guilty."

"Guilty."

The pale-eyed man gestured to one of the men who slung a rope over a thick branch and tied a hanging noose. They carried Conrado kicking and struggling to the tree.

"Your last good deed on earth is to serve as a warning that all do-gooders like you should stop trying to change things in Cuba," the man said. "If they don't stop, many will meet the same fate as you."

As the noose was slipped over his head and tightened around his neck, Conrado Benitez remembered that his nineteenth birthday was only a few days away . . .

Anita awoke from the nightmare with a jerk. Her mouth and tongue were utterly dry, her body trembling within the blanket. Tense and alert, she strained to hear sounds, strained to hear anything unusual. Croaking frogs. Rustling sounds that could be small animals scurrying through the undergrowth around the shed. Crickets chirping shrilly. There were vague sounds she couldn't identify at all. Anita began interpreting every sound as the disguised stealthy movement of rescuers sneaking up on the shed to ambush the guard. How would they overcome him? Despairing, she decided all the sounds were just ordinary sounds. *What if no one comes? What if they come, but things go wrong? If the guard sees or hears anything suspicious, he will use me as a hostage. Then what?*

The padlock clicked, and the door opened. She pretended to be asleep, letting her mouth drop open. *It must be the guard.* She felt him standing in front of her. *Don't touch me, don't touch me,* she prayed silently. He left. Click. *Just checking on me, gracias a dios.* Moments later, Anita heard the rumbles of snoring. An owl hooted nearby. Another owl hooted from somewhere else. Was it the same owl, flying about, hunting for mice or voles? Anita heard a strange grunt, then silence again. *What's happening?* Her heart began beating wildly. *Should I call out?* Then there were squeaking sounds at the door that she couldn't figure out. Suddenly cold air rushed in and a hand was clapped over her mouth. A man's voice whispered, "You are safe *señorita*. Keep totally quiet. Do not move."

TURNABOUT

Gun shots broke the silence. Anita's rescuer tipped the chair to the ground and protected her with his own body. Anita heard running footsteps, more shots, then shouting.

"He's hit, Captain. Shot in the leg. He's down, disarmed and surrounded."

Hands removed the blanket and the blindfold and were untying her hands and feet. Hands lifted her to her feet. Voices reassured her that she was safe, that her kidnappers had been apprehended. Anita's legs buckled. Hands supported her. Beams of flashlights swept around the shed. Pain shot through her upper body as she raised her arms to cover her eyes against the intolerable light. When her eyes focused, she saw several men dressed in black clothing, their faces smeared with something black. All were beaming at her, their teeth gleaming white in their blackened faces. A man in uniform entered, and all came to attention.

"Captain DaSilva, military police at your service, *señorita* Anita. I'm sure you want to see your parents before anything else. They are waiting at the schoolhouse. Are you able to walk to the vehicle?" Anita tried to move to take the Captain's outstretched hand, but her legs didn't respond. The ground rushed up to her face as she pitched forward.

When she came to, Anita was lying on the blanket on the dirt floor of the shed. One of the men dressed in black was kneeling beside her.

"How are you now, *señorita?*"

Anita sat up. "I'm fine. Thirsty, but fine. What happened? Are you police?"

"Military police," the soldier corrected. "You fainted. Probably stress-related. Here, drink this." He handed her a military canteen of water which she drank to the last drop.

"How did you find me?" she asked.

"You'll have to ask Captain DaSilva about that," he said. "We were only told how to conduct the rescue operation."

"How did you get in so quietly? The door was padlocked—with a combination lock, I think."

"I unscrewed the hinges and lifted the door right off."

"What has happened to the kidnappers? I heard shots."

"The three people that were here were captured and taken into custody. The Captain says that others are probably involved. The fellow guarding the door was knocked out but not seriously hurt. The other man in the house resisted arrest. He was armed and opened fire. He attempted to escape and was shot in the leg. One of our men was wounded during the operation, but nothing life-threatening."

"What about the man's wife? Is she alright?"

"She surrendered right away and was taken into custody with the others."

"She was forced to be part of this by her husband. She was very kind to me. What will happen to her?"

"Hard to say, *señorita*. The charges will be very serious. You are a lucky young woman to be alive. As you probably know, counter-revolutionaries who are willing to go this far in their hatred of the revolution are extremists. They have murdered others they kidnapped."

"Do my parents know I'm safe yet? And the Perez family, my learner family . . . Do they know? When can I leave here?"

"We're just waiting for Captain DaSilva to return. He will tell you if your parents and the others have been informed."

"Tell me honestly, do I look a fright? Do I smell bad?"

Even though the shed was lit only by the single beam of the flashlight in her rescuer's hand, Anita could tell the young man was blushing.

"That's really not my area of expertise, *señorita*."

Captain DaSilva himself drove Anita to the schoolhouse. On the way, he told her how they knew where she was being held.

"We questioned all the people who might have been on the road and side-roads leading away from the Perez family *bohío* the day you were abducted. A *campesino* told us he was passed on the road by a horse-drawn cart piled with hay. He greeted the driver, whom he recognized, and told us he heard some kind of noise as the cart passed."

"That was me kicking and trying to make any noise I could," interrupted Anita. "but I was gagged and tied so tight, and there was so much hay—I didn't think I made any noise at all."

"The noise you managed to make was very important, *señorita*, because it eventually led to the positive identification of your captors. The *campesino* said he didn't place any importance on those faint sounds he heard until we questioned him. He identified the cart driver, whom we arrested and interrogated for many hours. At first he wouldn't talk, but eventually he did. After that, it was a matter of observation and formulating the safest way to rescue you."

As the vehicle neared the schoolhouse, Anita could hardly contain her excitement. Captain DaSilva had told her that no one knew yet whether the rescue operation had been successful or not.

"Everyone's fear was that your captors may have already killed you, *señorita*."

Almost there, Anita could see many people sitting on the steps or standing around at the bottom. When they became aware of the car's approach, those sitting rose as one, all turning to await the approaching vehicle. There were her mother and father, illuminated in the beams of the headlights! Anita was out of the car before it had fully stopped. Running, stumbling, she flew toward her parents, into their outstretched arms. Everyone went crazy with joy observing the tearful reunion. To Anita's amazement, here was her beloved brother, a handsome, bearded, more muscular Mario! One by one, all embraced her, Marjorie, Pamela, Suzi, Dani, Claudio, all her *brigadista* companions, the supervisors, the campaign director. Anita forgot all about worrying about smelling bad and looking a fright.

"'Nita, 'Nita."

Anita turned to see Nataniel struggling in Ramón's arms to reach out to her. There was the whole Perez family waiting quietly to greet her, their eyes luminous, tears streaming down their faces. Anita hugged them all fiercely, apologizing for her foolishness.

Anita's father detached himself from the group, and walked to the military vehicle where Captain DaSilva stood leaning against the vehicle, smoking. He flicked the cigarette away as papá reached out to shake hands. In a spontaneous gesture, the whole group sprang forward to thank and congratulate the Captain. Bombarded by questions about the rescue operation, the Captain raised his hands up, shaking his head.

"We are fortunate to have the *señorita* here with us now, safe and sound. Tomorrow we will interview the *señorita*, and provide you with information about the kidnappers and rescue operation. We must question the three people taken into custody tonight to see how many others were involved. We will be looking for at least one other man. The *señorita* has told me she thinks she was able to do some physical damage to the hand and face of one, maybe two, of her captors at the time of her abduction. She may even have broken the nose of one of her abductors. That person, a man, is not among the four persons we have in custody."

"Bravo, Anita," people called out upon hearing this.

"For your assurance and safety," continued the Captain, "military police will maintain an increased presence in this region, but the threat to all the *brigadistas* remains serious. The campaign administration must exercise utmost caution and vigilance to protect them from harm. Tomorrow I will talk about all that with you, madam director, and your team of regional supervisors. Until then, *buenas noches.*"

With that, the Captain saluted the small crowd, got into the car and drove off. Military police guards that Anita hadn't noticed in the excitement took positions around the schoolhouse as everyone went inside.

"Were you scared?" everyone wanted to know.

"Yes, very scared. All the time. El Gallero, the head guy, was a brutal man. But you know what scared me the most?" Anita suddenly felt too shy to talk about the humiliation of being fondled, or worse, the fear of being raped . . . "Tied to the chair for hours on end, I was scared I would pee my pants."

"Anita!" admonished mamá, while all the others laughed. Anita glanced at Claudio. She was aware that he hadn't taken his eyes off her for a second. With Mario's arm around her shoulders and her hand clutched firmly within her mother's, Anita described her ordeal and answered questions until overwhelmed by exhaustion.

Scrubbed clean from top to bottom, wearing warm pajamas brought from home, Anita lay down for the first time in five days among clean sheets and warm blankets at the little hotel in Bainoa. At 3am, her mother and father had said goodnight, and were sleeping in the adjoining room. Anita thought about Mario, sleeping at the schoolhouse. He had to return to his assignment, so they would only have time to have breakfast together before he returned to Havana with their parents tomorrow to catch a flight east, back to his assignment.

Just about asleep, Anita's eyelids suddenly flew open. *Havana! Tomorrow!* She leaped from bed and knocked on the door of her parents' room. She heard her parents running to open the door.

"What's wrong, Anita? Are you alright darling?" Her father's face was anxious; her mother hastened to embrace her, making comforting sounds.

"I'm fine. Really I am," said Anita. "I just needed to tell you something important." Before her parents could ask what, Anita blurted, "No matter what you say, I'm not returning to Havana until the campaign is over. If you force me to, I'll never forgive you!"

She hurried back to her room before her astonished parents could utter a single word, locked the door and was asleep within minutes.

GETTING TO SECOND

O n a mild September day at the first seminar following her rescue, people treated Anita like some kind of celebrity. It got a bit boring answering the same questions over and over, so she felt relieved when the supervisors called everyone together. Anita and Dani sat cross-legged on the grass among all the brigadistas, listening to progress reports on the campaign. By this time, it was clear to those in charge that teaching a million people to read and write would not be accomplished by the end of the year at the rate things were going. Campaign organizers in Havana had come up with new strategies which the regional campaign director now explained.

"As many as forty thousand factory workers are going to be released from their jobs to be members of special literacy brigades called Do or Die Brigades. They will be assigned throughout the country to tutor where needed. Urban women are being urged to volunteer to tutor people in their own neighbourhoods. Local school boards will be required to supervise all literacy workers in their areas. And only yesterday it was announced that school re-opening has been postponed until January . . ."

Like everyone else hearing this news, Anita and Dani clapped and whistled until all the supervisors sitting amongst them stood up, holding up their arms to signal for quiet.

" . . . As I was saying, school re-opening has been postponed so that all professional teachers can join the campaign. A large group of teachers called study coaches will be sent out to do trouble shooting where it's most needed. In addition, all literate people are being asked to volunteer to pitch in teaching where they live. Put this all together, and Cuba will be one gigantic school. Now, before you leave for breakout groups, I have a special announcement. Some of you have complained that you're not getting enough social time, so the supervisors will be organizing a party, a real *fiesta,* with a live dance band."

The smiles all around would have lit up a cave.

During free time, Anita and Dani giggled about some of the stuff that had come up during the breakout groups. A girl named Silvia told about a serious on-going problem she had. Right from the beginning of her assignment, the wife in her learner family had been unwelcoming. Despite all Silvia's efforts, the wife became more and more unfriendly, making teaching very difficult. "I now realize that the woman is jealous and jealousy is making her nasty. She over salts my food; she orders me to do all the dirtiest work, and thinks up ridiculous tasks for me to do when her husband is home. Sometimes I hear her calling me ugly names under her breath."

"Quite likely, we will have to reassign you elsewhere," concluded Marjorie. At this, the *brigadista* burst into tears.

"But I have done nothing to deserve that," she protested. Reassuring her, Marjorie said, "This kind of thing is not unusual. The only solution is to assign a male teacher to this family. By the way, how did the husband behave? Did he reassure his wife there was nothing to be jealous about?"

"Are you kidding?" responded Silvia. "He loves all the fuss about him and struts about like a rooster." Everyone laughed, even the boys as they blushed to the tips of their ears.

The Year of Education,
September 15, 1961

Dear Mario,

The police found and arrested the guy I head-butted. I did break his nose! He revealed the names of others who were part of the rebel group, and they were arrested too. El Gallero was the rebel ringleader in the area. The kidnapping seems like a horrible nightmare, but I still have some technicolour bruises from the cart ride and sore wrists and ankles from being tied up to remind me how real it all was. Marjorie was right—Bainoa has been an adventure. Too much adventure!

I have a lump in my throat right now, because Marci leaves Cuba for Florida today—the day I lose my best friend. Zenaida and I are friends now, but it took a long time to overcome her surly ways. The supervisors organized a fantastic fiesta for all the brigadistas of the region, and I was able to bring Zenaida. She was the belle of the ball in the new dress and shoes mamá gave her. There was lots of flirting going on, which she enjoyed. My feet still hurt from dancing so much.

I feel shy to even write this, but I may have a boyfriend—Claudio, one of the brigadistas you met. I don't know if I want a steady boyfriend, but it's fun to be courted. You must have been told that we won't be going back to school until January. Aren't we lucky! I can't believe I've been here more than four months already. Three and a half months to go.

Love, Anita

Being around a pregnant woman was a completely new experience for Anita. She watched Clara's belly swelling, and sometimes Clara let her feel the baby moving. Clara was almost in her seventh month of pregnancy, and though she seldom complained, Anita could tell she was feeling uncomfortable. She worked as usual, but had to lie down to rest several times a day.

Anita was standing in the doorway one day enjoying the feel of the early morning sun on her face when Clara emerged from her bedroom yawning. Her face was blotchy and swollen.

"*Buenos días*, Clara. How are you feeling today?"

Clara moved slowly across the room, her hands cradling her belly.

"I will feel better in a few minutes, Anita, after I have had a *café-cito*." The interior of the *bohío* was still dim, so while Clara prepared coffee, Anita lit the lamp, a ritual she still loved, and turned the pages of *VENCEREMOS* to the day's lesson. Ramón entered from the yard bringing animal smells in with him.

"What's today's lesson about?" he asked, sitting down at the table.

"*CADA CUBANO DUEÑO DE SU CASA*—EVERY CUBAN WILL HAVE HIS OWN HOUSE," said Anita.

"The government is promising that we poor country people will have real houses?" said Ramón, expressing disbelief.

"Marjorie told me that in other regions, *brigadistas* are helping *campesinos* move their belongings into newly-built co-op houses and apartments, so I'm sure it will happen in the Bainoa region too."

"It would be nice to have a house with a real floor and running water inside," said Clara. "Will there be inside toilets, too?"

"I think so," replied Anita.

"I'll believe it when I see it," mumbled Ramón.

"Me too," said Zenaida, still rubbing sleep from her eyes.

When the simple breakfast of bread and *café con leche* was finished and the table cleared, Anita switched her conversational voice to teaching mode. "OK, unbelievers, let's begin the lesson now. Let's read and listen: *In the coming years, people will not be living in country bohíos or urban tenement houses . . .*"

As each one of her learning family read the paragraph after she did, Anita marvelled at how far her students had come. They could now sound out harder words and read simple sentences less haltingly. They could comfortably do fill-in-the-blanks exercises and write dictations making fewer mistakes. "I don't know when exactly, but soon everyone in this region will be taking the second test," Anita informed them at the end of the lesson. "How do you feel about that?" Anita was relieved to see they accepted this news without panicking.

"I want to be finished all the lessons by the time the baby is born," said Clara. "With two children, I may have no head or time for studying."

"Would you like to do extra lessons before the baby arrives?" Anita asked.

"That would be a good idea," said Clara, brightening.

"Could I too?" asked Zenaida.

"That's OK with me, if it's OK with Clara," Anita replied.

"What about me?" said Ramón, pretending to be offended. "Are all you women going to graduate and leave me behind?"

"Yes," said Clara, pushing him toward the door. "The man must go to work to put rice and beans and peanuts on the table."

Ramón pretended to tear out his hair. "You women are nothing more than tyrants, and men are your slaves." He placed his hands tenderly on Clara's swelling belly for just a moment, then left for work, whistling.

October 8, 1961

Dear Diary,

Claudio is so much fun! The muchacho makes me laugh. He asked me to spend free time with him at the next brigadista seminar. I don't think Dani will mind. She's always teasing me about Claudio. She says he's guapo, and if I don't take such a handsome fellow, she will. Today after the seminar, all the brigadistas were driven in trucks to help with the tomato harvest. Some tomatoes were split and juice was running up my arms. My hands got very numb with cold, but it felt good working

Now that the weather had turned cool, Anita was glad the next Sunday seminar was moved indoors at the unused, dilapidated school building in town. When the director announced that some *brigadistas* in other regions had already placed literacy flag above the doors where they teach, and that some places were close to raising the literacy flag in their town squares, Anita couldn't believe her ears. Nor could anyone else.

"How could that be!" the *brigadistas* exclaimed to each other. "Most of our learners haven't even taken the second test yet." Many *brigadistas* thought their learners couldn't do the test yet. The dismayed voices of the *brigadistas* ran back and forth along the rows of benches until gradually petering out. Gloomy faces regarded the director.

"*Muchachos,*" she said, "it's not about being first. It's about getting the job done in the time we have to do it. It's mid-October. We've still got nine weeks plus, and as teachers go, you're as good as any other group of *brigadistas*. A group from the Do or Die Brigades and some professional teachers will be arriving soon to help us. In your breakout groups today it's important that you be absolutely honest with your supervisor about evaluating whether you need additional help or not to get your learners ready to take the final test in December."

"Anita . . . Anita . . . What about you?" Anita looked up, startled. Everyone in the breakout group was looking at her. She hadn't been paying attention.

"I was asking if you want to arrange for extra teaching?" the supervisor repeated.

"No," Anita answered quickly. "I think I'm alright."

"You're sure? You seem a bit preoccupied," said the supervisor.

"I'm sure," Anita replied as convincingly as she could.

Swaying on Bufi as she and Ramón trotted home, Anita was lost in thought. *I should be able to manage with just three learners. Some brigadistas are teaching more . . . Dani for example . . . and think of Pamela, only eleven—no . . . she turned twelve recently—and she's teaching seven people.* Anita did wonder about Clara. Even with extra lessons, Clara wasn't doing as well as she had at first. Each day her belly ballooned out more, making her more uncomfortable and less able to concentrate. Anita was sure Zenaida could and would do it, even with the extra work of helping with the baby when it arrived in December. And Ramón? He worked so hard and was always exhausted, but maybe that would change now that harvesting was just about finished. Anita watched Bufi's shadow appearing and disappearing among the late afternoon shadows that lay across the road as they neared the *bohío*. Patting Bufi's warm flank, she hoped she had made the right decision to not accept help.

The second test had to be given before the next seminar. Any learners who didn't pass it would automatically receive extra tutoring. Ramón was already receiving extra classes at work from Do or Die Brigade tutors, so Anita felt she could relax about him. She would concentrate on helping Clara. She figured that if she took on more of the work around the *bohío*, Clara would be less tired during the classes, and so would be able to concentrate better.

First off, she insisted that Clara not do any more heavy laundry. "Zenaida can do the laundry, can't you Zenaida?" She was grateful that Zenaida nodded, for she hadn't asked her beforehand. And she herself couldn't help with laundry because she never left the property except with Ramón when he was armed.

Clara's ankles were always swollen, and ropy-looking blue veins bulged out on her legs. Looking at them made Anita feel slightly nauseous. She asked Zenaida if Clara's legs were that way when she was pregnant with Nataniel, but Zenaida said she hadn't noticed. Nataniel was always getting into things, so Anita spent as much time as she could looking after him. Something Anita had never done was cook, so now, when Clara and Zenaida prepared meals, she insisted on helping. She had never so much as cut a slice of bread before. Now she learned to chop onions, peel and mince garlic, shell peas.

"I have two announcements," she said one morning at the end of class before Ramón left for work. "One, today I will cook the evening meal for everyone. You must promise to eat it all and not hurt my feelings. Agreed?" Ramón said nothing, but looked at her with an amused expression on his face.

"That is very nice, Anita, but I don't think you know enough about cooking to prepare a whole meal," said Clara.

"Let's give her a chance," said Zenaida. "Even teachers need to know how to cook, right?" she said with a straight face. "I for one promise not to laugh, but I won't promise to eat everything."

Ramón and Clara looked skeptical, but they agreed.

"I'll settle for that," Anita said. "The second announcement is that the day after tomorrow, you will take the second test." The amused looks on their faces vanished.

"Do you think we are ready to take the second test?" Ramón asked.

"I don't think so, I know so," Anita answered, her fingers crossed behind her back.

When Anita began to prepare the evening meal, she insisted that Clara rest and let her do it herself. She had decided to make chicken soup, a Spanish stew with broad beans, rice and vegetables, and fried plantain bananas for dessert. Anita had seen these things prepared many times over the last months. *Shouldn't be too difficult*, she thought. She approached the chickens, determined to wring a hen's neck just as she had seen Clara do dozens of times, but she just couldn't make herself do it. Embarrassed, she asked Zenaida to do it for her. She did pluck the feathers and gut the chicken by herself, though she retched the whole time.

How do people do it? Anita asked herself as she worked through the afternoon. *No running water. Only this crude kitchen table to prepare the food on. Cooking on a small kerosene stove where you can't regulate the heat.* She pictured the kitchen at home—the long smooth counters, all the cooking utensils, the double sinks with their shining faucets, the modern electric stove. By the time everything was ready to serve, it was late, and Anita felt utterly frazzled.

"*La comida está servida*," she called out bravely. "Dinnertime."

Ramón washed up and sat down, his eyes twinkling. Clara tied Nataniel into the home-made high chair, then sat down herself, her belly pressed up tight against the table.

"It's about time," Zenaida teased. "I'm really hungry!"

They ate in silence. The soup was bland and greasy. The stew was watery. The rice tasted of burn. The bananas were burned. Anita put down her fork and looked up.

"Even I can't eat burned bananas," she said apologetically, pushing her plate away. They all burst out laughing. They laughed even more when they saw that Nataniel had eaten every bit of banana and wanted more.

What a mess there was to clean up! Anita relented and let Clara and Zenaida help.

"I'm not giving up," Anita said. "Next time will be better."

Ramón groaned and put his palms together in mock prayer. "God save us all from our teacher's good intentions," he said, rolling his eyes.

The Year of Education,
October 24, 1961

Dear mamá and papá,

How wonderful that Tomasa and Gladis passed the test! Will Fernando take the test again with more coaching? I hope so. My learners will be doing the second test tomorrow. They actually seem calmer about it than I feel. I may have to poke Ramón to stay awake because he is so tired these days. He is spreading manure, repairing fences and doing all kinds of other fieldwork. Papá, remember that you told me that Bainoa has the coldest micro-climate in Cuba? Well I'm feeling it these days. Please send me my warmest jacket by mail if you are not planning to visit again really soon.

You'll never believe what I am going to tell you. One of the brigadistas told Marjorie that the four-year-old boy in his learning family told him that he knows how to read too. He asked the child to read something from the workbook, and the child did. Marjorie was sure the kid had just been able to memorize it by hearing it repeated so she went to see the family. She said to the little boy, I hear you can read. Will you read for me? The kid said, Nobody believes I can read, but I can. I can even read in the dark with my eyes shut. Marjorie had brought the children's book The Sad Wolf with her. I remember reading it when I was small, but not four years old. Anyway, Marjorie asked the boy to read it to her. Guess what! He read the whole story without stopping. He had learned to read while the others were being taught. Isn't that amazing!

Did you know that I could read before you knew I could? I kept it a secret because I thought you might stop reading to me at bedtime.

Papá, you haven't written me even once since I've been here! I know you don't like writing letters, but you could scribble a few lines. Come on papá, just do it—please.

Love, Anita

Havana,
October 28, 1961

My dear Anita,

I kept meaning to write you, but as you know, I tend to leave a lot of things to your mother. Well, writing a letter shouldn't be too difficult for a newspaper editor. I know you are concerned about Fernando not passing the first test. He has been receiving extra classes from a volunteer teacher, a retired lawyer from the neighbourhood, and he is improving. He'll take the test again very soon. I think his problem was fear of failure. He's learning with more confidence now. I enjoy the classes, which I continue to give early in the morning (like you) before I leave for work.

Everywhere you go these days, there's teaching going on—in parks, in the cafeterias of factories and hotels, even in the lobbies of apartment buildings. The city of Havana is one big school! At the club, everyone is talking about what will happen when all these people learn to read and write. Will they quit their jobs as domestics and gardeners and junk and garbage collectors and delivery boys and a hundred other jobs done by the uneducated? Will they be expecting to "rise up" in life? The answer is obvious, or should be. Of course they will. Who will do all the work? they ask. Good question. Maybe I should be asking Fernando to teach me all about gardening, pruning trees, fertilizing plants. What do you think?

Everything is fine here, although some things are in short supply. The Yankees still refuse to trade with us and have influenced other countries to not trade with Cuba either. They call it "trading with the enemy". When things do arrive in the stores, mostly from eastern Europe and China, there are long line-ups. People grumble and get frustrated. I wonder how long we will have to endure rationing? At least, with rationing, everyone gets a share of whatever is available.

I know your mother is getting a package ready for you. We are planning to come to see you in two weeks. We pray that you will always be safe from harm. ALWAYS, ALWAYS be cautious daughter. Give the Perez family my best regards.

Much love, Papá

The Year of Education
November 4, 1961

Dear mamá and papá,

Even though you're coming soon, I can't wait to tell you that all three of my learners passed their second test. I was so worried that Clara was falling behind because of pregnancy and all, but she did well enough. I moved the small literacy flag closer to the door. In general, the supervisors are worried that Bainoa region is not advancing as quickly as it should, but everyone is working really hard. Like Mario, Dani is doing double duty now and jokes that she hardly has time to wash her socks.

Papá, I enjoyed your letter so much. Tell Fernando I am thinking about him and wishing him luck. How can you stand going to the club and listening to such selfish talk? It would do a lot of those spoiled people good to do their own work and get their hands dirty once in a while. I guess that goes for all of us, doesn't it?

When you come, I will introduce you to Claudio, a very nice brigadista who has become a special friend.

Affectionate regards to Tomasa, Gladis and Fernando (and a special hug for Tomasa).

Love, Anita

November 4, 1961

Dear Diary,

I mentioned Claudio in a letter to my parents. I just said he is a special friend, not a boyfriend. And he is special! We don't see each other very often, but when we do, we talk and talk and talk about anything and everything. My learners passed the second test. Hooray! I feel quite proud of them and myself. Everything seems to be speeding up. What a celebration we will have when Bainoa region raises the literacy flag in the town square!

Anita la cubana

★

Anita and Clara were in the chicken coop gathering eggs when Clara groaned loudly.

"*¿Qué pasa, Clara?* What's the matter?"

"The waters of my womb have spilled from me. My labour pains have started," Clara answered. "You finish gathering eggs. I must go to the *bohío* and lie down."

"But it couldn't be that. It's not time yet!" stuttered Anita. "The baby is not due until early December."

"Nature does not always pay attention to our appointments, Anita." Another pain made Clara cry out with pain, and she would have buckled if Anita hadn't supported her.

"Help me get to bed, Anita. Zenaida must go for Rosa."

As Anita and Zenaida were getting Clara into bed, Anita realized she knew nothing about how Clara had planned to have the baby. She knew premature babies needed special care. *Where had Nataniel been born? Who would deliver this baby coming weeks early?* Zenaida answered a few of these questions as they scurried about trying to make Clara comfortable.

"Nataniel was born right here in the *bohío*. Ramón delivered him, cut the cord and everything. I helped in any way I could, mostly just by letting Clara squeeze my hands. I will go get Rosa now."

The older woman soon arrived with her horse and cart, a worried expression on her face. She spoke a few words of encouragement to Clara, then spoke quietly to Anita and Zenaida. "When a baby comes too early, there could be many problems . . . complications. The baby will be small, so could come very quickly. I will go for the midwife. Zenaida, you and Anita must do your best to prepare things and make Clara comfortable until the midwife arrives." Nataniel, who had been crying the whole time, was swept up in Rosa's arms as she started for the door. "I will take Nataniel with me."

"But what shall we do?" said Anita, following Rosa outside. "I don't know what to do, and neither does Zenaida."

"Heat water in the biggest pot you've got. Get Clara to drink lots of water. Give her food if she wants any. Talk to her. Comfort her. I will return with the midwife as soon as I can."

Then she was gone.

Anita went back to Clara, who was quietly sobbing and repeating, "What will happen? What will happen?" Anita smoothed Clara's hair away from her anxious face.

"The midwife will come soon, Clara. Everything will be all right." Clara tried to smile, but her face contorted with a sudden spasm, and she cried out for Ramón. *What if the baby comes before the midwife arrives?* This was all Anita could think about.

Zenaida lit the kerosene stove and put a large pot filled with water on to heat. She heated some soup for Clara, and tried to give her some, but she wouldn't eat any, only sipping water now and then. Anita remained by Clara, holding her hand, babbling anything that came into her head to try to distract her between the pains. It seemed to Anita the contractions were coming closer together, but she wasn't sure. *Was the midwife on her way?* Between contractions, Clara seemed to sleep. When pain roused her, she wouldn't talk to Anita or Zenaida or respond to their questions. She just squeezed their hands hard.

Clara's hair became bedraggled and damp with perspiration, her face pale. She seemed very weak. The contractions were definitely coming closer together and it seemed to Anita that Clara's belly was clenching up like a huge fist. Anita's anxiety mounted with the passing of each minute. She asked Zenaida to go to the road to see if anyone was coming. *Oh come, someone please come*, prayed Anita, mopping Clara's perspiring face and neck with a cool cloth.

Zenaida came back, shaking her head.

LITTLE FISH

W hen at last Anita heard the clatter of a horse and wagon, she ran to the doorway. A small black woman came rushing in shouting, "No worries, Clara. Estela is here."

Anita collapsed on the stoop with relief.

"Get up girl," the midwife demanded. "This is no time to slack off." The midwife began taking things out of a large carpet bag she carried. "Help me get this rubber sheet under Clara. Zenaida, wrap these scissors in a clean cloth and put them in a small pot of boiling water to sterilize, then prepare a clean place to put the baby. And get something clean and soft to wrap the baby in. You, girl," she said, looking at Anita, "you stay right here with me. Now Clara, let's you and I get to work and have a nice baby."

Anita stood by Clara's side, holding her hand, giving her sips of water, cooling her face, neck and arms from time to time. Sometimes Clara slumped between contractions, frightening Anita, but the midwife didn't seem concerned. With each contraction, Clara groaned loudly, nearly crushing Anita's hand. Estela kept up a steady stream of encouragement, urging Clara to push hard when the contractions started coming closer together. Sweat drenched Clara's whole body as she pushed and pushed. The more she pushed, the paler and sweatier she became.

"The baby is coming, the midwife said quietly."

Anita smelled the blood before she saw any. Breathing through her mouth, she willed herself to stay calm.

"One more good push, Clara," said the midwife.

Anita saw the baby slither out of Clara's body into the midwife's waiting hands—slither out like a fish, a slippery little fish, dark and slimy and silent.

"¡Es una muchachita, a girl child!" the midwife shouted, flicking her fingers against the baby's heels and rubbing the body gently to make it cry. She placed the squealing, blood-and-mucous-streaked infant on Clara's deflated belly. Anita thought she would faint looking at the transparent, ropy-looking umbilical cord trailing from the little fish's abdomen. Clara gathered the covers around the squalling infant and kept repeating, "*¡Mi bebé! ¡Mi bebé!* The midwife washed her hands, then tied off and cut the cord, leaving a raw stub sticking out of the place where the baby's belly-button would be. She washed her hands again and gently searched the infant's mouth for any mucous. When the afterbirth came with another gush of bloody liquid, the midwife caught it neatly in a small pail. Anita saw the midwife's lips moving; she realized that Estela was saying something to her, but what? The midwife shook Anita's arm.

"*¡Muchacha!* . . . Go sit down before you fall down. You're whiter than the inside of a coconut."

Anita sat on the stoop of the *bohío* waiting for Ramón to arrive back from the fields. Inside, Clara slept deeply, exhausted from the labour of giving birth. She could hear Zenaida playing with Nataniel. The midwife had been a whirlwind, not only delivering the baby and cleaning mother and baby after, but directing everyone in cleaning and preparing the *bohío* so that all would be ship-shape.

"I will stay until morning to help the little *señorita* begin to suckle, and to watch for any complications," she said. Anita had watched, fascinated as the midwife gave the infant sweetened black tea, squeezing drops of the liquid into the tiny, pursed mouth from a little piece of boiled cloth. Clara's breasts were already swelling with milk. The tiny baby, swaddled warmly, slept in Clara's arms. Estela dozed on a chair at the table, her head slumped upon her skinny chest. Even now, hours later, Anita felt light-headed from witnessing the whole slimy gushy mess. She had been so afraid—afraid that Clara would die, that the baby would die; afraid that both would die before her eyes.

She jumped to her feet when she heard the approach of Bufi. Ramón hadn't yet dismounted when Anita was telling him in a rush of words that the baby had come early; that he had a daughter; that the baby was tiny but OK. As Ramón rushed past her into the *bohío,* all that she had experienced overcame her and she hurried in toward her hammock. The midwife was still asleep in a chair at the table, her head resting on her crossed arms. Anita glanced into Clara's and Ramón's little room lit by a single candle. Ramón sat in a chair, bent forward on the bed, one arm flung across his sleeping wife. The baby lie peacefully in the crook of Clara's arm. Zenaida was rocking Nataniel to sleep in his hammock. Too tired to even undress, Anita tumbled into her hammock, mumbling a prayer. *Please, please let Clara and the little fish be all right.*

Ramón didn't go to work the day after his daughter was born. The first thing he did was bury the placenta afterbirth in the garden: "to nourish the earth for the baby's future nourishment," he explained. Zenaida said he did the same with Nataniel's placenta. The midwife left, leaving instructions that the baby and Clara must be watched for certain problems, and that Clara was to remain resting.

"Tomorrow, class as usual," Anita said optimistically, but wondered if Clara would be able to resume.

She and Zenaida did all the household tasks. When Anita was gathering eggs from the hen house, she was surprised to see the hens had laid more eggs than usual. "Maybe the chickens got all excited too, Zenaida." Feeling sorry for Nataniel, who cried when his mother couldn't give him the attention he wanted, Anita played with him a lot. At supper, she sat him upon her lap to feed him.

"Anita . . ." began Ramón, in a tone of voice that made Anita wonder what was coming. "Clara and I have decided to name the baby after you. We are grateful for what you have done, and we want our girl to grow up to be just like you." Anita hid her face in Nataniel's curls, waiting until she could get control of her emotions. Nataniel reached up and pulled her hair. Disentangling his chubby fingers, Anita looked up with shining eyes.

"I'm honoured," she managed to say.

"We will teach baby Anita to call you *tía*, aunt Anita," said Clara. Clara looked over at her sister affectionately. "Both of you were wonderful. Thank you both for all you did for me and the baby."

"I guess Clara didn't notice that I was retching and nearly fainting the whole time she was giving birth," said Anita as she told Dani and Claudio all the details of Clara's labour and the birth of the baby before the seminar started. Dani's expression had grown more and more astonished as Anita described the birth. Claudio looked like he wished he were somewhere else.

"You actually saw the baby come out and everything!" Dani exclaimed. "Was it disgusting?"

"I wouldn't say it was *disgusting*, but it was kind of messy, but also really amazing. And you know what? They have named the baby after me."

"Wow, that make's the bond between you and your learner family really special!" said Dani. "I've been wondering about something, Anita. When the campaign is over, I wonder if many *brigadistas* will keep in touch with their learners. You probably will, right?"

"Of course I will, especially now that I have this special connection," Anita said. "Won't you keep in touch with your learner family?"

"I don't want to say I will. People are always saying they'll do things, like promising to keep in touch with friends you make at summer camp or someone you meet travelling. But then you don't actually do it. What about you, Claudio. Are there people you'll keep in touch with?"

"Maybe with Anita, if she wants me to," he replied, his eyes searching hers.

Heading toward the assembly of *brigadistas*, Anita linked arms with Dani and Claudio, grateful to have two such good friends.

"We have great news!" said the director when all the *brigadistas* had assembled. "Yesterday at noon, the town of Melena del Sur in the province of Havana was the first in the country to raise a literacy flag in the town square. Fidel himself attended the festivities."

Anita jumped to her feet with all the other *brigadistas* shouting "*Viva* the Literacy Campaign! *Viva* Cuba!"

"Other villages and towns are close to raising flags in November," the supervisor continued. "But there is also some not-so-good news. All the learners of Bainoa region have taken the second test, but a significant number didn't pass."

The "*vivas!*" turned to moans of disappointment.

"We are in the last stage of the campaign," the supervisor said, "and I know you're all working hard. But now we must work even harder. Classes must be given seven days a week to prepare as many people as possible for the third and final test. For that reason, there won't be another seminar until the last Sunday in November. Then we'll assess where we are at."

Anita and Dani looked at each other. Seven days a week . . . ! That meant no time for socializing, no time to see boyfriends and girlfriends, no time to just hang out. The whole group groaned like a wounded animal.

"Any questions?" asked the director.

Anita was surprised when Dani stood up. "When will we find time to wash our socks?" she asked with a straight face. Everyone howled and hooted.

"*Señorita* Dani, the day we raise the literacy flag here in Bainoa, I will personally wash your socks," the director replied.

"Mine too," yelled out everyone.

"Free time for an hour until the soccer game starts," said the director.

Anita and Claudio stopped to buy some roasted peanuts from a street vendor before going for a walk. The vendor scooped hot salted peanuts into small cones deftly fashioned from squares of brown paper. They tossed peanuts up for each other to catch in their mouths. Claudio never missed. When they reached the outskirts of town, they sat down on a low wall to talk. Nearby fields lay still and empty. Harvesting of all crops was complete for another year.

"We won't be seeing each other for a few weeks," said Claudio. "Will you miss me?"

"I *will* miss you," Anita answered without hesitation.

"Hey, I thought you would make a joke, or something," said Claudio.

"Why would I joke?" said Anita. "I'll really miss you. You make me laugh."

"Is that all I'm good for? You don't like me for my good looks or brilliant mind?"

Anita kissed Claudio, a real kiss. She hadn't planned to kiss him, but was glad she did. He became completely flustered—speechless, in fact. Anita pulled him to his feet. "*Vamos*, let's walk some more before going back." They held hands as they walked along.

"Some *campesino* musicians are coming to the schoolhouse tonight to play for a couple of hours. Do you think Ramón could bring you over and wait to take you back?" Claudio suggested.

"Not tonight, Claudio. Because of the baby . . . It's too soon to leave Clara and Zenaida alone for so long," Anita replied. When they got back, Claudio had to rush off to change into shorts for the soccer game, but not before stealing a quick kiss.

"Hmm, I see the romance has reached a new stage," commented Dani. "Was the boy being fresh?" she asked.

"No," Anita grinned, "but I was."

The Year of Education
November 10, 1961

Dear Mario,

> *I can't remember when I last wrote you. So much has happened. My family passed the second test. Clara's baby was born 6 weeks premature and I watched the whole thing! They named the baby girl after me. Zenaida and I are pitching in with the added work, but Clara seems to have lost her ability to concentrate during class now that she has two children to look after. I've decided to ask for help.*

> *How are you and your wild bunch doing? Are you still a bearded man? If so, the beard must be hanging down your chest, like old Rip Van Winkle. Our parents tell me that you have changed a lot. "He's an adult now," they say. They also said you are more handsome than ever—even with a beard. Don't go getting too "adult", brother. You won't be as much fun. Write soon.*

> *Love, Anita*

> *P.S. I think Claudio is my boyfriend now.*

"I have decided to stop the lessons Anita. I can't seem to concentrate during the lesson in the morning, and I'm just too tired at night," Clara announced one morning at breakfast not long after the birth of the baby.

Anita started to reply, but Clara interrupted her. "There are too many distractions, Anita. I know you are disappointed, but I just cannot do all that must be done and the lessons too. *Lo siento*, I'm sorry, but it's simply too much." Just then, Nataniel toppled over and began to cry. Clara hurried to pick him up.

Anita had been thinking about what she would say if Clara decided to quit the lessons.

"It is not only me you will disappoint Clara. You will be disappointed in yourself. At the end of the campaign, practically everyone will know how to read and write, but you won't, and you'll probably forget what you've learned so far. Don't you remember how excited you were thinking that one day you would be able to read stories to Nataniel and eventually to baby Anita? The new school being built in town for the district will open soon. Nataniel will go to that school, but you won't know anything about his studies. You won't be able to help him with homework."

As Anita spoke, Clara's body stiffened and her angular face hardened like stone as it always did when she was determined to resist.

"Zenaida will read them stories. Ramón will help Nataniel with his schoolwork," she said, getting up from the table.

"Clara, Zenaida will soon be seventeen," said Anita. "She will probably want to continue her education and get a job to earn her own living. It may seem harsh, but maybe you shouldn't count on Zenaida staying here."

"That is true," said Clara, standing rigid, holding Nataniel close, "and it is this literacy campaign that will take her away, that will break up my family."

Anita didn't know what to say to this. After all, Zenaida was all that was left of Clara's blood family. What Clara had just expressed was something like the fear expressed by the people at the country club: the literacy campaign, all the emphasis on continuing education . . . it was bound to change things dramatically. People wanting to improve their lives would leave their homes and families. She recalled her father saying that everyone would feel the campaign's impact in some way.

They are so close to becoming a literate family; I just can't let Clara slip back into the corner now. Anita thought back to certain pep talks the *brigadistas* had received at Varadero.

"Would you rather the campaign weren't happening, Clara? Would you rather that Zenaida remain illiterate . . . living with you until she marries or gets work as a domestic or a field hand? Would you want Ramón to remain illiterate, never to have the chance to do anything else except work as a field hand for the rest of his life—lead a donkey's life just like his father before him?"

Clara sank down onto a chair, hugging Nataniel close.

"Clara, I understand that you feel overwhelmed right now with the baby and all. But maybe we can arrange things to make it easier. I will ask Marjorie to arrange a teacher to come here to tutor you at the same time every day . . ."

"But what about the children?" interrupted Clara. "Whether I have lessons with you or some other person, I can't concentrate when the children need me, and there's always something going on with small children."

"Zenaida and I will take the children out during the lesson time. It will only be for one hour. We will stay outside so you can concentrate."

"But what if baby Anita needs to nurse? I can't let an infant be hungry."

"You will fill her to bursting before we go out. Besides, baby Anita almost never cries when she is being carried around."

"And what of the promise you made not to go anywhere by yourself, not to expose yourself to the danger of rebels?"

"Since the arrests, there has been no sign of rebel activity, but I promise we will not leave the yard. And think about this, Clara . . . If you do not continue, if you do not learn to read and write and pass the third test, that little flag cannot be put outside the door. Not even though Zenaida and Ramón do finish. What do you say?"

"I don't know what to say," said Clara. "I have never met anyone who can talk the leaves off trees as you do, Anita."

"Just say yes, Clara. At least try it for a while."

Just then they heard an uproar outside as all the chickens began to squawk. Zenaida ran inside screaming, "There's a big snake in the yard and it's got a chicken!"

AN OMEN

A nita and Clara ran to the doorway and saw a frantic scene. On the ground not five metres from the stoop was a huge snake, a chicken disappearing head first—feathers and all—into its gaping jaws. The rest of the chickens had retreated to the roof of the chicken coop and the lower limbs of trees. Alarmed and excited by the squawking chickens, the pigs were squealing, the mule was braying, and the goat was trying to break away from its tether.

Anita stared at the snake, more fascinated than afraid. "How repulsive!" she whispered. She had been told about these snakes everyone called the chicken snake. They mostly hung out in trees near old barns and sheds. Even though every school child learns there are no poisonous snakes in Cuba, every time Anita collected eggs, she feared coming upon a chicken snake. Anita estimated this snake was at least eight feet long. It was beautiful, actually, she thought, a brilliant yellow-orange colour with black bands and jet black eyes. The snake's muscles contracted and expanded as the chicken was drawn further into its body. Feathers lay scattered about on the ground.

"The snake will remain there for a long while," said Clara. "It will be too heavy to move after it eats. It's not the first time we've lost a chicken to the chicken-eating snake, and it won't be the last. God made the snake, so the snake must eat too."

"Clara . . ." Anita said, her eyes still riveted on the snake. "What about arranging for a tutor?"

Clara remained silent, staring out into the yard.

"I've always felt snakes are a good omen," she said eventually, as though talking to herself. "I will talk to Ramón. If he has no objections, I will try your plan." Anita relaxed. She was pretty sure Ramón wouldn't object. The snake lay completely still now, its upper body distorted, bulging with its meal.

"Why do you think the snake is a good omen, Clara?"

"Some say the snake represents temptation and evil, but I have heard others say that snakes are beloved children of the earth because they do not need feet to move and they touch Mother Earth with their whole body. I have also heard it said that snakes represent ancient wisdom. In the Bible, the snake encouraged Eve to eat fruit from the tree of knowledge, and she did, and she shared the fruit with Adam. Maybe the snake is a sign that I should be accepting knowledge so I can share that knowledge with my family."

Turning, she looked at Anita and said, "I believe in signs."

No one noticed when the creature slithered back to the bush, but eventually the chickens reclaimed the yard and resumed their scratching and pecking. When Ramón returned that evening, Clara told him about Anita's suggestions and about the chicken snake.

"What do you think of Anita's teaching plan for me, Ramón?"

"I think you should let the *maestra* do what is possible to put the literacy flag outside our door."

With Clara's consent, Marjorie arranged for a volunteer tutor.

A few days later, the tutor arrived in an open Jeep. After introductions—his name was Eugenio—Clara invited him to sit down and served him fresh coffee. "Please excuse us for a moment, *señor* Eugenio," Clara said, taking hold of Anita's arm firmly and propelling her outside.

What now? wondered Anita.

"I assumed the tutor would be a woman, Anita. I cannot be alone with a man. It's not proper," declared Clara in a whisper.

"But Clara, he's part of the campaign, a volunteer like me—part of the Do or Die Brigade," protested Anita.

"No, it is not proper. Ramón would not approve either."

Anita was taken by surprise. She knew Clara was modest and shy, but she hadn't realized such old-fashioned ideas would forbid this situation.

"Clara, this is completely different. Eugenio has not come to *visit* you when your husband isn't home. He's a teacher. When we were being prepared for the campaign in Varadero, we were told that our behaviour always had to be proper and respectful or we would bring shame upon the campaign and Cuba. I'm sure Eugenio will act properly and respectfully."

"You are leaving me alone with a man, a complete stranger. It is simply not proper," she repeated, her face beginning to take on its stubborn expression.

"Clara, you are part of the new generation of women *la revolución* is talking about. Many things from the past must be changed, including this old-fashioned notion. Now, do you want to learn to read and write or not? The teacher has finished his coffee and is waiting for his student."

"Good Lord! Is there no way to win any argument with you, Anita Fonseca? I know I am stubborn, but you . . . you are ten times—no, a hundred times—more stubborn. And you have a tongue a mile long! Take the children and go. Leave me to my fate today. But if Ramón objects, I definitely will not continue with a man tutor."

That evening, Clara asked Ramón what he thought about letting a strange man tutor her with no one else present.

"I think the special circumstances require me to trust *la revolución*, trust the tutor, and trust my wife."

"Well!" said Clara with a huff. "I guess you don't care about your wife's reputation. So Anita Fonseca, you get your way again. I see that from now on, I must protect my own virtue and reputation."

Ramón, Anita and Zenaida tried not to laugh, but couldn't help themselves.

Everyone was glad to be together again at the seminar the final Sunday in November, catching up on news and gossip. Copies of Bohemia magazine were being passed around. In it was an article about the literacy campaign featuring Marjorie and the *brigadistas* under her supervision. Much was made of the fact that Marjorie was an American. Anita had almost forgotten about the interviews, so many weeks had gone by since the reporters were around.

"Look at Marjorie, Claudio. How beautiful she looks! And look, there's Pamela teaching her students." Suzi was photographed with the pony and goat a *campesino* had given her early on to amuse herself while her mother taught. Anita was in a small group photo taken at one of the seminars, and one of Dani showed her at the schoolhouse playing the guitar surrounded by *campesino* musicians.

As everyone was assembling for the seminar, Anita noticed the director talking to Marjorie and the other supervisors. Marjorie's hand flew to her mouth, and a couple of the supervisors started to cry.

"Claudio, something terrible has happened."

Anita was right. When the director started to speak, her voice was grave.

"*Brigadistas*, a great tragedy has happened. I have just learned that a *brigadista* whose name is Manuel Domenech was ambushed and killed yesterday by counter-revolutionaries. He was eighteen. The counter-revolutionaries tortured and mutilated Manuel before hanging him. He had been teaching on a farm near the town of Trinidad in Las Villas. The counter-revolutionaries also killed a man named Pedro Latigua, one of the *campesinos* Manuel had been working with."

As the director spoke, the *brigadistas* sat in stunned silence, tears streaming down many of their faces.

"The sad thing is that Manuel had begged to be sent to the same area in the Escambray Mountains as Conrado Benitez," said the director, "so he was."

All around Anita, *brigadistas,* boys and girls alike, buried their faces in their hands. Voices were asking the same question: "Why? Why?" Anita remembered her own questions about why rebels had killed Conrado Benitez. She recalled her terrible nightmare. Now again . . . hateful people intent on ruining Cuba's plans to make the whole population literate . . . murdering to make the point dramatic . . . scaring people to keep them from participating . . .

"Anita . . ." Claudio was pulling her to her feet.

"During this moment of silence, let us send our thoughts to the families of Manuel Domenech and Pedro Latigua," said the director. All heads bowed, hands still wiping away tears. When the director raised her own tear-stained face she said, "I know you will want to talk, so take a fifteen minute break."

Anita didn't want to talk. She stayed where she was, feeling a mixture of sadness and rage. Claudio stayed beside her, holding her hand, squeezing it gently. They sat, not talking, until everyone was called together again.

"Despite this tragic happening, we must carry on our work here," said the director. "We will do it in the name of your fellow teachers, Conrado Benitez and Manuel Domenech. Security will have to be tightened even more." After a discussion about security measures, the director informed them about progress in the Bainoa region. "Those learners who didn't pass the second test received extra tutoring and took the test again. Most passed, but not all."

"How can that be?" the *brigadistas* murmured to one another.

"We have to accept that some people do not have the capacity to become literate," said the supervisor. "Not just here in Bainoa, but everywhere. There are many reasons why—old age, illness. Some people are mentally challenged. As well, in Oriente province there are groups of people living remotely whose first language isn't Spanish—for example, people from Haiti who speak French or a *patois*. And there are Jamaicans living in Cuba who only speak English or Creole. So Bainoa is not unique. We have doubled our efforts, so now we must triple our efforts, quadruple them if we must in order to get as many people as possible to pass the final test in the few weeks remaining. On the positive side, literacy flags are being raised all across Cuba, probably somewhere right at this moment.

"The date for the final test throughout the country has been set for December fifteenth." There was a sharp intake of breath throughout the room. Today was November twenty sixth. Less than three weeks remained. "You can give the test sooner if you think your learners are prepared—but not one day later. No exceptions," added the director. "Now, break into your groups, and we will figure out how to get the best results in the time we have left."

REFLECTIONS

*B*rigadistas who lived at the schoolhouse or in town were all assigned additional teaching tasks. "For sure my socks will rot right off my feet now, Anita. But we're nearing the end of the campaign. Isn't that exciting?" Dani asked.

"I suppose."

"You're feeling down about the murder, aren't you?" said Dani.

"Yeah . . . that . . . and the campaign coming to an end."

Dani looked at Anita with amazement. "You must be kidding, my young friend! I'm looking forward to soaking in my bathtub for three hours and watching the crust of dirt melt and slide off me. Then I will put on some makeup, a fashionable dress and pretty shoes and go out for ice cream at a café on *La Rampa*."

"Ramón will be coming for me soon, Dani. I'm going to find Claudio to say goodbye." Claudio was talking to a couple of his friends, so she hung back, not wanting to interrupt. When he noticed her, he left his companions and came toward her. Anita had to smile. Like so many of the boys, Claudio had grown during the many months in Bainoa. A lot of sock was showing below his pant legs, and his wrists dangled well below the cuffs of his shirt sleeves. *Some parents won't recognize their sons*, she thought. *They've grown up; their voices have changed; they've become young men.* Of course, the girls were changing too. She personally hoped her breasts wouldn't get any bigger. She didn't want to have the big breasts that most boys seemed so fascinated with.

The silence within the *bohío* and outside its walls was the kind of silence that seemed to find its way into your head—like when you hold a conch shell up to your ear. Anita sat in the stillness, watching the lantern's blue-yellow flame. Everyone was sleeping. Yawning widely, she sat a while longer thinking about the theme of the lesson she had taught that morning.

Usually she felt good about the lessons, but this one had left her feeling upset. The reading was about what a popular place Cuba has always been for tourists, and how every year huge numbers of tourists come to Cuba and leave behind thousands and thousands of dollars. Before the revolution, the beach resorts were restricted to white people, and many tourists came to Cuba to gamble and go to brothels. As Anita knew it would, talking about prostitutes and brothels had embarrassed her learners. *Oh, the look on Clara's face when I read those words!* She told them that brothels, casinos and gambling houses had been shut down soon after the revolution. She read them the letter her mother had written her about volunteers teaching literacy to the prostitutes. The reading went on to say that new tourist centres were being developed, and that now, any Cuban could go to any of Cuba's resorts. That's when things got upsetting.

"We've never been to a resort," Clara said. "We've never had enough money. We don't even have bathing suits."

Anita hadn't thought about this before; had never thought that most *campesinos* from this area had never been to a resort, maybe never even been to a beach. What else had they probably never done? She had never seen them receive any mail. They had probably never talked to anyone on a telephone. Had they ever gone to the movies? Watched TV? *I have so much, they have so little* she thought once again with a heavy heart. Yet, though they were poor, her learner family didn't seem unhappy. As she undressed, she wondered what a person really needed to be happy. She felt happy living with the Perez family now, but would she be happy if there were no home in Havana to return to?

> The Year of Education,
> Caimanera,
> November 25, 1961
>
> Dear Anita,
>
> Soon the campaign will be over, and we will return to Havana. Going home will not be easy for me. I mean returning to a situation where you are considered a child—well, not exactly a child. It's hard to explain. Here I am looked up to. I have real responsibilities. I learn something new, something practical almost every day. I am not treated like a "youngster". I hope when I return that our parents will understand that I am different now and that things between us will have to be different. How about you? How do you feel about returning?

I'm pretty sure my wild bunch will pass the third and final test. They have been amazing, working really hard. Even abuelo Carmelo will pass, though his handwriting is pretty weird. The Bible boys will pass easily. Everyone in Caimanera is tremendously excited about raising the literacy flag. I have told my learner family about you, and they want to meet my clever and brave sister. I will bring you here for sure one day. I hope all is going well with your teaching. I don't think I'll be writing again. See you in Havana brigadista Anita.

Love, Mario

Anita sat a long time with Mario's letter in her hand. The letter made her think about the thousands of *brigadistas* who would soon be returning home. Some would be eager to return to family and friends, school life and their familiar routines. Like Dani who was anxious to get back to Havana, back to city life. Others might feel like Mario, brooding about having to live under house rules when they had enjoyed independence for so many months. Would there be disagreements and slamming doors? *And what about you, Anita?* she asked herself, folding Mario's letter and putting it with all the others in the letter box. *Will mamá and papá understand that I'm not the same girl I was when I left?* As Anita crossed off another day on her calendar, she thought, *I won't know the answer to that question until I'm home again.*

THIRD AND FINAL

Nataniel had been sick for a few days with vomiting and diarrhoea, which had made it difficult for Clara to concentrate on her lessons. Despite Clara's protests that she didn't think she was ready, Anita convinced her to take the third and final test with the others.

"Just think of it as a practice test," she said. "There are still a few days until the deadline."

Baby Anita had been nursed and rocked to sleep, and Nataniel was already asleep in his hammock. Ramón had just finished smoking a cigar, which he did occasionally, and the pungent aroma still hung in the air. He had sharpened their pencils with his Swiss army knife, and now all three learners sat waiting quietly, bundled up in warm clothing as the December nights were quite chilly now. Outside the palm leaf door all was still except for occasional snuffling and snorting sounds coming from the pigpen. The lantern was lit.

"Let's begin. Open your workbooks to a fresh page and I'll explain how the test will go," said Anita. "First you will write your complete name and address at the top of the page. I will read you a short paragraph which you must listen to carefully because afterwards I will ask you questions about it. Then I will dictate the same paragraph for you to write. Are you ready? Does anyone need to get a drink or anything?"

All shook their heads, but then Ramón said, "Please, *maestra*. Don't go too fast."

"We can take all the time you need, but I can't help you. You understand that, don't you?" said Anita. All three nodded. "Then let's begin by writing your complete name, and below it, your address—just like we practiced."

Three heads bent and began to write. Zenaida wrote quickly and firmly. Ramón and Clara took more time.

"Now I will read the paragraph," said Anita. "Listen very carefully.

The Revolutionary government wants to make Cuba an industrialized country. Many new industries will be developed. Many jobs will become available. Unemployment will end.

Now you will write the answers to a few questions I will ask about that paragraph. Ready?"

"Anita, will you please read the paragraph again?" Clara asked, her voice quavering.

Anita read the paragraph again, slowly. "Ready now?" Clara nodded.

"Question number one. What does the Revolutionary government want to do?"

They wrote, and when all the faces were turned up to her again, Anita asked the second question. "What will be developed?"

The heads dropped, and they wrote. Ramón broke into a sweat as he always did when under a strain. Clara's face was visibly registering strain. Zenaida bit her lip but wrote steadily. Anita walked to the window so as not to be staring at them. Beyond the clearing, the trees were black silhouettes against a deep purple sky. When they all finished writing, Anita returned to the table.

"This is the last question. What will be the result?" *Would they understand the question? What if they didn't?*

Zenaida started writing, but Ramón and Clara sat looking at Anita.

"*Maestra* Anita, could you read the paragraph again?" Ramón asked.

Anita didn't know whether it was OK to read it again, but did anyway. Looking relieved, Ramón and Clara began to write. The baby stirred a bit. Anita hurried over to rock the cradle so Clara would not be distracted. Thankfully, the baby remained asleep. When they finished writing, Anita slowly dictated the same paragraph she had read. She watched with fascination as their hands moved across the page, still somewhat jerky, but so different from the way they had struggled to write when she first started teaching.

When she dictated the last word and said *punto*, period, she told them to lay down their pencils. "There is one final part to the test. Would you like to take a few moments to relax?"

Ramón went outside for air. Clara checked on the children and drank water. Zenaida remained at the table, creating decorative doodles along the edges of the page.

"How's it going, Zenaida?" Anita asked softly.

"It's easy," Zenaida whispered. *Shall I tell her not to doodle; that it's an exam paper?* Anita decided it didn't matter. When they were all together again, Anita explained the final part of the test.

"Our Prime Minister, Fidel Castro, asks that each learner write him a letter telling him what it means personally to have learned how to read and write. Carefully tear a clean piece of paper from your workbook and write Fidel a letter in your own words. At the top of the page put your address and the date."

Three incredulous faces stared at Anita.

"Write *Fidel Castro*?" said Zenaida.

"Yes. Write Fidel in your own words," repeated Anita. "Just tell him how you feel now that you know how read and write." Three faces continued staring at her in disbelief.

Oh, oh! This is really alarming them, Anita thought. She used her most encouraging tone of voice to say, "Just write a simple letter, a few lines—nothing complicated. There's absolutely no hurry. Take all the time you need."

Ramón sighed, tore a clean page from his workbook, and began to write. Anita watched his first words appear. Zenaida looked over at Ramón for a moment, then tore a page from her workbook and began to write. Clara sat unmoving, then suddenly stood up.

"No puedo," she said. *"No puedo.* I can't write a letter, especially to the Prime Minister." She left the table before Anita could say anything, and hurried to her bedroom. Ramón and Zenaida had stopped writing and looked at Anita with worried expressions.

"Don't worry," Anita said softly. "If the part that Clara has done so far is OK, she'll only have to write the letter. As I said, there's time. Go ahead and finish your letters." When they resumed writing Anita went to talk to Clara who was huddled on the bed, her face to the wall. Anita sat down and touched her shoulder.

"No puedo, Anita. *No puedo."*

"Maybe not tonight, Clara, but I know you can do it. Just relax now, and we'll practice tomorrow, OK?"

"OK. Maybe tomorrow," came the muffled reply. Anita breathed a sigh of relief. Ramón and Zenaida were still writing when Anita returned. Ramón was the first to put his pencil down. He pushed his workbook and the letter over to Anita.

"Do you want to wait here while I look at your test?" she asked.

"I will wait," he said.

"Here's mine," said Zenaida. "I want to wait too."

"First I will check Clara's test," Anita said, drawing Clara's workbook toward her. A few minutes later she looked up, relieved. "She has done the first two parts of the test well. I am sure she will have more confidence to write the letter when she knows this. Now let's look at your test, Ramón." As with Clara's test, there were a few minor errors, but his responses showed he had understood everything. As she read his letter to Fidel she had difficulty controlling her emotions.

> *Bainoa, Cuba*
> *December 11, 1961*
>
> *Dear Primer Ministro Fidel Castro,*
>
> *These are my words to tell you how proud I am to be able to read and write. I think now that I may someday be able to get a better job and be a better husband and father. Our family is grateful that you sent us brigadista Anita, the young maestra who has been so patient with us. We thank you and the revolution.*
>
> *Ramón Perez*

His writing bumped and jerked along, and not all the words were spelled correctly, but the words were there. Jumping up, Anita ran around the table to hug him. Getting the little literacy flag from where it was stuck in the thatch, she moved it closer to the doorway.

"Let's look at your test now, Zenaida." Other than some spelling mistakes and minor grammatical errors, it was just as Anita expected. She hugged Zenaida too. "Will you read your letter out loud?" Anita asked.

"Sure," Zenaida said.

> *Bainoa, Cuba*
> *December 11, 1961*
>
> *Dear Fidel,*
>
> *I never thought I would write a letter to a Prime Minister. At first I didn't want to learn to read and write at all. I didn't see the use of it for a simple guajira country girl. Now I feel different. I hope to go to the new school being built in Bainoa so that someday I will be an educated person. Then I will be able to help myself, my family and Cuba. Thank you for sending us maestra Anita. Tonight I am happier than I have ever been.*
>
> *Zenaida Maria Perez*

Beaming proudly, Ramón hugged Zenaida—something Anita had never seen him do. Now Anita moved the flag again, sticking it in the thatch just above the doorway. "I am sure this flag will go outside very soon—maybe even tomorrow," she said. Anita folded the letters, put them inside the workbooks, and put everything in her backpack. "Your letters will be placed with all the letters to be delivered to Fidel. *¡Caramba!* Just think of it! Thousands and thousands and thousands of letters!"

When Anita came out of the bedroom the next morning, she was greeted by three long faces. Clara stood looking at the flag stuck in the thatch above the doorway. "It is my fault that the flag will not be placed outside this *bohío*. It is my fault that our home will not be a territory free from illiteracy. I feel worthless, because now my husband and my sister will bear the shame." She started to sob, which set Nataniel to wailing and clutching his mother's skirt. Then the baby began to cry. Ramón tried to console his wife, but she turned away. Anita was about to reason with her, then decided she would do it when no one else was around. Right now, Clara was too distressed. The mood in the little *bohío* should have been joyful but instead it felt sour, like curdled milk.

How can I break this mood? Anita wondered. She did the first thing that came into her head.

"I'm hungry," she announced. "What about breakfast?" Her voice sounded bossy and rude to her ears. Ramón, Clara and Zenaida looked at her, startled, as though she had suddenly appeared out of thin air in their midst. As Clara prepared breakfast, Anita noticed her stealing glances at her from time to time. *Clara thinks I'm really mad at her. Well, maybe that's a good thing.*

Anita spread mango jam on her hunks of bread, then ate and drank her *café con leche* without uttering a single word. Nor did the others talk. As soon as Ramón finished, he went to tend to the animals and work on some repairs. Zenaida took Nataniel outside to play. Anita and Clara remained at the table.

"Please don't be angry with me, Anita," begged Clara, not looking at her, rocking the baby's cradle with her foot.

"What makes you think I'm angry?"

"You must be angry. The others have learned what you taught. They have passed the final test. I have not learned well enough, and now. . . . and now. . . ." She looked up at the little flag, her lips trembling.

"I'm not angry at all, Clara. I told you this could be a practice test. The deadline for finishing the test is still a few days away. You did well on the parts of the test you completed. That's the truth. So you only have to write the letter. I *will* be disappointed if you refuse to *try* to write the letter. It doesn't have to be perfect. Ramón's and Zenaida's letters were not perfect."

"But I do not know how to make things up in writing. All the lessons so far were repeated things, things we had heard or copied or fill-in-the-blanks exercises. I don't know how to make things up. *¡No puedo!*"

Anita had an idea. She motioned to Clara to wait, and went and got her box of letters.

"I have been away from home for almost seven months," she said, showing Clara all her letters. "You can imagine what these letters from my mother, my father, my brother and my friend Marci have meant to me. Some day your son or your daughter may need a letter from home, from you. Let's play practice by writing a short letter to baby Anita." Anita got a piece of paper and a pencil, and put them on the table in front of Clara.

Clara stared at the paper. "But what shall I write?"

"Tell baby Anita two or three thoughts that are in your head and heart right now."

Clara hesitated a little, then picked up the pencil and began to write. She pressed so hard the point of the pencil broke. Anita sharpened it with a paring knife and handed it back. Clara resumed writing, her brow creased with effort. She slid the paper with a few lines written on it across the table to Anita. Anita pushed it back.

"You read it to me . . . No, not to me. Read your letter to baby Anita."

Clara read, her voice pitched so low Anita had to strain to hear.

> *Mi querida niñita,*
> *Te quiero muchísimo. Pienso que eres la bebé más hermosa en el mundo. Me hubiera gustado leerte Los Zapaticos de Rosa, pero creo que no lo haré nunca. Lo siento.*
> *Tu mamá Clara*

My dearest baby girl,

I love you so very much. I think you are the most beautiful child in the world. I would like to be able to read you the story called Rosa's Little Shoes, but I don't think I ever will. I am sorry.

Your mother Clara

Anita put her hand on Clara's. "You see, Clara? Writing a letter is just talking with the pencil—putting the words already in your head on the paper. Now, let's pretend the campaign is over, that I am back in Havana and that you and I write each other letters. Turn the page over, and write me a very short letter."

This time Clara didn't hesitate. When she looked up from writing, Anita asked her to read the letter aloud. Clara read her words in a steady voice.

Querida Anita,

Nuestra casa parece vacía sin tí. Por favor, regresa pronto para visitarnos. Los niños se encuentran bién. Nosotros también. Saludos a tu familia.

Tu amiga, Clara

Dear Anita,

Our home feels empty without you here. Please come back and visit us soon. The children are well. So are we. Greetings to your family.

Your friend, Clara

Anita felt jubilant. "Clara, you see? You are literate. You have written new words from your head, and read them. They make perfect sense. Either of these letters would be acceptable to prove you have enough grammar and understanding to create something new. The letter to Fidel is a formality that all learners have to do. I will get a nice clean piece of paper so you can write a letter of your own to Fidel. If we aren't happy with it, you can do another one."

When Anita read what Clara wrote, she felt she would never, ever, feel prouder than at that moment.

Bainoa, Cuba
December 12, 1961

Primer Ministro Fidel Castro,

I am a simple campesina woman who never even dreamed of learning to read and write. The revolution sent us a young woman to teach my family. I have said no puedo more than a few times but this young girl always convinces me that yes I can. I am stubborn, but she is more stubborn than me so never takes no for an answer about anything. She says I am literate now, something I can hardly believe. My husband and young sister can now read and write too. When the literacy flag is placed outside of our bohío door my heart may burst with pride. Thank you for the literacy campaign and for Anita, our wonderful teacher.

Clara Mercedes Perez

A jubilant Anita wanted to place the literacy flag outside the door immediately, but restrained herself. "I have to get approval from a supervisor," she explained, and she didn't want to waste a minute. She knew where Marjorie would be teaching, so she begged Ramón to take her to Bainoa town. Ramón slung the rifle across his chest before leaving, and as they rode they reminisced about the months of studying and learning.

"Remember those first lessons, Ramón? I was afraid you'd chew your tongue right off."

As they neared town, they began to encounter people riding and walking, all calling out "*muy buenos días*". Anita waved back, grinning broadly. The *campesinos* looked the same as always—country people in simple country clothes coming and going on country errands. Yet today, things were very, very different. Seven months ago, most of these same *campesinos* couldn't read or write a single thing. Today, most of them could. She wished she could ask each person how it felt to be able to read and write. She wished she could read all their letters to Fidel.

They found Marjorie at the restaurant where they had eaten breakfast that rainy day months ago. The owner let the restaurant be used for special tutoring classes each afternoon.

"What brings you here?" Marjorie asked, surprised to see Anita.

"Because I'm so excited! My family has completed the final test. I know they have passed it, but I didn't want to put the flag outside the door until a supervisor gave me the go-ahead. Will you look at their tests to confirm we can celebrate today?"

As Marjorie reviewed the three tests, her face registered pleasure.

"*Felicidades,* Ramón. I congratulate you," she said. "You can be proud of yourself and your family."

"I am standing a little taller today, *señora* Marjorie, thanks to *maestra* Anita."

"I understand how you feel," said Marjorie, "Looking at these tests, I can see she has been a splendid teacher. Will you come to the flag-raising ceremony December sixteenth with the family, Ramón? The whole of Bainoa region will be celebrating its success."

"We will be there, *señora Marjorie.*" Ramón turned to Anita. "Before we return, I want to get some things," he said. Touching his fingers to his hat, he left, bidding *adiós* to Marjorie.

"Anita, I want to talk to you about something. Please wait here. I need to attend to the students for a few minutes." While Anita waited, many townsfolk passed as they went about doing their errands. Everyone smiled at her. Some stopped to talk to her, mostly asking her if she was excited now that she would soon be going home. *How different everything is from that day when Dani and I first walked around this town!*

Marjorie reappeared. "Just today the campaign office received word that there will be a huge rally in Havana December twenty-second. All campaigners will be leaving Bainoa on December nineteenth," she said. "Trains will be coming from the eastern provinces, picking up *brigadistas* and campaign personnel at designated stops along the way. Do you want to return to Havana by car when Luis comes to pick the girls and I up, or do you want to board the train to Havana?"

Havana . . . It was like talking about a different country.

"Is Dani going with you or getting on the train?"

"Only the supervisors know about this," said Marjorie. "You are the first *brigadista* I've told. What do you want to do? I must get back to the class."

"I'll go on the train," Anita said. "If Ramón gets back here before me, tell him I'll be back in a few minutes. I have to do something important. See you at the flag-raising ceremony."

When Anita and Ramón rode away from town, the sun was high in the western sky, but it was a winter sun so Anita welcomed Bufi's animal warmth. Usually she chatted to Ramón as they rode, but today her thoughts were all about leaving. *How will the work get done that I have helped with every day all these months? The animals? The laundry? There's so much more to do now with the new baby. And now that Nataniel is crawling about, he has to be watched more carefully. And Zenaida? How will she get to the new school? And when she is at school, there will be even more work that Clara will have to do by herself. How will Ramón and Clara continue to learn? They might forget everything if they don't keep going. Why haven't I thought about all this stuff before?* Anita desperately wanted to speak to Marjorie again, to get answers to these questions.

As they got closer to home, her thoughts brightened. She had accomplished her teaching mission and could hardly wait to celebrate. She was so eager to dismount that she didn't wait until Ramón had reined Bufi to a stop, but slid off the still-moving horse, falling hard on her fanny. Brushing herself off, she ran into the *bohío* shouting, "Clara, Zenaida, we can place our literacy flag outside right now. You have done it! You have all done it! Let's celebrate!"

Clara picked Nataniel up and threw him in the air, her face radiant. Zenaida and Anita danced and whirled each other around and around the small room. Ramón stood in the doorway looking from one to another, a big grin on his face.

"Has everyone gone mad?" he said.

Anita removed the flag from the thatch and the Perez family followed her outside. She had planned a little ceremony, but now found she couldn't speak, her throat was so clenched with emotion. Huddled together, Ramón holding Nataniel, Clara cradling baby Anita, Zenaida next to her, the family waited.

"This flag is the symbol of literacy in Cuba," began Anita when she felt she could. She stuck the small flag in the thatch above the palm-leaf doorway. "Placing this literacy flag above this doorway, I declare this home belonging to Ramón, Clara, Zenaida, Nataniel, and my namesake, baby Anita, to be a territory free from illiteracy from this day forward."

No one spoke. Even Nataniel, who was usually babbling, seemed to be aware that something special was happening, and was quiet in his father's arms. Anita shook each of their hands in a ceremonial way, then said, "I have a graduation present for each of you." Anita pulled three small packages out of her *mochila*, her backpack—gifts that she had purchased with saved allowance that each *brigadista* received monthly.

Ramón, Clara and Zenaida stood awkwardly holding their gifts. "Open them. Open them now," Anita said, eager to see their reactions. For Ramón, Anita had purchased a box of writing paper, a pen, some pencils, a pencil sharpener and an eraser. "I guess you're telling me I'm supposed to write you letters when you leave us to go home," said Ramón, his eyes twinkling. "And this?" he said, holding up the eraser.

"Just in case," said Anita.

Clara withdrew the classic children's book *Los Zapaticos de Rosa, Rosa's Little Shoes* from the wrapping. Speechless, she held it to her chest, then gave it to Nataniel but pulled it away quickly when he went to put the book in his mouth.

Anita felt anxious as Zenaida unwrapped her small package. *Would she like her gift?*

"Look Clara! Look Ramón! A diary! My very own diary! It's like Anita's except this one can be locked with its own special key." Zenaida asked Anita to write something in the diary, so they sat down on the stoop while Anita wrote an inscription on the flyleaf:

December 12, 1961
For Zenaida in The Year of Education
~ with affection from your teacher and friend,
Brigadista Anita Fonseca

Zenaida fingered the pages of the diary. "What kind of things do you write in a diary, Anita?"

"Things that are important to you; things that make you happy, that worry you or make you sad. And secrets, of course. The diary is a kind of friend you can confide in. Some people copy special things they want to remember from books they read. You will probably draw a lot in your diary." Anita showed Zenaida how each page was marked by day and month.

"When is your birthday, Zenaida?"

"Soon. January first," Zenaida replied.

"That's special! You will be writing your first words in your diary on your seventeenth birthday in the New Year."

"Come in for supper," Clara called out.

While Anita and Ramón had been in Bainoa, Clara and Zenaida had prepared a delicious meal. To make things festive, Clara had covered the rustic table with an ironed sheet. A glass jar full of colourful *croto* branches and a few wildflowers decorated the table. Even though the plates were the same chipped enamel ones used every day and the cutlery the same cheap metal ones, everything did look festive. Anita lit the lantern, and Clara served the celebration meal proudly. When they finished eating, Ramón went outside and returned to the table with his hands behind his back.

"A surprise," he said. "Guess what it is."

"A bottle of rum," Clara guessed. Ramón shook his head.

"Something sweet," guessed Zenaida.

"Yes, but what exactly?" said Ramón. "What do you think, Anita?"

"A cake?" she guessed. Ramón put two packages on the table.

"*¡Galleticas de almendra*! Almond cookies!" they exclaimed, "*y chocolate*!" It was the first time Nataniel had tasted chocolate and he cried for more, his salty tears mixing with the chocolate smeared all over his sweet face. They would have eaten all the sweets if Clara hadn't insisted on keeping some for the next day. Clara would not let Anita help clean up, so she sat at the table writing in her diary.

December 12, 1961

Dear Diary,

¡Caramba! I did it! My learners did it! I actually taught three people who were completely illiterate to read and write. I'm remembering how much I wanted to become a brigadista, how I pictured myself as the girl wearing the beret in the poster. Marjorie told me that one hundred thousand kids eventually volunteered as brigadistas, so tonight I'm thinking of the one hundred thousand different stories those kids have to tell.

I feel sad though, about Manuel Domenech and the other brigadistas who died. I think I will never forget how scared I was when I was blindfolded and tied up for those four days, and how lucky I am to be here writing this now. Mostly, I feel happy for Zenaida. I am sure she will want to continue to educate herself. I feel so close to the Perez family. When I was anxiously waiting to go to Varadero, I crossed off the days on my calendar looking forward to the day of leaving. Now I am crossing off the few days left until I leave for Havana. Even though I miss mamá and papá, I'm not really looking forward to that day. The thought of going back to my home in Miramar with all the super comforts that my learner family don't have . . . well, it just upsets me. I'm hoping mamá is not such a country club butterfly. That would bother me even more now than it did before. Maybe I will feel better by the time I climb on board the train with all the other brigadistas. What a scene that will be!

Anita la cubana

That night, Anita swung back and forth in her hammock, unable to sleep. She felt full—full of food, full of sweets, full of pride and satisfaction, but also full of regret that something so special was coming to an end.

CELEBRATION AND ENDINGS

People came flooding from all directions into the town of Bainoa for the flag-raising ceremony. They arrived on horseback, on mules and donkeys, in ox-drawn carts, crammed in the back of trucks and on foot. They came wearing garlands of flowers, waving literacy flags and singing. The town that had been so unwelcoming at the beginning of the campaign was noisy, festive, everyone eager to celebrate. Children swarmed among the adults, chasing each other, gorging on locally made peanut brittle available free at kiosks. A band played traditional songs in the town square. A raised platform had been built at one end of the park, and people scurried about setting up microphones, loudspeakers and chairs for speakers and special guests.

A truck had collected Anita and the Perez family mid-afternoon. Clara and Zenaida were very excited because they hardly ever went to town. The militiaman who sat in the cab with the driver for security got into the back with everyone else so Clara could sit up front comfortably with baby Anita. Swaying together as the truck bounced along, the *brigadistas* sang the *Brigadista* Anthem.

We are the Conrado Benitez Brigade
Books and lanterns in our hands
Helping lead our country forward
Teaching literacy throughout the land

There were several verses, and they sang them all several times. By the time they reached Bainoa, Anita's voice was hoarse. She arranged a meeting spot with her learner family for the ceremony, then went off in search of Claudio. Pushing through the crowd, she bumped into him as he was looking for her.

"Let's go somewhere where we can talk, Anita. We have a little time before the ceremonies begin." The only place they could find that was halfway quiet was the place set aside for hitching up the horses, mules and ox-carts. They jumped up on the rough boards of a cart, their legs dangling.

"Tell me your news," Claudio said. "Did Clara make it?" Anita told him about the final test, and how she had coaxed Clara to write the letter to Fidel.

"What about your learners?" she asked. Claudio had been teaching a group of eight Bainoa housewives.

"They all made it," he said, "and they almost knocked me over rushing to hug and kiss me all at the same time."

"You're coming to Havana for the big rally on the twenty second, aren't you, Claudio?"

Claudio's face clouded over. "That's what I wanted to talk to you about, Anita. I can't go. I received a telegram yesterday from my mother saying my father is sick—she didn't say with what—and that she needs me to come home right away to help in the store. I have to leave tomorrow."

Anita turned her head away. Another ending. Claudio put his arm around her shoulders. "We'll write," he said. "Cardenas isn't at the end of the world. I'll come to Havana to see you as soon as I can. I promise."

Anita wanted to believe that they would see each other again, that he would come to Havana, that her parents would like him, that they wouldn't mind his being mulatto. She wanted to show Claudio around the great city, to walk through the narrow streets of the old colonial part of Havana, go to a movie, sit on the sea wall of the Malecón swinging their legs! Somehow, she didn't believe it would happen.

She turned to face him, meeting his beautiful dark eyes with lashes longer than her own. As they hugged each other the band struck up the opening chords of the Cuban national anthem.

"We'd better get going," they both said at once. They ran back to the park where Anita joined the Perez family at the arranged spot just in time to join in singing the last verse. When the ceremonies began, Anita let her mind drift. In a couple of days she'd be leaving on the train. Would her brother be there to meet her? In a few weeks she'd be back at school . . .

Zenaida nudged her. "Anita, they're calling all the *brigadistas* to go up front."

Anita threaded her way through the crowd of seated people to join the *brigadistas* as they streamed together to the front of the platform. When they were all gathered, the people of Bainoa region rose to their feet and began to applaud and chant, *¡Que vivan los brigadistas!* Then the speeches began, one speaker after another heaping praise upon the *brigadistas*. One of the speakers compared the literacy campaign to a bumblebee.

"It is said that the bumblebee should not be able to fly at all since the surface area of its small wings compared to the weight of its body should make flight impossible. Fortunately, the bumblebee is not educated in the laws of physics, so it flies anyway." Laughter rippled through the crowd. "Being that Cuba is a poor country with limited resources," the speaker continued, "some people said the campaign was bound to fail. Fortunately these young people did not know that, and they made the campaign fly." Sweeping his hand toward the *brigadistas*, he said, "Join me in congratulating these magnificent young people." The crowd responded with many *¡Vivas!* while the *brigadistas* made jokes and noises about themselves being compared to bumblebees.

The town Mayor then thanked all those who had coordinated and directed the campaign and all the local groups that had provided services of any kind. Just as the crowd began to get restless, the Mayor announced that it was time to raise the literacy flag. He asked Pamela to come forward, and right after, Anita heard her own name called. Surprised, she made her way to stand beside Pamela and the Mayor.

"Pamela Moore Ríos came here to teach with her mother, *señora* Marjorie Moore Ríos, who is an American and a friend of Cuba," the Mayor boomed into the microphone. "Pamela is the youngest *brigadista* in the region. She turned twelve only recently. By herself, she successfully taught seven adults to read and write, and we honour her by inviting her to raise the literacy flag." The applause and whistles were deafening.

Turning to Anita, the Mayor said, "This young woman, Anita Fonseca, was kidnapped by a counter-revolutionary group and held captive for four days before she was rescued. Despite her ordeal, Anita refused to abandon the literacy campaign." The Mayor grabbed Anita's and Pamela's hands and raised their arms while the crowd cheered. Then the mayor called upon *señora* Flor Tamayo to come forward. A wiry old woman, erect, bright-eyed and smiling, her face pruned with wrinkles, came to the stage on the arm of a young man.

"*Señora* Flor Tamayo is our oldest student," explained the Mayor. "She says she's ninety–two years young, and she wants to read you the letter she wrote Fidel Castro. Speaking with the quavering voice of the aged, Flor Tamayo read her letter.

Dear Fidel Castro,

No one in my poor family has ever been able to read and write. Thanks to you, thanks to the revolution, an old lady, her six children and sixteen grandchildren are able to read and write now, ending generations of ignorance. May God bless you and all the people of Cuba. If you would come to Bainoa to visit me, I would be the happiest woman in the world.

Flor Tamayo

When the applause died down, Pamela, Anita and *señora* Flor Tamayo were led to the flagpole. Together they raised the literacy flag bearing the words:

BAINOA: TERRITORIO LIBRE DE ANALFABETISMO*

Men threw their hats in the air, children jumped up and down, crazed by the cheering which went on and on. The *brigadistas* hugged one another and their supervisors. They even hugged the Mayor. Anita forgave him for not being around to meet their group the day they arrived in Bainoa that rainy day seven months ago. Over the din, the Mayor struggled to make himself heard, inviting everyone to stay for the banquet and street party.

Anita ate and danced until she felt she could neither eat another tamale nor dance another cha-cha-cha or danzón. The musicians, decked out in polished cowboy boots, broad-brimmed hats and bright bandannas knotted around their throats, showed no sign of tiredness. The combo of seven played atop a long cart decorated with a bower of palm leaves, flowers and hundreds of small literacy flags. Anita lounged with Claudio against the side of the cart. *This may be our last time together for a long time—maybe even forever—*she thought, while watching the celebrants eating, drinking and dancing. Militiamen and militia women armed with rifles stood around the edges of the crowd. Many of the enemies of *la revolución* had been caught and arrested throughout Cuba during the campaign. There hadn't been a threat in the Bainoa region since she had been kidnapped, but following the ghastly murder of Manuel Domenech, the militia had continued to stand on guard.

---

* Bainoa: Territory Free From Illiteracy

"Look, Claudio. Look at *señora* Flor Tamayo dancing." The old woman passed in front of them, her hips swinging sedately to the tempo of a traditional *danzón*. "It was fun watching Clara and Ramón dance, wasn't it?"

"That Nataniel is one squirmy little kid," said Claudio. He had held Nataniel, and Anita had held the baby while Ramón and Clara enjoyed a few dances. When they returned to collect the children, they were flushed and happy.

"And look at Zenaida," said Anita. "She hasn't stopped dancing since the band started playing." Anita caught Zenaida's eye, and winked. Zenaida winked back. She had been dancing with the same young *campesino* for some time. "Who knows when Zenaida will have another opportunity to dance and have fun with people her own age?" Anita said aloud, talking to herself really.

"Hi, you two," said Dani, flushed from dancing. "Do you know I'm going to Havana tomorrow with Marjorie and a couple of other supervisors? We'll be delivering the students' letters from this region to Fidel."

"Lucky you!" exclaimed Anita. "Where is it happening?"

"At the Field of Champions baseball stadium. Fidel will be there to receive the letters."

"How are you getting there?" asked Claudio.

"In a van. We're being picked up at seven in the morning and will be back here by evening. So I think I'll just stay up all night tonight and party."

"How come you're coming back? Why not just stay in Havana since the assignment is over anyway?" said Claudio.

"*¡Hombre! ¿Estás loco?* Are you crazy, man? I'm not going to miss the train ride to Havana with all the *brigadistas*. It will be historical."

"And probably *hysterical* too," Anita added.

"I wish I didn't have to go home so I could be on the train too," said Claudio, becoming glum.

"Well, you can't, but you can dance this salsa with me," Anita said, yanking Claudio off his feet into the throng of dancers.

Kissing Claudio goodbye was the first of many emotional goodbyes to be made over the next couple of days. As the truck pulled away from the town square, she waved until she could see him no longer, hoping it was not the last time. Reaching into her pocket, she fingered the folded piece of paper with his address and telephone number. All around her, *brigadistas* chattered and sang, still excited by the day's festivities. Anita joined in, but only halfheartedly. Before climbing into her hammock, she crossed another day off her calendar. Only two more days remained until she left for Havana.

She flopped into the hammock, and started it swaying. She had forced herself join in the festivities, had made herself dance and have fun, but since the evening of celebration with her learner family, she felt weird, not herself.

As the hammock swayed, the rope rubbed on the hooks it was suspended from. Tonight each back and forth rubbing movement seemed to be saying: o-ver, o-ver, it's-all-o-ver, o-ver, o-ver, it's-all-o-ver. Tears brimmed, spilled over, streaking across her temples then falling into the cupped hollows of her ears. O-ver, o-ver, it's-all-o-ver . . .

"Anita . . . Are you crying?" whispered Zenaida.

"I guess so," said Anita.

"What's the matter? Did you and Claudio fight?"

"Nothing like that, Zenaida."

"Then what?" persisted Zenaida.

"Can't you guess?"

"Is it because you'll be leaving?"

"It's that, but it's more than that," Anita said, her voice ragged. "For seven months I have had a goal, and every day was dedicated to achieving that goal. Now that goal has been reached and the campaign is over . . . what now? Return to Havana to do the same old same old? Get up . . . go to school . . . do homework . . . sleep . . . get up . . . go to school . . . do homework . . ."

"I wish I could do that," said Zenaida. "Tomorrow and the next day, and every day I will be doing my same old same old right here—cleaning, washing, cooking, taking care of Clara's children . . ."

"Zenaida, you must try to get to the new regional school somehow. You heard the announcement didn't you? The education campaign is not stopping just because the *brigadistas* are leaving."

"I know," said Zenaida, "but I'm not sure I'll be able to go. Clara and Ramón need me here. And what about Clara and Ramón? How will they continue to learn?"

"I don't know how exactly, but I talked to Marjorie tonight and she assured me that the education of adults will not stop when the campaign ends. The Perez family will be able to continue studying if they really want to."

"I wish you could stay and teach us, Anita." Zenaida's voice was wistful.

"Let's not talk about it anymore. I'll just start crying all over again."

Anita rolled out of the hammock for the last time and dressed quickly. Yesterday Anita had gone around in one of Ramón's work shirts because Clara had insisted on washing and ironing both of her uniforms and mending the holes in her socks. Ramón had cleaned her boots—not only cleaned them, but made them gleam. He had polished the scuffed leather with some sort of grease. *Probably pig fat*, Anita thought, smiling as she pulled them on and laced them. As she put an **X** through the number **19** square on the December page, her throat tightened. Leaving day.

Her bulging duffel bag sat waiting by the palm leaf door. She and Ramón were to ride to the schoolhouse where she and the other *brigadistas* going to Havana would be picked up in a truck and taken to the place where the train was scheduled to stop. Knowing how much Anita loved coconut, Zenaida had prepared a bowlful, freshly-grated and sweetened with honey, especially for her.

Except for Nataniel's baby-talk chatter and the clinking of cups and cutlery, this last meal together was a sad affair. Ramón drank the last of his *café con leche*, slung Anita's duffel bag over his shoulder and went to saddle Bufi.

The time to say goodbye arrived. Anita held baby Anita gently for a moment, then hugged and kissed Nataniel. Coached by Zenaida, Nataniel put his chubby palm to his mouth and blew Anita a kiss. Delighted, Anita kissed him again.

"Hasta luego, muchachito precioso. So long, dear little fellow."

Clara hugged her fiercely, whispering, "We will never forget you."

"Nor I you," responded Anita, struggling not to cry. When she turned to say goodbye to Zenaida, she said, "Hey, remember how you hated me when I first arrived?"

"I remember," Zenaida said. The two girls hugged affectionately.

"Remember, Zenaida, we have a bet."

"I won't forget," Zenaida said.

"I left you my book about Anne Frank. Some day when you have read it, we will talk about it. Now, before I go, I want to take one last photograph. Everyone go stand near Bufi."

Anita's camera lens opened and shut on the Perez family doing their best to smile.

"*Tenemos que irnos*, Anita. Time to go," Ramón said quietly.

Riding out of the clearing, Anita looked backward, waving goodbye to the little group clustered in front of the *bohío*. She felt like a deserter. She was heading toward the luxury of her home in Miramar, while the Perez family remained as they were the first day she met them—still living in a simple hut with an earthen floor, no electricity, no toilet, no shower, no running water, few comforts. She remembered the lesson she had taught: "*In the years to come, people will no longer live in bohíos or tenement houses . . .*" She remembered Ramón's sceptical reaction to this claim.

Oh please let everything we read and talked about around the table by lantern-light come true! As she mouthed these words silently and fervently, she heard Clara's voice shouting, "Anita, Ramón . . . wait . . . wait . . ." Ramón reined in Bufi.

"You forgot the lantern," Clara called out breathlessly, running up the path, the lantern swinging from her hand.

"No, Clara. I left it for you, for the family."

Just before turning onto the road, Anita heard Clara and Zenaida call out what she was to hear many more times that day. "*¡No nos abandones! ¡No nos olvides!* Don't abandon us! Don't forget about us!"

As they neared the schoolhouse, Anita saw that the transport truck was already there and could hear the hubbub of excited voices. Anita dismounted. Ramón remained in the saddle. She stroked Bufi's flanks. After a few moments, Ramón handed down her duffel bag. "You heard what Clara and Zenaida said, *maestra*. Don't forget us. Now go. I don't like sad goodbyes."

"I'll write, Ramón. Don't forget to go to the post office once in a while." Ramón nodded, wheeled Bufi around and trotted off, his arm raised in a farewell gesture.

RETURN

Anita stared at Ramón's receding back, then hoisted her duffel bag and headed toward the noisy cluster of *brigadistas*, her eyes searching for Dani. She found her sitting on the steps trying to comfort Suzi who was crying pitifully because she had to leave the goat she had become so attached to.

"Hi, Dani. Tell me about delivering the letters to Fidel,"

"*¡Qué bola!* It was a gas! The letters were in thousands of boxes placed in a huge pile. Marjorie said there were around 700,000 letters, maybe more. Fidel opened some of the letters and read them over the loud speaker. It was fantastic! You could tell Fidel was really moved. He said the government is going to establish a Literacy Campaign Museum, and that all the letters will be kept there."

Just then Marjorie and Pamela came down the steps hauling boxes and duffel bags.

"OK everybody," Marjorie called out. "It's time to go. Everyone going on the train get on the truck."

Suzi started wailing again.

I know just how you feel, Suzi, Anita thought, as the truck pulled away. She and Dani continued waving until the small group left on the schoolhouse steps disappeared from view.

Greetings of "Hi Anita. Hi Dani. How did your assignments go?" greeted the two girls the minute they boarded the train and began pushing their way through the crowd of *brigadistas* standing in the aisle. *Brigadistas* were already jammed together on the slatted wooden seats, so those just getting on had to stow their duffel bags wherever they could, then stand squeezed together in the aisles. Some girls sat on empty laps. The train was a raucous carnival of noisy reunions, everyone talking, exchanging stories of where they had been and what they had experienced.

"Dani, I'm going to look for Dominga and the twins," said Anita. Two passenger cars along, Anita came across the twins who nearly strangled her by both hugging her at once.

"Is Dominga on this train?" Anita asked.

"No, we already looked. Maybe she'll come on the next one," one of the twins answered. *Vanesa, or Vera?* Anita felt too embarrassed to ask. They talked awhile, then Anita left them to continue going through the train to look for others she might know from Varadero. As she passed through the cars, she caught snatches of conversation.

"Would you believe it! The men of the family were almost never without a cigar in their mouths, and the women smoked cigars too!"

"My assignment was in Oriente province in a cabin near the top of Pico Turquino, the highest mountain in Cuba."

"I grew out of my uniform and had to wear borrowed clothes the last three months."

Hundreds of different stories right here on this train—as many stories as there are brigadistas, Anita thought. Moving through one passenger car after another, Anita stopped now and then to greet kids she recognized. Amidst all the raucous chatter she heard some *brigadistas* saying that they didn't want to leave; that they didn't want the campaign to end. Each time she heard that, Anita felt better knowing she wasn't alone in feeling that way. She heard too that many had left their lanterns behind with their learner families.

Someone tugged at her uniform as she passed. It was Betina, the ten-year-old *brigadista* she had met at Varadero.

"Hi there, Betina. How did it go?"

"It was great!" Betina said. "I was in Cienfuegos. I helped two *brigadistas* teach a group of adults. They all learned. And because I was the youngest *brigadista* I got to raise the flag. I'm eleven now." Anita told her about Pamela raising the flag too.

"Have fun at the rally, Betina. Maybe I'll see you there." When she got back to her car, Dani was singing and playing her guitar, surrounded as usual by an admiring crowd.

Dust was blowing in through open windows, but nobody seemed to care. As the long train advanced through the countryside, *campesinos* stopped whatever they were doing to wave. They seemed to know about the special trains carrying *brigadistas* to Havana, to the rally that would celebrate the successful completion of the campaign.

The train made only one stop after Anita boarded. When the train halted, the *brigadistas* hung out the windows waving literacy flags and singing the *Brigadista* anthem. Anita observed the farewell scene taking place outside. People of all ages embraced departing *brigadistas*. Many were crying. Children clung onto *brigadistas'* legs like baby monkeys. As the *brigadistas* boarded, the gathered crowd surged forward spreading out along the length of the train. As the train pulled away, they began calling out the same refrain that still echoed in Anita's ears:

"*Adiós. Adiós*. Please don't forget us."

Anita felt anew the pangs of parting from the Perez family. The newly boarded *brigadistas* pushed down the already crowded aisles, boys and girls alike wiping away tears without embarrassment. Soon though, they joined in the gaiety, singing and swapping stories, deliriously happy despite the sadness of goodbyes.

As the train entered the outskirts of Havana, the excitement on board doubled, then tripled as they passed through the city that was home to so many on the train. When the train began slowing down, everyone craned their necks to peer out the windows on the station side. As they pulled into the station, Anita couldn't believe what she saw—a throng of hundreds of people packed the entire platform, all waving handkerchiefs, flowers or flags.

"*¡Caramba!* What a welcome! How will we ever find our families in this crowd, Dani?"

The train squealed to a stop. As soon as the steps were lowered, the *brigadistas* poured off the train, greeted by the crowd with hugs, claps on the back, handshakes, flowers, even gifts.

"*¡Dios mío!*" exclaimed Anita. "We are getting a hero's welcome."

"So we are, darling girl, and we deserve it," responded Dani.

As they were about to descend the steps, Dani gave Anita a quick hug and kissed her on both cheeks. "Call me tomorrow," she said, and holding her guitar above her head, she stepped down and started making her way through the crowd. Surprised by Dani's sudden departure, Anita hesitated on the steps, looking around, but was soon pushed from behind.

"Anita . . . Anita . . . Over this way." Her father's voice. *Amazing how you can tell the voice of someone dear to you, even in a crowd,* marvelled Anita. She shoved and threaded her way through the throng following the direction of her father's voice. "This way, Anita. Keep coming. This way, this way . . ." People patted her on the back as she waded through the throng. Someone thrust a bouquet of flowers into her arms. Finally she inhaled her father's familiar scent as his arms enveloped her in the jostling crowd.

"Safe," he said. "You're home, safe and sound."

Anita embraced her mother who held her as though she would never let her go. And then, here was her brother beaming at her, still bearded, his hair brushing his shoulders. Anita shrugged off her duffel bag and leapt up, almost knocking him over, her arms clasped around his neck, her feet off the ground.

"*Hermano mío*, how I missed you!"

On December 22, *brigadistas* by the thousands converged into a huge mass fronting the raised stage in Havana's gigantic civic square. Singing and chanting, wearing clean, pressed uniforms, many *brigadistas* carried giant pencils, the symbol of literacy. Though it was drizzling rain, that didn't stop thousands upon thousands of people in a festive mood from pouring into the square from every direction for the celebratory rally. Many of the celebrants beat every kind of percussion instrument known to Cuba.

Anita, Mario and Dani stood squeezed together among the thousands of *brigadistas* in the crush of the jubilant crowd. Waiting for the ceremonies to begin, Anita reflected upon the last couple of days. Being home, celebrating the success of Tomasa, Gladis and Fernando with the family, swapping stories with Mario, seeing a few friends—all that had been great. But Anita felt out of sorts. She had tried to help Gladis with the laundry, but Gladis had smiled shyly and said, "Oh no, *señorita Anita*, that wouldn't be right." She made her own bed every morning, but when she insisted on helping Tomasa clear the table after meals, Tomasa became flustered and flushed deeply. To her credit, her mother said nothing, but Anita could tell she disapproved. She wanted to be helpful, but nobody needed or wanted her to do anything. Agitated, she had called Marjorie. "Relax," Marjorie said. "There will be lots of opportunities in the bigger world to get involved in. Some things change by revolution, Anita; others by evolution." Anita felt better when she hung up.

Mario's voice called her back to the moment. "Look, Anita."

She followed the direction of Mario's pointing hand. A skinny man was climbing up a really tall lamp standard. Anita focused her camera on him, following him through the viewfinder to the top. When he swung one leg over, and sat straddling the disc-shaped metal cover surveying the tremendous crowd, Anita snapped the shutter.

When the ceremony finally started, the Minister of Education was the first to speak.

"We estimate that a million people are united here this day to declare Cuba a territory free from illiteracy." The people cheered as if with one great throat. The Minister then read the names of participants in the campaign who had died, most from something as innocent as an allergic reaction to a bee sting, and one the victim of brutal and calculated murder at the hands of counter-revolutionaries. Name upon name . . .

Manuel Domenech . . .

Alberto Alvarez Serpa . . .

Rogelio de Armas Ruesca . . .

Pedro Blanco Gomez . . .

Jesús Cabrera Fraga . . .

Catalina Vidal Arjona. . . .

José Antonio Sánchez . . .

Oscar Zayas Ugarte . . .

When the last of the hundred names was read, the multitude bowed their heads for a moment of silence to honour the dead. At the end of his speech, the Minister proclaimed, "Above all, bravo to the three hundred thousand volunteers, youth and adults, who taught over 707 thousand illiterate adults to read and write!"

The applause was thunderous.

"We're applauding for you, Clara, for you, Ramón and for you Zenaida," Anita murmured.

Hand over hand, the Minister of Education raised an enormous flag up the tall flagpole. Raised high, the wind caught the blue cloth and spread it, displaying the bright yellow lettering:

CUBA: TERRITORIO LIBRE DE ANALFABETISMO

The throng roared and millions of hands clapped to the throb of beating drums. Anita felt she would burst with pride knowing that she had been part of something so big, so important. Some *brigadistas* began to chant the *Brigadista* Anthem, which soon spread to all the others.

We're teachers
Young teachers
Illiteracy we did fight
Cubans by the thousands
Have learned to read and write

When Prime Minister Castro came to the microphone, the *brigadistas* surged as far forward as they could. Fidel called seven-year-old Élan Melendez to the front of the platform, shook his hand and introduced him as the youngest volunteer teacher in the campaign.

"Dani and I heard about him on the train," Anita told Mario. "He helped his brother teach."

Then Fidel brought forward a tiny black woman whose name was Maria de la Cruz Semanat. He said she was 106 years old and had been born and raised a slave. When Fidel explained that the *señora* was the oldest person to participate in the campaign and was now literate, the crowd went crazy. The old woman blew kisses to the crowd with both hands.

"Today, Cuba salutes all the campaign volunteers," Fidel said, "but especially we must honour the more than one hundred thousand *brigadistas,* mostly teenagers, who left the comfort and security of their homes for months on end to do a difficult job. Sweeping his gaze over the multitude of *brigadistas*, he said, "By your combined effort, you have helped end four and a half centuries of ignorance in Cuba."

In the seconds following Fidel's words, something unexpected happened. A boy *brigadista* near the front shouted out loudly, "Fidel, tell us what else we can do. Tell us what to do next." Immediately, those *brigadistas* near the boy began repeating his last words. The words spread, becoming a demanding chant taken up for minutes on end by Anita and the thousands of gathered brigadistas. The *brigadistas* carrying the giant pencils lifted them up and down in rhythm with the chant.

Tell us what to do next!
Tell us what to do next!
Tell us what to do next!
Tell us what to do next!

Anita, Dani and Mario linked arms with those around them as they chanted. Anita felt she would burst. The *brigadistas* had done something extraordinary for their country—so why stop now? Like a speeded up movie passing before her eyes, Anita remembered her mother and father finally signing the consent form, remembered practicing to be a teacher at Varadero, remembered the unfriendly look on Zenaida's face when they first met that changed to sisterly affection over time. She remembered lighting the lantern for the first class, how its light leaped to illuminate the table and the dark room beyond it, the tension of the first test, the joy and relief of the final one. She remembered how it felt to be called *maestra*, the birth of the little fish, the smell and taste of fear those four awful days when she sat bound and blindfolded. But best of all she remembered placing the little paper literacy flag outside the door of the *bohío*. That flag would soon fade and curl in the sun, but her memories of the seven months that put the flag there and helped raise the big one here today would never be forgotten. Never! She just had to keep on doing something meaningful.

Yes, Fidel. Tell us what to do next.

IN THEIR OWN WORDS

January 1, 1962

Dear Clara, Ramón and Zenaida,

I think I'm probably the first person to write you a letter. It's wonderful to be home with my family, but I miss my life with the Perez family more than I can tell you. My father said something wonderful the other day when we were talking about the campaign. He said that during the campaign, the campesinos discovered the world of words, and the brigadistas discovered the forgotten people of Cuba. Now that I have "discovered" you, I don't want to lose you, so I hope you will write me back and tell me your news. Please don't worry about making mistakes.

There were a million people or more at the rally. When the people cheered, I imagined they were cheering for you. I hope you will be able to participate in the Seguimiento, the Continuing Education program. My mother has decided to keep on teaching. I am so proud of her! Gladis, the laundrywoman my mother taught to read and write, has decided she wants to keep studying so she can train to be a childcare worker. Tomasa doesn't want to continue studying, but she is happy that she can read and write. This morning she proudly showed me the grocery list she wrote out by herself. Yesterday I helped Fernando, our gardener, write a letter to his family in Oriente province.

The photographs are really nice, aren't they? I have framed the last one I took the day I left, and it sits on my bedside table so I can see you before I turn off the light each night and first thing every morning.

I'm not the soft little city girl I was when you first met me. I grew up a lot living with you those seven months. I'm a lot stronger in every way; I learned what hard work is and that I am capable of doing it. I know I can manage without all the privileges I was used to. Above all, I saw for myself the many things that need changing in Cuba so that life will be fairer and better for everyone. What I learned during the campaign will stay with me my whole life. I do need more cooking lessons though, don't I?

School starts again in a few days, so I will once again become a student. At the rally, the brigadistas asked Fidel what we could do next. He said that we should study hard and educate ourselves to become what our country needs—teachers, doctors, nurses, agronomists, engineers, researchers, scientists—people with skills. I'm sure he would say the same thing to you, Zenaida. Today is your birthday, Zenaida, and I hope you are having a wonderful day. Did you start writing in your Diary? And don't you worry, I will bring my handsome brother to meet you someday soon.

I hope all of you are well. Kiss the children for me. My mother and father send their best regards and wish you a Feliz Año Nuevo. I wish you a Happy New Year too.

Yours always, with great affection,
Anita

Bainoa
January 15, 1962

Dear Anita,

Remember my pretend letter to you saying the house seems empty without you? Well that is true. I think even baby Anita looks around for you. Your letter is the very first one we have ever received. I hope there will be many more. We are well and happy but we would be happier if you were still here teaching us. In September Zenaida will go to live with people in town and attend the new school. Ramón and I do want to continue classes. If we can find a way, we will study with the Continuing Education program you talked about. Now I say Sí puedo, not No puedo. Anita, being able to write this letter was worth all the trouble and tears. You mean the world to us, and we will never forget you. Please give my greetings to your family.

Yours with affection, Clara

Bainoa
January 15, 1962

Dear Anita,

I will be living in town and going to school next September. Isn't that great! It looks like you might win that bet we have after all. Will you send us a photograph of you in front of your house? And one of Mario to see if he is as good-looking as you say. I want to ask you for a favour. Please send a letter just to me. I want to put it in my diary. I did start writing in it. I will confide to you what I first wrote. I said I used to be a nasty girl, but now I'm not, thanks to a special person named Anita. I hope you like the picture of me lighting the lantern that I drew on the back of this letter.

Affectionately, Zenaida

Bainoa
January 15, 1962

Dear Anita,

It is good that we are writing letters. Perhaps my thick head will not forget so quickly what you taught us, *maestra*. Clara has already told you about Zenaida. We will see what the future holds for Clara and me. I keep the piece of paper with the words *Plantation Foreman* on it to keep my dream alive. Nataniel is a laughing boy, full of fun and mischief. Your namesake baby Anita is growing and becoming more beautiful each day. We miss you—but not your cooking. I think the pigs miss you too. Forgive me for making jokes. My hand is tired now, and my tongue half-chewed off. I remember you once told us we were making history. I look at what I have written and it seems a miracle. The Perez family knows the miracle has a name—it's Anita.

Your friend forever, Ramón